DEADLY
ENCOUNTER

DEADLY ENCOUNTER

M A COMLEY

2017

New York Times and USA Today bestselling author M A Comley
Published by Jeamel Publishing limited
Copyright © 2017 M A Comley
Digital Edition, License Notes

All rights reserved. This book or any portion thereof may not be reproduced, stored in a retrieval system, transmitted in any form or by any means electronic or mechanical, including photo-copying, or used in any manner whatsoever without the express written permission of the author, except for the use of brief quotations in a book review or scholarly journal.

This is a work of fiction. Names, characters, places and incidents are a product of the author's imagination or are used fictitiously, and any resemblance to actual persons living or dead, business establishments, events or locales is entirely coincidental.

ISBN-13: 978-1977857484

ISBN-10: 1977857485

OTHER BOOKS BY M A COMLEY

Blind Justice (Novella)
Cruel Justice (Book #1)
Mortal Justice (Novella)
Impeding Justice (Book #2)
Final Justice (Book #3)
Foul Justice (Book #4)
Guaranteed Justice (Book #5)
Ultimate Justice (Book #6)
Virtual Justice (Book #7)
Hostile Justice (Book #8)
Tortured Justice (Book #9)
Rough Justice (Book #10)
Dubious Justice (Book #11)
Calculated Justice (Book #12)
Twisted Justice (Book #13)
Justice at Christmas (Short Story)
Prime Justice (Book #14)
Heroic Justice (Book #15)
Shameful Justice (Book #16)
Immoral Justice (Book #17)
Unfair Justice (a 10,000 word short story)
Irrational Justice (a 10,000 word short story)
Seeking Justice (a 15,000 word novella)
Clever Deception (co-written by Linda S Prather)
Tragic Deception (co-written by Linda S Prather)
Sinful Deception (co-written by Linda S Prather)
Forever Watching You (DI Miranda Carr thriller)
Wrong Place (DI Sally Parker thriller #1)

No Hiding Place (DI Sally Parker thriller #2)
Cold Case (DI Sally Parker thriller#3)
Deadly Encounter (DI Sally Parker thriller #4)
Lost Innocence (DI Sally Parker thriller #5)
Web of Deceit (DI Sally Parker Novella with Tara Lyons)
The Missing Children (DI Kayli Bright #1)
Killer On The Run (DI Kayli Bright #2)
Hidden Agenda (DI Kayli Bright #3)
Murderous Betrayal (Kayli Bright #4)
Dying Breath (Kayli Bright #5)
The Caller (co-written with Tara Lyons)
Evil In Disguise – a novel based on True events
Deadly Act (Hero series novella)
Torn Apart (Hero series #1)
End Result (Hero series #2)
In Plain Sight (Hero Series #3)
Double Jeopardy (Hero Series #4)
Sole Intention (Intention series #1)
Grave Intention (Intention series #2)
Devious Intention (Intention #3)
Merry Widow (A Lorne Simpkins short story)
It's A Dog's Life (A Lorne Simpkins short story)
A Time To Heal (A Sweet Romance)
A Time For Change (A Sweet Romance)
High Spirits
The Temptation series (Romantic Suspense/New Adult Novellas)
Past Temptation
Lost Temptation

KEEP IN TOUCH WITH THE AUTHOR

Twitter

https://twitter.com/Melcom1

Blog

http://melcomley.blogspot.com

Facebook

http://smarturl.it/sps7jh

Newsletter

http://smarturl.it/8jtcvv

BookBub

www.bookbub.com/authors/m-a-comley

ACKNOWLEDGMENTS

Thank you as always to my rock, Jean, who keeps me supplied with endless cups of coffee while I punish my keyboard. I'd be lost without you in my life.

Special thanks as always go to my talented editor, Stefanie Spangler Buswell and to Karri Klawiter for her superb cover design expertise.

My heartfelt thanks go to my wonderful proofreader Joseph for spotting all the lingering nits.

And finally, to all the wonderful Bloggers and Facebook groups for their never-ending support of my work.

M A Comley

PROLOGUE

Fifteen years ago...

Fear clawed at Anne's throat. She glanced over her shoulder for what seemed like the hundredth time in five minutes to find the man was still chasing her and getting nearer.

Why didn't I cry for help when I was able to? No one is going to hear me out here. The muscles in her legs burnt and felt as heavy as concrete. Doubt clouded her mind. *Have I got enough energy to outrun him?* Her lungs were on fire, and her breath had been labouring for a while. She scanned the industrial unit the man had forced her to turn into and shook her head. Nothing. No form of help.

No one is going to find me here, not at this time of night. Please, God, if it's my time to die, make it swift and painless. Let me drop down dead from a heart attack rather than let this beast get his hands on me.

Beads of sweat trickled down her forehead and dripped into her eyes. She coughed, her throat parched from her exertions. The inkiness of the night sky grew blacker the deeper she ventured into the unit. *Should I confront him? Ask him what his problem is? Why is he chasing me?*

Distracted by her thoughts, she stepped on something, and her ankle buckled immediately. Her fall felt as if it were happening in slow motion. The palms of her hands slid along the hard, uneven pavement, and she wasn't quick enough to prevent her chin from hitting the ground. Tears of pain mixed with frustration quickly formed. Within seconds, her stalker was standing over her, his own breath ragged.

She turned to face him, shocked to see a familiar face. *No, it can't be. I must be wrong!* As her eyes adjusted to the dark, she peered closer then gasped. "Why? Why were you chasing me?" Anne sat upright and pushed herself up on her feet, only for the man to shove her back onto the ground with a mighty force. She'd never suspected he was so strong.

"Stay there, bitch."

Her fear escalated, threatening to cut off the air to her lungs. She'd known him for years, and he'd never spoken to or treated her so roughly before. "What… what do you want from me?" her voice trembled. *Did I really say that?*

"It's obvious, or are you truly that dense?"

"Why are you talking to me as if I'm a piece of dirt?" Her concern wasn't with what was about to happen to her, only why.

"I'm in charge here, not you. Just shut up for once. You've always liked the sound of your own voice, haven't you?" He bent down and swiped her hard across both cheeks.

She gulped. His rage confused her to the point that she really had no idea what to say or how to act. If she shouted and showed anger, the punishment he was about to mete out might be that much worse. She'd read somewhere that if a woman spoke gently to a man who was intent on attacking her, it would likely baffle him or make him come to his senses and realise that he was making a huge mistake. "Please, why are you doing this? Let's talk this over before you do something that you'll regret."

He leaned down, placing his face inches from hers. Hot breath tickled her cheek. "You talk too much—you always have. Why do you insist on making this worse than is necessary?"

Petrified, Anne decided another tack was called for. After all, she had nothing to lose, except her life. Her gaze met his. "I'll do anything you want, but please don't hurt me. Think of the children. They need me. I need them. I want to be there when they move up into secondary school. When they start dating or consider getting married."

He struck her again, harder than the previous time. The blow took her breath away. "I told you to shut up." He withdrew a knife from his jacket pocket. Its blade glinted with reflected moonlight.

She raised her hands in front of her. "Please, please don't hurt me. For the children's sake, I beg of you."

"Your children will be better off without you. I assure you."

Tears began to cascade down her cheeks, and she brushed them away swiftly with the back of her hand, refusing to show him how broken and weak she had become. "How can you say that? No child should be without their mother to guide them through the early part of their lives. Please, take what you want from me and let me go home to my babies. They need me."

He took a step forward. His gaze never left hers as he towered over her. The knife rose into the air at the same time a blood-curdling scream left her mouth.

Please God, let someone hear me.

She felt the tip of the knife puncture her neck then sink into her chest. Several thrusts later, her body could stand no more, and she fell backwards, smacking her head on the ground. With her children's adorable faces prominent in her mind, she took her final breath.

CHAPTER ONE

Arriving at Wymondham Station, Norfolk, on a sunny June morning, DI Sally Parker greeted her partner, Jack Blackman, with a smile. "Blimey, you look terrible. Dare I ask what's wrong?"

"Nothing a little sleep wouldn't put right."

"Still teething, is she?"

"Yep, and some. How long are we expected to put up with this?" he replied, looking sorry for himself.

"Not so easy the second time around, old man, eh?"

"Less of the 'old man' if you don't mind, boss. I've only just celebrated my forty-second birthday. What the heck was my teenage daughter thinking when she set out to make me a grandfather at the tender age of forty?"

Sally chuckled. "I doubt you came into your daughter's mind when she did the deed. Anyway, the baby should be past that stage any day now, I'm presuming. Not that I know anything about babies and how much it takes to care for one. Give me a puppy to handle any day of the week."

They walked through the entrance, greeted the desk sergeant with a smile and a nod, and continued their conversation on the way up the stairs to the incident room. "The experts in all the books I've read reckon around two. I'm sick to death of not having a full eight hours' kip. It's like someone switched on the 'punish this guy non-stop for two years' button. I'm getting close to snapping."

Sally shrugged. "If things are that bad, then you're going to have to ask Teresa and her boyfriend to find alternative accommodation, matey."

He sighed wearily. "Right, and I can see that going down well with Donna. If anything, she'd rather tell *me* to pack a bag and move out instead of Teresa and her tribe."

Sally smiled and sympathetically rubbed the top of his arm. "Sorry, Bullet," she said, calling him by the nickname he'd brought with him from his time serving in the army. "I wish I could offer you wise words and a solution, but, as usual, I'm *totally* out of my depth on this subject."

"Not your problem, boss. You might have to elbow me during the day to wake me up if I drop off to sleep over the paperwork I have lined up."

Sally raised a finger. "Unless another case has come in overnight, you mean."

"Crap, yeah. that. We've only just completed the last case. It would be nice to have a breather in between."

"Wishful thinking on your part, Jack." Sally made her way over to the vending machine, bought two cups of coffee, and deposited one of them on her partner's desk before she walked into her office. The room felt stuffy, and the warmth of the morning sun covered her desk. She opened the window a fraction then picked up one of the many envelopes lying on her desk. Before she had a chance to tear it open, her landline rang.

"Hello. DI Parker. How may I help?"

"Ah, glad you're at your desk bright and early, Inspector. I should have called you last night, but something cropped up and distracted me."

Sally groaned inwardly. DCI Green was constantly on her back, demanding to be kept informed about cases as they progressed. The man never gave her the room to investigate a case without sneaking a peek over her shoulder. As for praising her and her team when they solved a case, well that was absolutely non-existent. Though she had accepted his ignorance for what it was over the years and it didn't affect the way she conducted her job, the last thing she needed was a call first thing from her DCI. "Good morning, sir. What can I do for you?"

"We have a very important visitor arriving this morning. Chief Constable Stockard, no less."

Sally automatically looked down to assess the suit she was wearing and breathed a sigh of relief. For some reason, she'd possessed the foresight to don her best suit for the day. "Oh, right. Any particular reason why he's coming to see you, sir?"

"It's not *me* he's coming to see, Inspector. It's *you*."

Sally's mouth hung open, and her mind raced at a hundred miles an hour. Her last case whizzed through her brain. *Did I do something wrong? Is he about to reprimand me about a case?* She hadn't stepped out of line, not that she could remember. *What the hell could the chief constable want with me?*

"Parker? Are you still there?"

"Yes, sorry, sir. Me? He's coming all this way to see *me*? May I ask why?"

"You'll find that out when you meet up in my office. He's due here in ten minutes. Leave it five minutes for him to get comfortable, and then come and see us."

Sally gulped down the bile that was tickling her throat. "I'll see you in fifteen minutes, sir." She hung up and stared at the phone for a second or two. "Jack, get in here, quick."

Her concerned partner rushed through the door seconds later. "What? Jesus, the colour has drained from your face. Is it your parents?"

"No. Sit down."

"Crap, is it Donna or one of my kids? Damn, why did I spend ten minutes complaining about them earlier, when—?"

"Hush. If you'll let me get a word in, man. It's nothing like that."

"What's up then? Another case?"

"The truth is, I don't know."

Jack's brow furrowed. Exasperated, he said, "You're not making any sense, boss. If you don't know what's wrong, then why do you look like shit?"

"I've been summoned by the DCI," she replied flatly.

"And? In connection to what?"

"That's just it. I don't have the foggiest idea. I thought you could help me out."

Jack placed a hand over his chest. "Me? How the fu… how can I help? Boss, you're talking in riddles. Just spit it out."

"Green should have rung me last night. Actually, I'm glad he didn't, or I probably would have joined you in the not-sleeping department if he had."

Jack sighed. "You know how annoyed you get when an interviewee goes around in circles about something? I know how that feels now. What's going on?"

"The bloody chief constable is on his way to see me—that's what's frigging going on. To see *me*? Why?"

Jack collapsed into the chair opposite her, tilted his head back to look up at the ceiling, and let out a deafening whistle. "Holy crap. What the effing hell have you done?"

Sally's mouth gaped open for the second time in as many minutes. Recovering, she said angrily, "Me? I haven't done anything. At least, I don't think I have. Can you think of a case I haven't solved by the book lately? Anything along those lines?"

"Nope. Jesus, Sally, this sounds major."

"No shit, Sherlock! I was kind of hoping that you would reassure me—you know, persuade me to put any doubts I had to one side—but I guess I was wrong about that."

"Umm... sorry about that. Just speaking openly, boss."

Sally shook her head, reached for her handbag, and headed for the door. "I might as well make myself look presentable for when they sack me. I'll be in the loo."

Once she was standing in front of the mirror in the ladies' toilet, she opened her handbag, withdrew her mocha-coloured lipstick, and applied it to her thin lips. *Can't think what I've done that warrants me being raked over the coals.* She pulled a comb through her shoulder-length blonde hair, yelping when it snagged on a knot at the end. Her apprehension was teetering on the edge of being deemed out of control. *Stop it! What good is it going to do you to get wound up about this? Que sera, sera!* After one last lingering look at her reflection, she inhaled a large breath to steady her nerves then rushed back to the incident room to dump her bag in the office. Sally retraced her steps through the silent room, aware that Jack had obviously filled in the rest of the team. "Well, wish me luck, guys. I think I'm going to need it."

"Good luck, boss," the team said in unison before she left the room again and began the long, torturous journey up the hallway to the DCI's office. The closer she got to her destination, the weaker her legs became, as if they had turned into jelly. She fought the urge to run back to her office and ring her fiancé, Simon. *Crap, why didn't*

I think to ring him rather than nip to the loo? He would have offered me the comforting words that Jack failed to deliver.

"Hi, DCI Green is expecting me," Sally said to Green's petite secretary, Helen.

"Hello, Inspector. Go right in. They're waiting for you."

Sally gulped a large breath. "That sounds ominous."

Helen gave her a half-smile. "You'll be fine. Go through."

Sally kicked out each leg, trying to boost her circulation before she knocked lightly on the door and poked her head into the room.

"Hello, sirs. You wanted to see me?"

It was obvious she had disrupted their conversation, which made her feel a hundred times worse.

"Ah, there you are, Inspector Parker. Well, come in," DCI Green ordered, remaining seated behind his desk. "You remember Chief Constable Stockard, don't you?"

The chief constable leapt out of his seat and crossed the room to greet her with an outstretched hand and the broadest of grins. "So nice to see you again, Inspector. Join us, please." She noticed his carrot-coloured hair first and wondered if he had a fiery temper to match.

"The pleasure is all mine, sir." She studied the man's green eyes, searching for some kind of insight as to why she'd been summoned. She found nothing but reassurance within their depths. The pair of them walked towards the DCI's desk and sat down. Sally tried to read the DCI, but even after working under him for five years or more, she found him a hard man to judge.

"There's no need for you to look so terrified, Inspector," Green said, reclining in his chair a little.

"There isn't, sir?"

The chief constable swivelled ninety degrees in his seat, his knees barely four inches from her left leg. "Let me explain, Mike. Do you mind if I call you Sally? Can't stand all this pomp and formality in my presence."

Sally smiled and nodded, appreciating the way he was trying to put her at ease. "Not at all, sir."

"Good. Then I'll begin. We've been watching you over the past few months."

When the chief constable paused, she didn't know whether to reply or to keep quiet. Luckily, he broke the silence before the situation became awkward and continued his explanation.

He beamed, reminiscent of a small child full of expectation on Christmas morning. "I like what you do, Sally, or should I say *we* like what you do? You're exceptional in your role. That last big case you solved—the one regarding the death of the serving police officer's wife—that was just sublime. Not only that, but the other cases you've solved over the past year or two have also been superb. I seem to recall that you even had to work alongside another force on one of those cases?"

"Yes, sir. It was an absolute pleasure working alongside Lorne Warner from the Met in London, though, sir. She's a dear friend of mine and has taught me so much over the years. It's always difficult taking on the role of an inspector and being a female, to boot. Her guidance has been invaluable to me."

"Nonsense, you're doing yourself an injustice. You're a very strong woman, especially since that debacle with that warped husband of yours. I'm going to quickly pass over that. I just wanted you to know that I'm aware of that particular period in your life. My admiration for you exploded when you dug deep into your resolve and came out on top. To display such character the way you did when you went on to arrest the bast… brute, well, I have to applaud your tenacity on that front."

Sally had very little control of the tears misting her eyes during his speech. "Thank you, sir. That means a lot."

"Okay, I digress. As I was saying, we've kept a close eye on you for a while. I've been asking Mike to report back to me every time you've solved one of your tougher cases. You're tenacious and never give up. I wish the rest of my force had half the drive and determination you have. We'd be at the top of the chart for arrests in the whole of the UK. I'm waffling, I know. Have patience with me. I'm rarely placed in such a position, and I feel it's just as important to praise someone's excellent policing skills as it is to tear an officer off for cocking up, shall we say."

"Thank you, sir. Your words of praise mean a great deal to me," Sally said, not letting the opportunity to have a dig at Green slip by.

"Credit where it's due—that's my motto. Anyway, Mike and I have been discussing you at great length over the past few months. An opportunity has arisen that stems from the last case you solved, the cold-case. You're aware—of course you are—you're the one who discovered the fact that the leading investigator on that case failed miserably to carry out his duties correctly. You're also aware that the same officer arrested and convicted over a hundred criminals in his time with this force. The powers that be have decided that those convictions need to be scrutinised and dealt with appropriately. In other words, we'd like you to head up a new cold-case team." His eyes lit up with excitement as he awaited her response.

Sally's gaze darted between DCI Green and the chief constable. "You've caught me off-guard, sir. I just don't know what to say."

"It's simple. One word. Yes. It needn't be a permanent role. We're probably talking maximum of a year or slightly more than that, at the end of which, you would return to the post you have now."

"But who will take over the role I have now, sir?"

"No one. This is the only area in the country where it appears the crime rate is actually decreasing. You know how these things work, Sally—the ones dealing with statistics at head office will probably suggest job cuts in this area pretty soon anyway. Look at it this way: all you'll be doing is safeguarding your future."

"Okay, sir. In that case, what about my team? After all, I'm nothing without them. They do most of the legwork for me. They're the ones who have succeeded in making me look good in your eyes."

"I don't believe that for an instant, Sally. Mike and I have discussed this at length, and we're not averse to you remaining with the team in this new capacity. Do you think your fellow colleagues would be willing to go along with this opportunity?"

"We're a solid team, sir. I'm sure they'd jump at the chance to correct any unjust convictions, in light of them possibly losing their jobs if they don't agree. Can I have a word with the team before I accept the role on behalf of everyone else?"

"Of course you can, with these words of endorsement ringing in your ear, Sally. There is no one out there better suited to this valuable role than you. No one that DCI Green and I could trust to investigate these crimes as thoroughly as you and your team. There's no *I* in *team,* as I understand. Can you give us an answer by the end of the week?"

"How about by the end of the day, sir? DCI Green is aware of how incensed I was when I uncovered the truth of how Falkirk's policing skills—or lack of them, should I say—had convicted so many people. It grieves me to think that some of those people who protested their innocence might have been subjected to up to fifteen years in prison. That breaks my heart in two. I've never knowingly convicted any criminal if there has been an ounce of doubt about their conviction."

"I understand entirely. Which is why Mike and I feel you're the right person to take on this challenge. The sooner we get your decision, the better, so the end of the day would be just perfect. But please, the last thing I want you to feel is that you *have* to take on this new role. DCI Green and I will fight tooth and nail to keep you and your team in jobs, should my premonition become a reality in the future."

"I appreciate that, sir. I truly do. Will that be all?"

"For now. Thank you for taking the time out of your busy schedule to meet with me."

"It was an honour, sir. Shall I give the result of my consideration to DCI Green?"

"Yes, do that, then Mike can ring me straight away. Think long and hard, Inspector. You'll have our backing either way."

"That's reassuring to hear, sir." Sally stood up, extended her hand, and smiled as the chief constable also rose to his feet and walked her to the door.

"Goodbye, Sally."

Sally walked out of the room and closed the door behind her. She leaned against the wall and expelled a large breath.

"That bad, eh?" Helen asked, amused.

"No, not really. I think I worked myself up into a state before I got in there. Thought they were going to sack me."

"Never! Not you, Inspector!"

Sally pushed away from the wall and crossed the room. "I'm glad so many people have such confidence in my abilities. Wish I felt the same way. See you later."

She felt like kicking her heels together in the air like the comedian Eric Morecombe used to do in some of his sketches with Ernie Wise, but reconsidered when she pictured herself lying in a twisted heap on the floor if the stunt went wrong. Sally returned to the incident room. When she pushed open the door, a sea of concerned faces turned to look at her. It was then that she decided to wind her colleagues up. She stormed past them and began banging the drawers to her filing cabinet. Before long, Jack appeared in the doorway.

He cleared his throat. "Everything all right, boss?"

"Do I look all right, Jack?"

He shrank back. "Sorry I asked."

Sally burst into laughter. It really wasn't in her to mess with her team's heads. "I'm joking. Call the team together and get me a coffee, will you?"

Jack tutted and left the room. She heard him cussing her just before he shouted to the team.

Sally picked up the phone and dialled a number. "Hi, is Simon available?"

"He's not. Sorry, he's just started a PM," one of the female lab assistants at the mortuary replied.

"Never mind. I'll call back later. If you could, tell him Sally called, thanks."

"I'll do that for you."

Sally hung up and stepped over to gaze out the window at the car park. There were no real views to see in this part of Norfolk. The area was as flat as a punctured tyre. But her love for the area never wavered. She was disappointed she wouldn't be able to share the exciting news with her fiancé before the rest of the team. *Never mind, a few hours aren't going to make that much difference.* She sighed. There had been a time when her parents would have been her first port of call; now it was Simon who dominated her thoughts. *But isn't that the way it should be?*

She would ring Simon first then call her parents after. She knew exactly how her mum and dad were going to react. They had always been so proud of her achievements—from the first day she'd marched through the gates of the police training college at Hendon, in fact.

Smiling, Sally walked back into the incident room to find the team gathered around the whiteboard. She walked towards the board, pulled out a nearby chair, and took a sip of coffee from the paper cup Jack had placed on the desk.

"As you know, I've just had a meeting with the DCI and the chief constable. I was a tad nervous, and Jack will attest to that. However, I needn't have been. The thing is, the chief constable handed me an opportunity."

"Crap, you're not talking about a promotion?" Jack interrupted quickly. "You're leaving us?"

"No, Jack, I haven't been offered a promotion. I wouldn't leave you guys, anyway. Actually, what was discussed in the DCI's office concerns you, too."

"Me? What the heck?"

"Calm down. Don't look so worried. Let me rephrase that: this concerns *all* of you." Sally paused, casting her eyes around the room. She recognised expressions of interest and curiosity staring back at her. "Seriously, I think this is a huge opportunity for all of us. When the chief constable first mentioned it, I wanted to run for the hills. Good job there aren't any around here. But you know what? The more the idea settled in my mind, the more excited I became about it."

"Are you actually going to tell us what this 'amazing opportunity' is, boss, or do you intend on keeping it to yourself?"

"You're an impatient sod at times, Jack Blackman."

"It's taken you long enough to figure that out, boss."

"Four long years," she teased. "Anyway, as I was saying before I was rudely interrupted by my impatient partner, I think this opportunity is something we should really think long and hard about going forward. Okay, I suppose the idea has come about because of a recent case we solved and what we uncovered concerning that case."

"Do you have to keep going around in circles? Can you not just tell us what the heck you're getting at?"

Sally shook her head, not in disgust at his continuous interruptions but more out of amusement. "All right, you win. I've been asked to head up a cold-case team." She scanned the room, watching her team's reactions to the news, until her gaze came to a halt on Jack. "The chief said that I could choose my own team. I'm asking you guys if you want to join me in this venture."

"Is this because of the Aisha Thomas case?" Joanna Tryst, a bright young detective constable, asked.

"You've got it, Joanna. What do you reckon?"

"I enjoyed doing the research on that case, I must admit."

"I sense a *but* in your tone. Come on, we need to speak frankly about this; it's got to be a team decision."

Joanna smiled. "No *but* from me, boss. I'd relish the challenge. Will we be asked to go through all of that idiot Falkirk's convictions?"

"That's what I took from the meeting, Joanna. I hate the thought of all those people sitting in prison if they're innocent."

"Me, too. Then it's a big fat yes from me."

Sally's gaze drifted to thirty-year-old, Detective Constable Jordan Reid, another keen member of her team, whom she respected. "Jordan, what say you on this one?"

"I'm up for it, boss. It's a no-brainer after working the Thomas case. You do realise that some of the convictions will be tough to overturn if they were wrong, though, don't you? We were lucky with the Thomas case, being able to trace all the witnesses surrounding that one, but it won't always be that simple."

"You're right to raise that point, Jordan. Thanks for the feedback. Glad you'd be up for it, all the same."

"You know me, boss. I love a challenge."

"How about you, Stuart? What's your take on this?"

One of the quieter members, Detective Constable Stuart McBain, had been with the team as long as Jack. Sally sometimes had trouble understanding the broad Scot, who was a lot broader than her fiancé at times, but she still loved listening to his accent.

"I'm as easy as a Sunday morning. Happy to go with the flow. Whatever is good for the team."

"Thanks, Stuart, that's good to know." That left only one member of her team to consult. "Jack? How do things stand with you?"

Jack sat back in his chair and folded his muscular arms over his taut chest. Since leaving the army, he'd tried to stick with his rigorous fitness regimen to maintain his muscular build. He gave people the impression he was a real bruiser, but inside, he had a heart of gold and was a genuine softy. Judging by the frown contorting his features, Sally doubted he was thinking gooey, mushy thoughts, though.

"It's like this: while I agree in principle, what I'd really like to know is, what's the alternative?"

Sally bit the inside of her mouth. Did she tell the team or not? She'd never kept anything from them before. Believed in complete transparency at work, especially involving her team. Inhaling a large breath, she replied, "I'm not sure, to be honest with you, Jack. You know as well as I do that the government is always expecting the police force to make cuts where possible. You're also aware of the crime rates decreasing in this area. To me, that can only mean one thing. That's why I believe we should leap at the chance to set up this new team. However, I can't force you to join me and the others. That decision will be yours to make."

"It's a tough one. I know we're up against things manpower-wise, but why a cold-case team?"

Sally hitched her shoulders. "Perhaps someone from the government has suggested it to someone high up in the force, thinking that if some of the innocent people have their convictions squashed, it will alleviate the overcrowding in prison. I'm in the dark as much as you about that, partner."

"It just seems a little suspect to me. That's all."

"Jack, if you're in any doubt about this, then you should take time out to consider your choices. I'm not here to persuade you all to transfer with me. That choice is down to you guys. I would state that I'd be delighted if you did agree to join us, though. I'd be lost without my long-standing partner by my side."

"That's it, plant the guilt trip on me."

Sally laughed. "I'm doing nothing of the sort." She could hear the phone in her office ringing. "I need to answer that. Think over what I've said for a few minutes. Voice any doubts you have with the rest of the team, see if they can sway your decision," she shouted as she rushed out of the room to answer the call. She threw herself in the chair behind her desk. "DI Parker. How can I help?"

"That's one thing we haven't discussed yet. Whether you intend taking on my name after we've tied the knot."

Sally leaned back in her chair and smiled the second she recognised her fiancé's sexy voice. "Well hello, you. Blimey, I haven't given that much thought. Mind you, I suppose I'm desperate to get rid of Darryl's name, so I think you should take that as a definite maybe."

"Only a definite maybe? Let's try it out: DI Sally Bracknall. It sounds far more sophisticated to me," Simon stated, sounding triumphant.

"Hmm… I see one problem with that. My partner's name is Blackman. Let me just try this out: 'Hi, I'm DI Sally Bracknall, and this is my partner, DS Jack Blackman.' We could run into difficulties."

"Nonsense, they're not the same at all. I hope you're not putting obstacles in the way, young lady?"

Sally cringed every time he called her that, mainly because it reminded her of the thirteen-year age gap between them. Other times, that insignificant fact didn't affect her at all. "I wouldn't dream of it. How did the PM go?"

"The usual. Why did you ring so early? Anything wrong?"

"No, nothing. I wanted to run something past you, really."

"Personal or work?"

"Work, but I suppose it will also impact on my personal life."

"Blimey! Let's hear it."

"I was called into the DCI's office this morning, only to find that the chief constable was there to see me."

Simon whistled. "Wow, are you in trouble?"

"That was my first thought, but he was quick to dismiss that. They've offered me an opportunity to start up a new department."

"Sounds intriguing. Doing what exactly?"

"Delving into cold-cases on a full-time basis."

"I see. And how do you feel about that, Sal?"

"At first, I was a little apprehensive, but then my conscience pricked and reminded me how outraged I felt when I tackled the last case we worked on. I'm quite excited by the prospect now."

"What will happen to your team? Will another DI be drafted in to take over your role?"

"I'm just discussing that with my team now. Word is that my team as it stands will be disbanded." Sally looked up to see Jack standing in the doorway, his jaw dropped open. "Sorry, Simon, something has come up. I have to go. I'll ring you later, love."

Before her fiancé could reply, she hung up the phone and motioned for Jack to sit down. "Jack, everything all right?" she asked, hoping against hope that he hadn't heard her conversation but knowing full well that he had.

Her partner fell into the chair, shaking his head in disbelief. "Why? Why couldn't you have told the team that?"

"That's not fair, Jack. I would have told you all eventually. I was testing the ground. Seeing what you all thought about the idea first. Please don't be angry with me."

"I'm not angry—disappointed, yes, especially when you've always prided yourself on not keeping secrets from us regarding the job."

"I know. Please believe me, I had every intention of telling you all. I promise."

"So, what you're saying is either we agree to change over to the cold-case department, or we lose our jobs? Have I summed that up accurately enough?"

"There's nothing definite in that statement, Jack. What we're talking about is a high probability. Can I ask what your objection would be, if we, as a team decide to go down that route?"

He sighed heavily. "I can't give you a definitive answer to that, boss. It just doesn't sit right with me for some reason. I can't help wondering if the same passion would be there raking over old evidence and clues."

Sally shook her head. "I really don't see what the difference is, Jack, whether the evidence is old or new. All I can say is I believe, from a personal perspective that I had the same desire, passion and determination to solve the Thomas case as I attributed to any other case I've solved over the years."

"I get that. But I still have a niggling doubt that is going to be hard to shift."

"Then how long do you need to consider the proposal?"

"How long are you prepared to give me?"

"Until the end of the day. That's when the chief is expecting my answer. Look, why don't you use my office to ring Donna, discuss all your concerns with her? Perhaps she'll be able to guide you in the right direction."

"I wouldn't mind, thanks. I'm sorry to have such a downer on this."

Sally pushed back her chair and moved towards the door. As she passed, she squeezed her partner's shoulder. "I need you to be behind this one hundred percent, Jack. I can't carry people or argue with them when the need to solve the case will be even greater than normal. We'll be trying our hardest to get innocent people released from prison."

"Maybe that's where the dilemma is for me. Perhaps at the back of my mind, I'm deliberating whether those people are truly innocent or not. What if we release someone and they go on to commit a similar crime, or a more heinous one after listening to the psychos regaling their gruesome crimes on the inside? How the hell will I be able to live with myself then?"

"We could say that about every crime we solve. If there is an ounce of doubt that the person we're fighting for carried out the crime, then that's when we stop the investigation. Nothing is set in stone on this, I promise. Your problem is that you're a compassionate human being. There aren't many left in this vile, twisted world of ours, so I'd hate for you to alter. Talk things over with Donna, and we'll thrash out any other concerns you have afterwards, okay?"

"Thanks for understanding, Sally."

She winked at him and left the room. She went around the rest of her team to see if they had any lingering doubts. They all seemed really excited at the prospect of having a new challenge to look forward to. When she arrived at Joanna's desk, Joanna leaned forward and whispered, "So, what happens if we don't agree, boss?"

Sally smiled. Joanna had always been bright, and she reminded Sally of herself at times. The young constable would go far if she pushed herself hard enough. "I wasn't told that, Joanna. I think we can guess, though, right? I'm having a hard time convincing Jack at the moment. He's in there running it past Donna now."

"Why the hesitation?"

"He can't put his finger on it. Maybe there's more to it than he's letting on. He hasn't had the easiest of times at home lately, what with looking after his granddaughter and all that entails, such as lack of sleep on a regular basis."

"It must be hard. Can't see me having kids because of that very thing. I enjoy my sleep too much."

"I'm inclined to agree with you, although Simon and I have yet to broach the subject about having kids. I'll certainly do my best to dissuade him. Talking of which, I better ring him back." Sally moved to the nearby desk and rang the mortuary.

Simon picked up the phone as soon as it started to ring at his end.

"Hi, it's me. Sorry I had to end the call abruptly; a minor incident occurred."

"No problem. You've just caught me about to start another PM. Why don't we go out to our favourite restaurant tonight for dinner?"

"Deal. Okay, see you later." Sally hung up and smiled dreamily out the window. She was lucky to have Simon in her life. He was the only man who truly understood her and the importance of her work, being in a similar field. He had never once asked her to do anything that she didn't want to do in their downtime, unlike Darryl. Her ex had constantly planned most of their time off together, not giving her the option to object to a venture or to utter the words that she was tired and needed a break. The two men were extreme opposites in many respects, thankfully. She could always talk to Simon and have intelligent conversations about police—or pathology—related subjects. Darryl had never shown a molecule of interest in her work at all. Being a pilot, he was used to having a bunch of adoring air hostesses hanging off his every word and flirting with him every second of the day.

She shook the damaging thoughts from her head. She'd moved on with her life and was blissfully happy with her new beau while her ex was still confined to a prison cell for raping her. It had taken all her strength to arrest Darryl for the crime, but she'd had Jack by her side when she'd done that. She prayed he would be by her side going forward, as well.

Jack reappeared in the doorway and motioned for her to join him. He had a sheepish look on his face. Her stomach churned into knots as she walked towards him. Sally closed the door behind her.

"What did Donna have to say?" she asked, dropping into her chair.

"She listened to my apprehensions and raised some valid points that I hadn't thought about." He held his hand up in front of him when she opened her mouth to speak. "I'm not divulging what they are."

"Okay. So where do we go from here? Are you with me—us—or not?" She struggled to read the expression that clouded his features, then worried, she prompted, "Jack?"

Another huge sigh expanded his chest. "Go on then. What have I got to lose?"

Relieved, Sally picked up her pen and threw it at him. "You bugger. You had me worried there for a moment. I'd be lost without you by my side."

"Let me rephrase that for you: the thought of having to mould another partner into my way of doing things was crucifying me."

Sally sniggered. "You know me too well. Maybe the transparency issue needs adapting a little before we continue our working relationship."

"Nah, you'll never change, and I wouldn't want you to. I love working with you and the rest of the team. I'm sorry for my indecisiveness. It doesn't mean to say I won't have a few doubts going forward."

She nodded. "I can understand that. If I'm honest, I think we'll all have those in the coming months. We need to voice our concerns openly and be honest with each other, all right? We've always done that in the past, so there should be no reason to change that in the future."

"Okay, I'm in. So, what next? Do we have a new case to get us started?"

"One thing at a time. I've just spoken to the rest of the gang. They're confident they want to do this. Now that you're on the same page, I'll contact the chief constable and get the ball rolling. He'll probably tell us to wrap up any cases we're working on over the next few days and start trawling through the cold-cases then, I suspect. Go, get back to work and make me a proud DI once more."

She watched Jack leave her office, his shoulders no longer slumped in dejection, then she picked up the phone and took a few deep breaths to steady her nerves before she rang the chief constable on his personal line.

"Hello, sir. It's DI Sally Parker."

"Ah, the inspector calls. I take it you're calling to accept the position offered you earlier?"

"Well, in a nutshell, yes. I've discussed it with my team, and they'd be honoured to be considered for the opportunity, sir. *We'd* be honoured. I want to thank you for thinking of us."

"Not at all. Given your experience dealing with such matters, it was a foregone conclusion that I should ask you."

"Can I ask when this is likely to take place, sir?"

"Now that you've accepted, I have a few such cases sitting on my desk at present. Give me until tomorrow morning to organise things a little better, and I'll get back to you. How's that?"

"It sounds like a good plan to me, sir. We'll crack on with tying up any loose ends to our ongoing cases today then. Thank you again for showing your faith in me, sir."

"No—thank *you* for doing such an outstanding job. It's my privilege to reward such tenacity and determination. I'll speak to you in the morning."

"Thank you, sir. That means a lot to me. Goodbye."

Sally sat back, thinking she was having the most satisfying day so far in her police career. To have the backing of a high-ranking commanding officer, when she had battled so much over the years in a male-dominated environment, was a huge achievement—definitely something she would look forward to celebrating with Simon later.

CHAPTER TWO

On the drive into work the following morning, Sally reflected on the wonderful evening she had spent with Simon the previous night. When he'd looked at her across the table, her heart had fluttered. His eyes were full of admiration and pride about the job offer, something she'd never witnessed in any of her other relationships. *Why couldn't I have met him years ago? Why did we both have to waste so many years apart? Hold your horses, lady. Things might change significantly when he places a wedding ring on my finger—just like it did when I married Darryl.*

Another part of her argued, *don't be silly! They're poles apart.*

She listened in amusement as her inner voices argued with each other. Simon had treated her like royalty, the way he always had. He'd also insisted on dropping by her parents' house on the way home from the restaurant to share the news with them in the flesh. Although her father and Simon soon began discussing the joint project they were embarking on in their property-developing business.

Sally's mum had squeezed her so hard that when she got undressed and ready for bed, Simon noticed bruises on her arms, but it was worth it. To see both her parents with huge smiles on their faces, proud of her work achievements, instead of wrinkles of worry on their foreheads, meant a great deal to her. They'd been through the mire over the last few years, what with the evil neighbours opposite making their lives hell twenty-four-seven before the council had finally moved them on to a different house. Then her father had been forced into bankruptcy after one of his clients left the country without paying for the work he'd completed. All the turmoil had led to Sally moving back home and taking over the mortgage payments for her parents. She was still paying it today, even though she'd recently moved in to Simon's beautiful home. He'd insisted that she shouldn't contribute to his bills, that it wasn't a condition when she had accepted his invitation. She even got to have Dex, her golden

Labrador, stay with them at the weekend. Yes, Simon truly was one in a million and a real keeper.

Joanna and Jack were already at their desks when she walked into the incident room. "Morning, you two. Everything all right?"

"Just tying up a few loose ends, boss," Joanna replied.

"Anyone for coffee? I'm buying."

"No, you won't. I'll get these. Call it an apology for doubting your sanity yesterday," Jack insisted, leaving his chair and walking over to pop a couple of coins in the vending machine.

"That's news to me." Sally chuckled. She heard her phone ringing in her office and sprinted the short distance to answer it. "DI Parker, can I help?"

"Ah, Inspector. DCI Green here. Care to join me in my office? I have something for you."

"Morning, sir. I'll be right there." Sally shot out of the office. "Keep mine to one side, I've been summoned. Be right back." She rushed along the corridor and into the DCI's outer office. His secretary, Helen, smiled at her. Not any ordinary smile—it was a smile that said she knew what was going on and found it highly amusing.

"Go straight in, Inspector."

"Hmm... sounds ominous. Can I have a hint of what awaits me? Good or bad?"

"You'll find out soon enough."

"Is he alone?"

"Sort of. Go through and see for yourself."

Sally rolled her eyes. "Gee, thanks for your help."

Helen laughed, and Sally knocked on the door and pushed it open when she heard Green beckon her. Her eyes, along with her chin, nearly hit the floor when she spotted the boxes.

"Morning, sir," she said once she'd recovered from the surprise.

"Good morning, Inspector. You might need a hand shifting those."

Sally stepped towards the twenty or so archive boxes lining the far side of his office and shook her head. "Is this all for me and my team?"

"Yes. That lot should keep you busy for a day or two, right?"

She'd never seen the DCI look so amused before. When he smiled, he bared almost-straight, brilliant-white teeth, making him look kind of handsome. "Day or two? You jest, of course. I think it'll be more like a year or two, looking at this lot. These are all Falkirk's cases, I take it?"

"Every last one of them. No doubt you'll be able to deal with some of them briskly—i.e. if the sentence has already been spent or the convicted person has died during their stay in prison—whilst others will need you to dig deep between the pages. Just do your best. Let me know which case you'll be dealing with first."

"What? I have to wade through them all before I decide which case needs my attention first? The chief constable said he had a couple sitting on his desk he felt were urgent. Any idea what they are, sir?"

"Nope, I think he was pulling your leg. They all need to be reinvestigated, Inspector. There's a spreadsheet on top there with a brief summary of all the cases. Cast your eyes over that first and then decide. That would be my suggestion. Can you get them removed from my office within the next hour or two? I'm a tad anal when it comes to my office being littered with things not concerning me directly."

Sally just stared at him. *How ridiculous!* Because he was her superior, any of the cases connected to her would indeed be something to do with him farther down the line. "Yes, sir. I'll get the boys to shift them ASAP." She left the office and let out a huge breath once she'd closed the door.

Helen chuckled. "Nice situation to be handed first thing in the morning, eh?"

"It's all right for you to laugh. Crap, how am I going to explain this lot to my team? They're going to wonder what they've let themselves in for by agreeing to transfer to the cold-case team, and they're not the only ones. Jesus, what have I done?" She hit her temple with the heel of her hand.

Helen placed a hand over her mouth to prevent herself from laughing. "Sorry, wish I could help, Sally. I think you're going to need dozens of pairs of hands to help you with that lot. Maybe they have a trolley downstairs you can use."

"I'll nip down and check. I'm guessing that it's still going to take Jack and a couple of others all morning to collect them." She pointed over her shoulder and whispered, "That'll piss Green off. He's laughing about it now. I bet he'll be tearing his hair out in a few hours."

"I think you're possibly right about that. Try not to make him too upset. I'll be the one taking the brunt of his frustrations."

Sally smiled. "Really? Now there's a thought. That'll teach you to laugh at my predicament."

"Touché, Sally."

After going downstairs, she returned to the incident room with the trolley to find the rest of the team had arrived and were all sitting at their desks.

"Jack, Jordan and Stuart, can you drop what you're doing and go to DCI Green's office, please? He needs a hand shifting a few things."

Jack frowned. "From us? What aren't you telling us, boss?"

"Is this my coffee? Thanks for that, Jack. I'll be in my office, dealing with the morning post, if anyone wants me. Oh, and the trolley will come in handy, so take that with you." She rushed into her office without another glance in her team's direction, suppressing the laughter that was itching to break free.

Ten minutes later, Jack entered her room, his face like thunder. "You're kidding me, right?"

Sally let out a full belly laugh. "Nope. I bet you're regretting your decision now, aren't you?"

He shook his head in disgust. "And some. Where are we going to put it all?"

"It's going to take us a good week or so to sort through it all. We'll need everything to hand. Pile it up at one end of the room. I'll quickly sort this lot and join you as soon as I can."

"Yeah, right. Take your time. I think we'll be ferrying the files all morning."

Sally chewed her lip. "Sorry, matey."

"I have a feeling we're all going to regret our decision if that lot is anything to go by."

"Don't be such a sourpuss. According to Green, we should be able to give most of the cases a cursory glance. Let me get this paperwork out of the way. I'll be with you in say half an hour."

"The boys and I will still be carting the files back to the office, but feel free to start going through the files without us."

"Joanna and I will do just that. I'm never one to pass the buck, Jack. You know that."

"Yeah, we'll see." He turned and walked out of the office, leaving Sally wondering if she had indeed forced her team into a situation that could see them drowning in paperwork for years to come.

Over the next half an hour, the men wheeled boxes into the incident room, huffing and puffing and shouting the odd curse word. For once, Sally was glad to take refuge in her office to deal with her nightmarish paperwork. Thirty minutes whizzed past, then she was forced to confront the torrent of abuse, if only in the form of death stares, coming her way when she re-joined her team.

Jack entered the incident room, carrying another heavy file. Even for a fit, walking bag of muscles, he was clearly getting a good workout from shifting the boxes. Sweat on his brow was coursing down the side of his face. "Jack, take a break. There's no need to strain yourselves getting them all moved in one go. I'm sure Green doesn't expect that from you guys."

"You might want to tell that to his face. He looks daggers at us every time we enter his office."

"Sod him. I'm ordering you to take a break." Sally stepped into his path, preventing him from going back to Green's office.

"All right, you win. I'll take five when the boys return—we all will." He breathlessly slumped into his chair. "Thank God we've got that trolley. We'd be on our knees by now, otherwise."

Sally winked and pointed to her head. "Used my brains on this one, partner. I couldn't see you boys struggle. I knew the desk sergeant had one tucked away downstairs."

"Smartarse," he mumbled under his breath, giving her the impression that he wouldn't have thought about tracking one down if she'd left him in charge of shifting the files.

Any other inspector would have taken him to task over the name-calling, but Sally was thrilled about the banter they shared between them as a group. That was why the team got on so well and achieved so much.

Picking up the spreadsheet, Sally ran her finger down the cases. "That bloody Falkirk has a lot to answer for. What an idiot he was. Still, his ineptness has put his pension in jeopardy in the process. Let's hope he didn't screw up every case he touched. Joanna, you and I will search through the database, check off all those found guilty, see if their time in prison has been spent yet or not. These files go back fifteen years from what I can see. I'm presuming that most of the people he convicted will have had their sentences fulfilled by now, and they'll be walking the streets again. If that's the case then the pile will be whittled down a fair bit from the outset. Then there will no doubt be cases where the prisoner has perhaps died during his or her time in prison. That'll mean there are less to wade through. Okay, let's get cracking and leave the boys to finish transporting the rest of the files." She flashed Jack a smile. Her partner shook his head and marched towards the exit, dragging the trolley behind him.

"You're such a wind-up merchant, boss," Joanna said, fighting the urge to laugh.

Sally placed a hand over her chest. "*Moi?* I don't think so. Have you felt the weight of one of these files?" She stood over an archive file and tried to lift it. She managed to raise it two inches off the floor before she dropped it again. "They weigh a bloody tonne. Still, Jack and the boys can look on the bright side."

"There's a bright side?" Joanna asked, perplexed.

"Yeah, just think how much money and time I've just saved them by skipping a gym session."

Joanna laughed.

Within seconds, Jack came back into the room, wheeling another two boxes.

"A few more trips should have you sorted." Sally beamed at him.

Jack ignored her smug smile and hoisted the boxes on top of the others already in situ. "Only eight more to fetch."

~ ~ ~

Sally settled down at the spare computer beside Joanna, and between them, they rattled through the cases, placing either a *D* for 'dead' or an *A* for 'alive' next to each of the names. Then there was a matter of tallying up the files inside the archive boxes with the list and putting each of the files in the appropriate pile.

The whole process took them the rest of the day to accomplish.

Wearily, Sally stretched out the knots in her back and announced, "Right, why don't we all go home and get a good night's rest and begin in earnest on this lot in the morning?"

The team agreed to the proposition and quickly dispersed. Only Jack remained behind. By the look on his face, she sensed she was in for an earbashing. "All right, let's hear it."

Jack perched on the desk beside her. "Hear what?"

"You're obviously pissed off about something, Jack."

"Nah, what's the point?" He nodded his head towards the archive boxes. "Looks like we've got enough cases to see us through to our retirement."

"Don't be daft. Joanna and I have already highlighted some of the cases that can be returned to the storage unit."

"Great, and who's going to be granted that chore?"

"Why are you being such a grouch about this, Jack? You had the option to opt out if the job didn't appeal to you."

"I know. Maybe it's just me wondering if I've done the right thing after all. Looking at that lot, we're sure going to have our work cut out for us. You know how much I hate the paperwork side of things. Isn't that what looking into cold-cases is mostly going to be about?"

Sally sighed. "Not necessarily. Is that what this is all about?"

Jack frowned. "What?"

"The paperwork? Is that why you're still having lingering doubts? I need you to be fully onboard with this, partner, or it just isn't going to work. I feel as though you're putting unnecessary obstacles in the way."

He shrugged. "Maybe I am. I'm trying to summon up some enthusiasm but…"

Sally felt her frustration building. She stood up and walked into her office to collect her coat and handbag. When she returned, she stopped in front of Jack and locked gazes with him. "Think things over properly tonight and let me know your decision in the morning, all right? Think of the job security aspect before you rule it out, Jack, for Donna and the girls' sake."

His head dipped, and he mumbled, "Okay, sorry to be a pain, Sally."

"You haven't been, yet. But if you accept the job and begin to doubt whether you're up to the task or not, then that is going to really piss me off, matey. If I were in your shoes I'd be thinking more along the lines of seeing how I go for a month or so, and jack it in—excuse the pun—if I can't get my head around the new regime. You need to decide quickly, though, mate. I haven't got time to waste on this—you've seen the massive task ahead of us."

They left the incident room, descended the stairs, and left the building in silence. "We'll talk tomorrow."

"Okay. Have a good evening."

"You, too. Think long and hard about your future—and for goodness' sake, make the right decision for yourself, Jack. Don't do it for me."

Sally jumped inside her car. Watching her dejected partner walk away, she had a sinking feeling that he would show up the next day with a resignation letter in hand.

When she arrived home, in spite of Simon's best efforts to make her laugh, she found herself distracted and worried about what the morning would bring.

"Want to talk it over?" Simon asked, sidling up to her on the large leather couch.

"Not really. I don't think it would help. It's in Jack's hands now."

"I'm here if you need to vent, you know that. Maybe he'll reconsider his options overnight and surprise you with his decision in the morning."

"Either way, I think tomorrow is going to be a bugger of a day. I need a cuddle."

Simon happily obliged. He hooked an arm over her shoulder and pulled her close. She felt his lips touch her forehead and travel down her face until he grazed her lips gently with his own. She moaned softly as his kisses carried her off to a deserted island, where only two inhabitants existed. All the stress of the day dispersed instantly.

That was what she loved about this man: his ability to put things right immediately. Though he was a doctor, constantly dealing with corpses, his skill of casting a healing spell over her only reinforced her understanding of what a truly compassionate man he was.

Their passion escalated, and it wasn't long before she was unravelling herself from his arms. She leapt out of the chair and held out her hand to him. He slipped his hand into hers and allowed her to lead him up the stairs to bed.

CHAPTER THREE

Despite listening to Simon's assurances over breakfast, Sally drove into work with her nerves taut. She glanced around the car park, searching for Jack's car. He hadn't arrived yet, and she wasn't sure if that was a good or a bad sign. It would at least give her a chance to get an extra coffee down her neck before meeting with him.

A full ten minutes passed before Jack sauntered into work. His demeanour came with a warning that constricted her stomach muscles until they became painful.

"Morning, boss. Can I see you in your office?"

Sally smiled and turned on her heel, expecting him to follow her. She settled in her chair and waited as he closed the door and sank into the chair opposite. "Thought long and hard overnight, have you?"

He pulled the skin around his right eye down. "Yep, I guess the bloodshot eyes are a bit of a giveaway."

Sally was at a loss for what to say next. She could tell what was coming, and she didn't have a clue how to prevent it. "And your decision is?"

He shook his head. "I can't do it, boss. I thought I could handle it yesterday, but the more the day progressed, the more the proposition refused to sit well with me."

Unexpected tears clouded Sally's vision. She coughed to clear the lump in her throat. "And what about Donna? What does she have to say about this, Jack?"

He shrugged. "She's okay about it. Says that I have to do what feels right for me, and I'm sorry—this just doesn't feel right."

"So, where do we go from here? Do you want me to have a word with DCI Green?"

"If you wouldn't mind. If I can get a transfer, that would be the icing on the cake. I really don't want to leave the force after the amount of time I've invested in it. I just can't handle looking into cold-cases for the reasons I stated yesterday. I hope you understand and my decision won't damage our friendship in any way."

"It won't, and I totally understand. You might have to work with us for a week or two until an alternative position arises. Will that be okay with you?"

"Of course. I'm sorry to let you down, Sally."

"You haven't let me down. The truth is, none of us know how this new set-up is going to pan out. We might all be joining you in another team soon—you never know."

"I doubt it. Once something sparks an idea with you, you usually see it through to its conclusion. You'll make this work, with or without my input. You still have an excellent team around you. The four of you will crack those cases wide open. To be honest, I'd probably be surplus to requirements."

"How do you make that one out?"

"Will you really need a partner going forward?"

"I hadn't given it much thought. I suppose I will. Never mind. One of the other members will have to suffice. Seriously, Jack, I'm going to miss having you by my side. If things don't work out for you once you get transferred, promise me that you'll let me know. There will always be an opening for you on my team."

"Thanks, Sally. I'm going to miss you and the rest of the guys. I'll still be around the station, hopefully, so we can have a catch-up now and again. Damn, who am I going to complain to now about my lack of sleep?"

She smiled. "You'll find some mug whose ear you can bend."

"That's why my decision has been so hard to make. Friends like you don't come along that often, even if you have been a tyrant of a boss over the past five years or so."

"Right. I bet you'll be calling me a bloody angel once you've worked under someone else for a while."

Jack laughed. "I bet you're right about that." He pushed out of his chair and headed towards the door.

"I'll ring the DCI now, put the ball back in his court about a transfer. I'll let you know what he says. Maybe you'll change your mind again if an opening in the vice squad is the only available option open to you."

"I doubt it." He closed the door behind him.

How she prevented herself from breaking down, she would never know. Jack had been like a brother to her since they'd become partners. That kind of working relationship only came along once in a blue moon. *I can't force him to work with me. Best to let him go and get on with his life.*

She pushed the thought aside for the next half an hour while she dealt with the post. Now, fully composed once more, she picked up the phone and called DCI Green.

"DCI Green."

"Hello, sir. It's Sally Parker. Are you free for a quick chat?"

"Over the phone or in my office?"

"The phone will do, sir."

"Very well, fire away, Inspector."

"It's about my partner, DS Blackman, sir. He's had a change of heart since yesterday and no longer wishes to join me and the rest of my team in the new department. I was wondering if you would look into offering him a transfer. He's an excellent officer. One that, in my opinion, we should hold on to. I've tried my hardest to try and persuade him, but he's adamant that he doesn't want to remain with us in our new venture."

"Give me until the end of the day. I'll get back to you, but I can't promise anything. Make sure you pass that snippet of information on to him for me, will you?"

"Thank you, sir. I'll tell him what you said. Goodbye." She held the phone away from her ear as the line went dead. *Bugger! That's pissed him off now.* She left her office to join her team and beckoned Jack over to the vending machine to apprise him of the situation.

"Damn, that doesn't sound too good."

"It's not too late to change your mind. Have you told the others yet?" Sally inserted a pound coin in the slot and selected the white coffee option.

"No, I thought you could tell them."

"Still expecting me to do your dirty work for you?" He opened and closed his mouth quickly, seemingly stunned by her quick retort, until she dug him in the ribs. "I'm joking. I thought you knew me better than that, partner."

"I do. Sorry, my mind is in turmoil. This hasn't been an easy decision for me to make, Sally. I can assure you, it's knocked me for six."

"I know. Forget it. Let's grab everyone a drink and get on with some work."

With the team supplied with hot coffee, they began searching through the files in earnest.

Sometime during the morning, Joanna let out an excited squeal. "Oh, my God, I think I've stumbled across something major, boss."

Sally rushed over to Joanna's desk. "What's that?"

"One of the names on this list has been matched to an alert." She angled the monitor towards Sally so she could read the alert. "A Craig Gillan."

Sally turned to face Joanna, her mouth wide open in awe, and shook her head. "My God, the remains pulled out of the river were identified as Anne Gillan's only last week. What year did she go missing?"

Joanna ran her finger down the file. "In 2002."

Sally stood upright and raked a hand through her blonde hair. "Yes, fifteen years she's been missing. Does it say who the pathologist dealing with the corpse is?"

Joanna nodded. "It's Simon Bracknall, boss."

Sally thought it strange that Simon hadn't mentioned the case the previous week. She put that down to his busy schedule and wanting to spend quality time with her after work. He rarely discussed cases that she wasn't linked with at home anyway. "Let me give him a ring. Find out what you can about Craig's conviction, Joanna. I'll be right back." She marched into the office, perturbed that she wasn't aware of the case, but then chastised herself for being silly. The same time last week, neither she nor Simon would have known that she and her team would be asked to run a cold-case department. She picked up her landline.

A female member of his staff answered.

"Hi, is Simon available for a quick chat?"

"I'll check. Hold the line." There was a slight pause before she picked up the phone again. "Sorry, no. He's just started a PM. Can he call you back in an hour or two?"

Looking at her watch, Sally decided it would be best to go see her fiancé in person. "Can you tell him I'd like a meeting with him at around twelve? Tell him it's really important."

"Sure, can I ask who's calling?"

"Sorry, I should have said. It's Sally Parker. Tell him it's police business, not personal. Thanks."

"I'll tell him."

She hung up and re-joined Joanna. "Fancy a trip out to the mortuary later?"

Joanna pointed at her chest, her eyes wide with shock. "Me? Won't Jack want to go with you?"

"It's not his scene." Sally looked over her shoulder at Jack. "He'll be leaving us soon. I need you to keep that to yourself for now."

Joanna gasped. "No. I can't believe it."

Sally placed her finger to her lips. "I want him to tell you guys himself, later. Back to the case. What do we know? I'd like to spend the next hour and a half going over the details of the case before we head off."

She pulled a nearby chair close to Joanna's, and together, they sifted through the case notes. "Bloody Falkirk strikes again by the looks of things. Do we know what evidence he found against the husband?"

"I've seen the evidence sheet somewhere." Joanna rifled through the pages and withdrew a sheet. "Here it is. Blood on Craig Gillan's cable-knit jumper. States here that it was deemed incriminating because it looked as though someone had tried to wash the garment to hide the evidence."

"Okay, maybe I was too quick to come down heavily on Falkirk this time. Have you got Gillan's statement there? What did he say about the stain?"

Joanna placed the statement in front of Sally. "Here you go."

"Right, he said his wife used to have a lot of nosebleeds. That's feasible, I guess."

"If she was prone to having them, then they can strike at any time. My poor mum used to suffer dreadfully from the damn things."

"How awful. I've never had one myself, that is, without someone's fist inflicting an injury." She thought back to her life with Darryl and the couple of times he'd bopped her on the nose. She shuddered.

Joanna rubbed her arm, as if sensing what she was thinking about.

"I'm fine. What other statements do we have in there? Anything to say he was an abusive partner?"

"Plenty of statements. No mention of any abuse. Seems a tad strange to me."

Sally cushioned her chin between her forefinger and thumb. "Hmm… that seems very odd. Did they have any children? I really need to brush up on the case. Let's see what the newspaper archives can tell us."

Joanna tapped away at the keyboard until the monitor brought up a clip from *The Norfolk Post*, a local newspaper that had, unfortunately, since folded. Together, Sally and Joanna read through the article. The first fact that Sally jotted down in her notebook was that Craig and Anne Gillan had a son of five and a daughter of eight at the time of her death. "What happened to the children? Who brought them up?"

Joanna looked through the case notes again and tapped her finger. "I've got a Patricia Millward listed down here as being Anne's mother. Maybe she took on the job of raising the children."

"Search for her address. It seems a good place to start to me."

Joanna brought up the electoral roll and located the woman's address instantly. Sally handed Joanna her notebook so that she could jot it down.

"Can you give her a ring? See if she has time for a quick chat this afternoon. Say, around three? That will give us enough time to talk with Simon before we go over there."

Sally's enthusiasm for the case grew exponentially. What a great case for the new team to begin with. According to Craig Gillan's statement and the newspaper article, the man had always insisted he was innocent. Sally studied the picture they had on file of him. Looking deep into his grey eyes, she found an overwhelming sadness. If Falkirk had refused to listen to Gillan's alibi and accused him of killing his wife, then Craig wouldn't have had the time to grieve properly for Anne before Falkirk threw him in prison. Of course, there was every chance that he was guilty of the crime, but considering the other case Inspector Falkirk had messed up, she would rather assume Gillan was innocent until she found something damning enough to put the rubber-stamped guilty mark on his file.

"All sorted, boss. Three o'clock this afternoon. She seemed astounded by the call."

"I'm not surprised. Let's see what else we can dig up before we visit her."

An hour and a half whizzed past. The next thing Sally knew, Jack was standing over them, clearing his throat. "Did I hear you right? That you had an appointment with Simon coming up?"

Sally glanced up at the clock on the wall and leapt out of her chair. "Damn, we were so engrossed, I forgot the time. Are you ready to go, Joanna?"

"Yep, I'm good to go."

They pulled up outside the mortuary department at the hospital twenty minutes later. She hated being late. Luckily, they had a few minutes to spare before that happened.

Simon was still dressed in his operating greens when Sally and Joanna walked through the corridor. "Looks like we're both running behind a little. Wait in my office. I'll just get changed."

Sally moved two chairs from against the wall and positioned them in front of his desk. When he entered the room a few minutes later, he placed a tender kiss on Sally's forehead, and she felt her cheeks colour up.

Then he extended his hand to Joanna. "I don't think I've had the pleasure. Simon Bracknall, and you are?"

"DC Joanna Tryst, sir."

Simon frowned. "Simon will do. I'm not your senior, Joanna. Where's Jack?"

Sally shifted in her seat. "I'll fill you in later. Unfortunately, he's decided not to come on this exciting journey with us."

"Really? Wow, I didn't see that coming."

"Neither did I. Simon, I need to ask you about the remains that were found in the river last week."

He shook his head. "Dreadful case. Gosh, are you dealing with it?"

"Yes, looks like it. Can you tell us how they were found, by whom?"

He reached for a file on his desk, passed it to Sally, then bounced back in his chair and steepled his fingers. "The remains were found at Acle, when the river was being dredged. As you can imagine, the woman's corpse was nothing more than a skeleton after all these years in the water. The lab identified her from dental records."

"She's definitely been in there for fifteen years then?"

"Yes, in my expert opinion.

"How was she killed?"

"Several wounds to her chest and neck. Looks like a large knife. The attack was vicious and personal. Again, that's just my opinion."

"Is it likely that the husband did this, Simon?"

"Attacks like this usually determine that as a conclusion. I looked into his case. He's always pleaded his innocence and has kept his nose clean whilst inside."

"Well, we're taking the case on. Fifteen years that man has been sitting in prison, separated from his children. Why didn't her body resurface after a few months or years?"

"Because it was weighted down with a hessian sack full of bricks."

Sally's brow furrowed. "So, it was a premeditated murder. Who in their right mind carries around with them a sack and bricks just in case?"

"Hard to believe, right? Which is probably why the SIO at the time pointed the finger at the husband as opposed to a stranger out on the prowl."

"Hmm… in that case, we'll need to question all the family and friends again, in the hope that someone will remember something that was said back then. Or if any of them show any signs of guilt when we interview them. Either way, we have a challenging time ahead of us. Was there anything else that we should know about?"

"Not really. I can't tell you for definite how many times she was stabbed, but after studying the nicks in her ribs and sternum, I counted at least fifteen stab wounds. There could have been a lot more than that if the knife was thrust between the ribs, et cetera. Either way, my take is that someone was determined to kill her for whatever reason, and they succeeded."

"Thanks, Simon. We're just going over to see the victim's mother now. Not sure what state she's going to be in after all these years and being confronted with the news that her daughter's remains were found last week. I'll see you later."

Simon walked them to the door of his office, his hand rubbing up and down Sally's back. She found his touch comforting and was dying to feel his lips on hers, but she restrained herself admirably in front of Joanna.

"Good to meet you, Joanna. Look after her for me."

Joanna laughed. "I think it'll be the other way around, Simon. Hope to see you soon."

"Not too soon," Sally said, briefly kissing Simon on the cheek.

"Nice perk to lift my day. Take care."

"Oh, one last thing. Have you informed Anne's mother when her daughter's, er… remains will be released?"

"I have. The funeral home is due to pick her up this afternoon."

"Thanks."

Sally was sure that Patricia Millward would be tearful during their visit and so she tried to prepare herself on the journey.

She pulled up outside a retirement bungalow situated at the end of a quiet cul-de-sac and applied the handbrake. "Deep breaths, here we go. It'll be hard for you to deal with this side of things to begin with, Joanna. Don't think you're letting me down if the emotions take over and get the better of you in there, all right?"

Joanna sighed heavily. "I can feel the back of my eyes heating up already."

"Try and keep a lid on it, if you're able to. There will be times when that'll be difficult. Just remember this happened fifteen years ago."

"Yes, boss. I'll try."

CHAPTER FOUR

A grey-haired lady was tending to her roses in the garden of her home. "Hello, you must be Inspector Parker. I've been looking out for you."

Although the woman smiled, Sally noticed that her eyes were full of sorrow. "That's right, and this is my partner, Detective Constable Joanna Tryst. It's kind of you to see us at short notice, Mrs. Millward."

"Let's go inside. I hate the nosey neighbours knowing my business."

Mrs. Millward led them inside her spacious bungalow and into the lounge, where they found her husband sitting in an upright armchair, reading a daily newspaper. He tucked the paper behind him and stood up to greet Sally and Joanna. Sally saw that the man had a cane resting beside his chair and that he had a slight curvature of the spine.

"Hello, Mr. Millward. I'm DI Sally Parker of the newly formed cold-case team, and this is my partner, DC Joanna Tryst. It's a pleasure to meet you both."

"Thank you for coming, Inspector. Won't you take a seat?"

Sally and Joanna sat on the fabric couch as instructed.

Mrs. Millward had remained by the door. "Can I get you both a drink? It won't take me long; the kettle is already boiled."

"That would be lovely. Coffee for me, white with one sugar. Joanna?"

"The same for me. That's very kind of you."

Mr. Millward returned to his seat, and he winced as he lowered himself into the chair. "Darn hip is playing up again. I'll be glad when they call me in for the operation to replace it. Don't ever get old, lasses. It's a bugger when your body starts breaking down."

"Sorry to hear that, Mr. Millward."

"You calling me that doesn't help, either. It's Fred, and my wife is called Patricia. We're not one for all this pomp and ceremony. We're down-to-earth folks who miss our daughter terribly."

"I can imagine." Sally swiftly left her chair when Patricia walked into the room carrying a fully laden tray. She took it from the lady and placed it on the coffee table in between all the chairs.

"Thank you. It was heavier than I anticipated. I brought you each a slice of my fruit cake; only came out of the oven a few hours ago. Baking relaxes me, you see. Helps me to put things into perspective. You'll have a piece, won't you?"

"I'd love some. Totally forgot to eat at lunchtime, so it will fill a hole, thank you."

Sally waited until Patricia had handed everyone their mugs of coffee and a slice of cake before she broached the subject of Anne. "I was sorry to learn about your daughter's case. As I said, we've only just been assigned the task of looking through a batch of cold-cases that have come to our attention. I wasn't aware of your daughter's case until this morning. It was a shock to learn that her body had been discovered only last week. For you, too, I should imagine."

The couple glanced at each other, and a silent message passed between them. It was Patricia who cleared her throat and spoke first. "We're not sure how to feel, Inspector. We're still rather numb about it. It's difficult to grieve without a loved one's body, I suppose. I don't know what's worse: her being missing for fifteen years, not knowing whether she was dead or alive, or them finding only her bones."

Sally's heart felt as if a giant hand was squeezing it. "I'm sorry. It must be hard. Remember her as she was."

Patricia withdrew a tissue from the box sitting on the side table beside her and wiped a stray tear from her cheek.

Sally smiled gently. "Are you up to going over the case with us? Or would you rather leave it for another day?"

"No, I'd like to get this over with as quickly as possible, dear, if it's all the same to you. Agreed, Fred?"

Fred nodded and reached out a hand to her. Patricia slipped her hand gently into his. "Yes, wholeheartedly."

Sally could tell the couple loved each other deeply and thought the pain and heartache they had been subjected to had probably drawn them closer together.

"Feel free to stop at any time. Before you begin, perhaps you can tell me what your relationship with Craig Gillan was like first?"

Patricia smiled. "We loved him as if he were our own son. Knew he was innocent. From the second that bumbling inspector—sorry if that sounds disrespectful—turned up and jubilantly announced that he'd arrested Craig for her murder. We told him instantly that he had made a dreadful mistake. He seemed dumbstruck at the time. I can remember his jaw dropping open. It obviously wasn't how he'd expected us to react when he broke the news. Craig loved Anne with all his heart. He would never have laid a hand on her, and he knew what would have happened if Fred had ever found out he had. He just wasn't—sorry, *isn't* that kind of chap. He abhors any form of abuse, verbal or physical. I remember one day we were at the park feeding the ducks on a family outing. He saw a man and a woman arguing. The man suddenly grabbed hold of the woman's hair and was threatening to bash her with his fist, until Craig shot over there and gripped him round the throat."

"He had a violent streak then?" Sally asked, her heart sinking a little.

"No, not in that sense. Only when someone was doing something drastically wrong to someone else. He would never have treated Anne like that. He loved her to bits. Had done since they were at school together."

"Have you remained in contact with Craig since his imprisonment?"

"Oh, yes. We raised the children as our own and reported to him monthly by letter how they were getting on. He's always thanked us for that, says it's the one thing that kept him going in there. I dread to think what the poor boy would have done if we hadn't stayed in touch."

"What about the children? A boy and a girl, I believe. Did they visit their father frequently?"

Patricia's smile diminished, and her head dropped a little. "Molly always visited her father. Still does, every month without fail. Jamie has always refused to go with her, couldn't get past his father's conviction. He was fine up until the day he discovered the jury had found Craig guilty. Jamie broke off all contact with his father from that day. No matter what I say to him, every time we discuss his father, he leaves the room in disgust. It's pitiful, really. We're all in Craig's corner, except Jamie. That hurts Craig more than anything else in this world. He's suffered untold abuse and beatings inside, but none of that compares to the hurt he's had to contend with because his son refuses to speak to him."

"I'm so sorry to hear that. It must be hard for both parties concerned. How old was Jamie when his father went to prison?"

"Only five. Molly was eight, just that little bit older and able to cope with things far better. But then, girls grow up quicker than boys, don't they? The outcome might have been different if Jamie was the eldest, but I guess that's something we'll never know."

"Terrible situation. I'm so glad you took them under your wing," Sally stated before taking a sip from her coffee and tearing off a little piece of the scrumptious cake to nibble on.

"It was hard to cope with him, and we debated letting Social Services have him at one point, only for the briefest of moments. He's been in terrible trouble with the police over the years. He went into his shell, refused to discuss either of his parents, as if they had let him down. Which I suppose they had, but it was none of their choosing. They both didn't deliberately go out of their way to either be killed or to be put in prison. Some people get set in their ways, and nothing you say or do will put things right in their eyes. That's Jamie all over."

"Do both children still live with you?"

"No. Jamie left us as soon as he turned sixteen. Not sure where he is now. I think Molly has a rough idea of his whereabouts, but she keeps it from us rather than upset us. That boy has put us through hell over the years. Don't get me wrong, we haven't cut him out of our life. It was his choice to leave and never to get in touch with us again. We have to accept that. Otherwise, we'd worry ourselves sick with what he's up to now. Molly said that she told him his mother's body was discovered last week, but she was very cagey about how he'd reacted to the news. Hopefully, it will mean closure for him. However, I don't suppose that will come until he learns that his father is exonerated. That is how this will end, Inspector?"

Sally placed her mug and side plate on the coffee table. "The last thing I want to do is raise your hopes, as it's very, very early days into the investigation. Too soon to say if Craig is innocent or guilty, but we'll be doing our best to put any wrongs right in the investigation. A few months ago, we solved another cold-case that had a surprising outcome. The case had originally been investigated by Inspector Falkirk. That's why my team have taken on this new role in a brand-new department. If the clues are there, we will find them. My team are like dogs with bones, determined little blighters." Sally turned to face Joanna and winked at her.

"It would be wonderful to see him out of prison. Fifteen years, though! You're aware that he's up for parole in two years?"

"Yes, we read that in his file. Of course, nothing is written in stone there. He would only get parole if he's been a model prisoner. We'll do our best to get him out of there before then if we find evidence that he's innocent."

"We understand, and we'll certainly keep our fingers crossed until that day arises. Are you aware that both his parents have died since he went to prison?"

"That's a shame. No, I wasn't aware of that. Through ill health?"

"His mother died of a broken heart, refused to believe that her son was guilty, but didn't have the strength to continue to fight for him after several cancer scares over the years. Not long after Jill died, Stan, his father, passed away from a heart attack. He had an exceptionally stressful job working in London on the stock markets, something like that anyway."

"Very sad. Was Craig allowed to attend the funerals?"

"Yes. Jill's funeral was the first time we'd seen him for years. I was appalled by his appearance. Prison hasn't been kind to him over the years."

"May I ask why you stopped visiting him?"

Patricia looked at her husband for a split moment then back at Sally. "Neither of us could bear going there. I know how dreadfully selfish that sounds, but we just couldn't overcome the anguish of sitting in the visiting room with the thought of all those murderers on the other tables close by."

"I can totally understand that. How did Craig react to the news?"

"He was devastated, as you can imagine. We just couldn't brush the thought aside and continue our visits."

Fred placed his empty mug back on the tray. While his wife sipped at her drink, he replied, "I don't know how Molly does it, going so often. She's such a loving child, unlike her brother. We allowed her to start visiting her father once she'd turned eighteen. Her first visiting order came through on her eighteenth birthday. It made Craig's day to see her on that special day." He wiped a stray tear from the corner of his eye as he spoke.

Sally felt a lump growing in her throat. "Let's hope we'll be able to reunite them properly in the outside world again soon. My team and I will do our best to achieve that. You have my word. Would you mind going over the events of that day, as you remember them. I know it's asking a lot of you."

"Not at all. It's something we'll never forget." Patricia placed her cup on the coffee table. "Anne had been at work, she had changed shifts that week, to cover for a friend."

"Where did she work?" Sally looked at Joanna and nodded for her to note down what was said.

"At the Norfolk Sponge Factory. She wasn't on the production line; she wouldn't have stood working on that. No, she worked in the canteen, catering for the staff who were on duty around the clock. She had recently cut her hours down, so she only worked twenty-five hours a week usually. The week she went missing, she had agreed to help out and work full time. She was going to put the extra money aside to go towards a weekend away camping with the kids. They rarely went on holiday, couldn't afford it."

"I see. What shift was she doing that day?"

"Three to eleven. That's right, love, wasn't it?" Patricia asked Fred, her brow furrowing as she thought.

"Yes, that's right. Stupid shift if you ask me."

"The incident occurred when?"

"It was as she was walking home, we believe. According to Craig, Anne rang him at nine o'clock on her break and said she couldn't wait to get home."

"How did Anne usually travel home from work? Via public transport?"

"Good Lord, no. She only worked ten minutes from the house, so she always walked there and back."

"Even at that time of night? Did she usually stick to the main road?"

"Usually, yes. Craig was beside himself when he learnt that she'd gone missing. If she worked her normal shift, sometimes he would drop by and give her a lift home. But at that time of night, there were the kids to consider. There's no way he would have left them alone in the house while he went to fetch her, even if it was only a ten-minute round trip."

Sally's mind began to whirr. "So, he would have shown signs of guilt at the time for that reason alone, I take it. Maybe that's what the original investigating officer picked up on when he questioned Craig—his guilt manifesting in that way. Falkirk misread the signs and thought he was guilty of doing the deed. Sorry, my mind is working overtime there."

Patricia's hand covered her mouth for a few brief moments. "My God, you've probably hit the nail on the head. I've never thought about that before. Neither of us had."

"It's just an assumption on my part at this stage, a logical one." She turned to Joanna and asked, "Do you recall the officers finding any signs of a struggle anywhere?"

Joanna nodded. "Down by an industrial unit close to her home. They found traces of Anne's blood. No other DNA at the scene, from what I can remember."

"Thanks." Sally smiled and asked Anne's parents, "I take it the investigation team arrested Craig as soon as they found the blood. Is that right?"

"Yes, that's right. They got a warrant to search the home and found a cream cable-knit sweater thrown in the bottom of his wardrobe. It had traces of blood on it. When they tested it, the blood matched Anne's and they arrested Craig on the spot. That's when we took the children into our care."

Sally bit the inside of her mouth, thinking that she would have probably done the same given the evidence. "They didn't check out his alibi?"

"No, he had no witnesses. The kids were in bed asleep. They only had his word on the matter. It's such a mess. Tell us you can work your way around this, Inspector."

"We're going to do our best. If Craig was innocent, then the real culprit has lived his life freely up until now. That can't be right. Which is why I need to ask you more questions. I'm sorry. If it all gets too much, just stop me, and we can pick it up another day."

"Nonsense. Ask away. We want to help in whatever way we can."

"Going back to Craig and Anne's relationship, are you sure they never fought or had a cross word with each other?"

"No, never. In our eyes, they were the perfect couple. I knew my daughter inside out, Inspector. If she had lived a charade all her married life, I would have known about it. My daughter never, ever kept secrets from me, and I understood her every mood. I would have recognised the signs of any discomfort immediately."

"What about any of their acquaintances? Did either Anne or Craig mention that they'd fallen out with anyone at all, either in their personal lives or at work?"

Patricia thought the question over then shook her head. "Not that I can remember. They just weren't the type to fall out with their friends or colleagues. It's unthinkable that should happen to either of them. Genuinely, you couldn't wish to meet a more laid-back couple, I promise you."

Sally hesitated before asking her next question. She swallowed hard then asked, "Do you think it would be possible to talk to Molly and Jamie? See what their recollections are from around that time?"

"Molly, I have no doubts about. She'll do anything to help get her father off—sorry, that came out the wrong way. I wasn't implying that she would lie for him in any way."

Sally smiled reassuringly. "I get your drift. What about Jamie? If we managed to track him down, do you think he would be open to speaking with us?"

"You can certainly try. What kind of reception you'll get, heaven knows."

"Does Molly still live with you both?"

"No, she's just moved out, bought a house of her own. She won't be home until gone five thirty. She works for a solicitor's firm as a conveyancing secretary. Good pay but not challenging enough for her, she says, but it's helped her to get on the property market. That's what she's been desperate to do for years. Maybe I can get her to ring you. Make arrangements when to set up a chat."

Sally pulled a business card out of her jacket pocket and placed it on the tray. "I'll leave that there. Please tell her not to be worried about the interview."

"That'll put her mind at rest. She can tell you how to get hold of her brother, too."

"Can you think of anything that would help the fresh investigation? Maybe there's something that has bugged you over the years that you thought the investigating officer back then should have been told?"

Patricia and Fred glanced at each other, but both of them shook their heads.

"Okay. Then I think we should begin our investigation from the beginning. We'll try and keep you informed as we proceed. I'll need to visit Craig in prison to get his take on the events that occurred back then. I hope he's up to meeting me."

"He'll welcome the chance for the case to be reopened. He rang us last week when Anne's body was discovered…" Patricia paused to hold back the tears welling up in her eyes, then added, "He was as relieved as we were, but then the questions set in. Why? How? Where? When? Back to why again."

"It must have been, and probably still is, something very traumatic for him to have to contend with. We'll go now. Thank you for the refreshments and wonderful cake."

Mr. Millward tried to stand up but slumped back in his chair, defeated.

"Stay there, sir, there's no need for you to get up. It's been a pleasure to meet you." Sally shook his hand.

"And you, Inspector. Do your best for us."

"We will, sir."

Patricia opened the front door, and a cool breeze wafted into the hallway. "Thank you for your kindness, Inspector. We realise the case is in safe hands now. We never had that much confidence in the rabble dealing with the original case. You seem a very caring person."

"I like to think so, Patricia. Keep the faith; we'll do our utmost to get Craig out of there if he is indeed innocent. I'll keep in touch as promised. Goodbye."

Sally and Joanna waved as they left the house. In the car, Sally blew out a relieved breath. "Well, that was pretty intense. Those poor people. When they should have been enjoying life, they put their lives on hold to raise their grandchildren. How heartless of the boy not to keep in touch with them after all they sacrificed for him. Sorry for venting. You'll get used to that after a while. It goes with the territory of being my partner."

"Am I? Your new partner? I thought this was a one-off."

"Stop that. I'll get a complex if I think you don't want to accept the challenge. I haven't driven Jack away, if that's what you're thinking."

Joanna laughed. "I wasn't thinking anything of the sort, boss. I've worked alongside you for three or four years now. I think I know you a little better than that, not much granted."

"Ditto. Maybe we can get to know each other on our way out to the prison."

"You're heading out to see Craig Gillan now? Wouldn't it be best to ring ahead and arrange a visit first?"

"Strike while the iron is scorching—that's my motto, as you'll soon learn. So, what made you sign up to the force? Have any members of your family been coppers over the years?"

"Dad was a constable in his early days. Didn't like it. Too much paperwork for him, he used to tell me. What tickled me was that he went back to uni to become an accountant."

They both laughed. "That's hilarious. Definitely one job I wouldn't entertain being thrown into. I hate the amount of paperwork I have to deal with daily as it is. Maybe that'll change with the new role I've taken on. I can live in hope anyway. What about your mum? What does she do?"

"Mum works in a retirement home, on the night shift. She loves her job and devoting her time to care for others. It really upsets her when yet another story focusing on the brutality of care assistants in some care homes breaks in the press, because she and the staff at the Nightingale Home would never allow anything bad to happen to any of their patients."

"I suppose it's like everything else in this life—there is good and bad in everything. Look at what we're dealing with now. Going over cases that were screwed up by a bad copper."

"Yep, never thought of it that way."

"While I'm driving, maybe it would be a good idea to ring the prison, just to check it's all right for us to visit Gillan today. Tell them it's a matter of urgency, and that should do the trick."

CHAPTER FIVE

Sally had mixed feelings when the prison, built in 1887, came into view. Her ex-husband was serving his four-year sentence there and was due to be released in a few years. She was hopeful that her imminent marriage to Simon would put an end to his fixation with her. Only a few months ago, he'd arranged for someone to cause havoc in her life, vandalising her car and abusing her beautiful dog, Dex. She shook her head to dispel the vile image of her baby being trussed up like a chicken with silver tape wrapped tightly around his muzzle.

Joanna appeared to pick up on her trepidation. "Damn, I forgot. He's here, isn't he? Are you all right about this, boss? Should I go in instead of you?"

Sally tapped her on the knee and smiled. "No way. I'll be all right. There's no chance of me meeting my ex—at least, I hope there isn't. Let's not tempt fate by mentioning the pillock, eh?"

She drew the car to a halt in the car park, and together, they walked towards the intimidating arched entrance. The building was huge and reminded her of one that she'd seen featured in a film about the KGB in Russia years ago, *Gorky Park*. She shuddered as the door opened and a stern-looking gentleman in a suit greeted them with firm handshakes.

"Inspector Parker. I'm Governor Wilkinson. I was a little put out by your call, if I'm honest." His tone reminded her of the strict headmaster she'd had at school.

"I'm sorry. We've only just taken on the case, and I felt it would be best to come and see Mr. Gillan before the true investigation got under way. Sorry if that has inconvenienced you at all."

"I accept the situation for what it is. Despite the inconvenience, I've arranged a special room for you to interview Gillan. You'll be away from the other prisoners; therefore, it'll be easier on him once he's back amongst them."

"Are you saying that he's likely to be terrorised by the other inmates if they learn that we're here to question him?"

"Don't look so shocked, Inspector. I can't predict what will occur, but it has been known to happen in the past in such circumstances. The police have a bad reputation within these walls, as you can imagine."

"Ah, I see what you're getting at now. Thank you for doing all you can to avoid such behaviour. May I ask what sort of prisoner Gillan has been over the years?"

"A model one. He's kept his nose clean, and there's every chance that when his parole hearing comes up in a couple of years, he will be released on good behaviour. Providing he keeps out of trouble in the meantime."

"In your opinion, do you think he was guilty of killing his wife?"

Governor Wilkinson stopped walking. "It's not my opinion that counts, Inspector. Twelve jurors found the man guilty."

"I know that. But surely you have an opinion about the men serving time in your prison, Governor?"

"Nope. I'm here to ensure the running of this prison goes like clockwork. I have enough filling my day without getting involved in every prisoner's personal life." He set off again and stopped outside a metal door on the right of the long, narrow corridor. He pushed open the door and stepped back to allow Joanna and Sally to enter. "Take a seat. The prisoner will be along shortly. May I point out that there is a camera in the corner? We will monitor what is going on at all times, although there is no recording apparatus set up in the room."

"Thank you. Hopefully, Gillan won't be tempted to strike us, but if he does, it's reassuring that you will be on the other side of the camera."

"Not me personally, but a member of my staff will be." He closed the door, leaving them alone in the stark-white room.

"Not sure how I'll feel questioning Gillan whilst being on *Candid Camera*," Sally remarked, smiling at Joanna, who was also looking ill at ease.

"Seems a little bizarre to me. Makes me feel a lot safer, though, so that's a plus."

"There's no need to be scared. From what we've heard about Gillan already, I'm sure he'll turn out to be a pussycat. Although, who could blame him after being cooped up in this place for fifteen years if he's altered. Will you take notes for me during the interview?"

"Of course, boss. I think we're, or should I say, *I'm* worrying unnecessarily."

They manoeuvred the two chairs so that they would be sitting close together and sat down. They waited a full five minutes until the door opened. A prison officer built like a gorilla, with a stern facial expression led a chained man into the room. He shuffled because his feet could only move independently for around eight inches, no more. The officer pushed Gillan into his seat and attached the cuffs around his wrists to the metal loop on the table.

Anger mounting, Sally's eyes narrowed at the way Gillan was being manhandled by the goon. "Excuse me, is that truly necessary?"

The guard backed up to the wall, glaring at her disdainfully.

"You can leave us alone. I'm sure we'll be perfectly safe."

His lips parted and Sally could see that a few of his front teeth were missing. "It ain't gonna happen, lady."

She got the impression the officer was intentionally winding her up and decided to slap him down. "That'll be 'Inspector' to you when you address me."

The officer smirked as if her reply had amused him.

Deciding it would be best to ignore him altogether, Sally turned her attention back to the broken man in front of her. A quick study told her that there was no sparkle in his steel-grey eyes. His skin was a faint hue of yellow from lack of vitamin D, and his relatively broad shoulders were rounded, making her want to reach over and force him upright to give him a dose of self-assurance that he was obviously lacking. In other words, she couldn't prevent her heart aching for the man. Her instincts told her there and then that he was as innocent as a new-born lamb, and he hadn't even opened his mouth yet.

"Hello, Mr. Gillan. I'm DI Sally Parker, and this is my partner, DC Joanna Tryst."

The man's head lifted slightly, he flicked back a clump of long, dark grey hair and gave her the briefest of smiles. "What's this about, Inspector? Finding my wife's body last week?"

"It wasn't originally, but it is now. We're part of a cold-case team, and your conviction was amongst the cases we were tasked with tackling. We were just starting our investigation when our database highlighted that Anne's body had been discovered last week." She noticed the way he winced when she'd deliberately mentioned his wife's name.

"Thank God. Now she can be laid to rest in peace. Every time I've closed my eyes over the past fifteen years, I've seen her terrified face, reaching out, begging for me to help her. Which of course was beyond me, stuck in here. I would have moved heaven and earth to find her, had I not been falsely arrested." He lifted his hands and rattled the chains restraining him to the table.

The officer standing by the door grunted. "Keep your hands still, Gillan."

Sally shot the prison officer a venomous glare. He smirked again and shrugged as if to say, "Whatever, bitch."

"This is why we're reinvestigating your case. We recently dealt with a cold-case that was, shall we say, dubiously dealt with by Inspector Falkirk. The original suspects were exonerated in that case. We're hoping that will be the outcome in your circumstances too, providing you're innocent, of course."

He placed his chest closer to his chains and covered his heart with one of his hands. "I swear to you that I did not, could not have, killed my wife."

"Would you mind going over the events of that evening with us?"

He exhaled loudly. "Of course. I won't be able to tell you anything different to what I told that chump back then, though. Sorry, I didn't mean to sound disrespectful to a colleague of yours."

Sally raised her hand. "I've called him a lot worse than that over the last few months. Please, in your own words, tell us what occurred that evening. My partner will be taking notes, if that's okay?"

"Of course. It's like I told Falkirk. I was at home that evening. I'd put the kids to bed at about eight and prepared the dinner for when Anne… got home from work. She always told me not to bother with a dinner when she was on the late shift, but I refused to listen to her. We always shared our mealtimes together. I didn't care that I'd have to wait an extra five hours to eat compared to normal. It was something we always did, had done since we got married."

"How long were you married?"

"Ten years, although we'd never been with anyone else since the day we got together at secondary school. We only had eyes for each other. We were inseparable, until…"

"I can see how much she meant to you. I'm sorry that you've had to endure this atrocious ordeal." She sighed. "Going back to that night, did you alert the police?"

"Yes, when she hadn't arrived home by eleven thirty, I rang them right away. They chastised me, told me how foolish I was to report her missing after only fifteen minutes. But I just knew, felt it in my heart, that something dreadful had happened."

"Maybe your wife decided to go out with colleagues that night."

"No way. She never socialised with friends or work colleagues. We spent all of our time together apart from when we had to work. We were soulmates through and through. Thought what the other one thought, finished off each other's sentences. For anyone to believe that I would be capable of such a heinous crime is just unthinkable. I can't tell you the number of times I've contemplated committing suicide over the years, but the thought of her still being out there prevented me from doing that."

Sally lowered her voice and leaned forward. "And now that her remains have been discovered? Are you tempted or have you been tempted to go down that route in the past week or so?"

"The thought has constantly crossed my mind," he said quietly.

Sally suspected he feared saying it louder in case the officer reported back to the governor. "Please, don't do anything rash. Think of your children. Molly and Jamie, isn't it?"

"That's what has stopped me so far. I'd do it in a heartbeat if I didn't have them. I couldn't put them through losing both parents. Not that Jamie cares one iota about me. He's cut me out of his life because he believes I killed her. I could put up with the fifteen years of hell living in this place, but that one fact, that my son believes I'm guilty, has torn me apart over the years."

Sally covered his hand with hers. "Then let's work together and prove the jury and Falkirk wrong. Let's do this for Jamie's sake. How's that?"

"How? How can I prove my innocence sitting in this shithole?"

"Through me." She turned to face Joanna and pointed. "Through us, me and my team."

He fell silent. Where Sally had thought she would see relief in his eyes, she saw something else that she found difficult to recognise.

Suddenly, his voice became choked, and his head sank to his chest as he said, "Do you know what it's like to grieve for a loved one, Inspector?"

"Yes, a grandparent. It's awful. I hear that everyone grieves differently in this life."

"A grandparent," he repeated quietly. "It's not the same as losing a spouse, but you'll appreciate the magnitude of the raw emotions and pain a person goes through during the grieving process."

Sally nodded, wondering where his statement was leading.

"Now imagine living through fifteen years of hell, not knowing whether to grieve or rejoice in the fact that a loved one's body hasn't been found. Then thinking possibly that she might have run off and even done the unthinkable and staged her own death."

Sally's mind raced. She felt sorry for the man and the torment he'd put himself through during his imprisonment. "I can't imagine how that must feel. I'm so sorry."

He went on with his speech as though she hadn't spoken. "If you could, I'd tell you to multiply the feeling by a million, and it still wouldn't come close to what I've been subjected to over the years." He rattled his chains as he pointed to his head. "It messes with this. Fifteen years!"

Sally found herself in search of the right words to respond, but it proved impossible. She couldn't begin to understand what he'd been through. He would have had little to no sympathy from the prison officers; that much was evident if the goon in the corner was anything to go by. He'd obviously been through a living hell during his spell behind bars.

She reached across the table and touched his hand again. Her glance shot up to the guard as defiance rippled through her. "Craig, I promise you this: we'll do everything in our power to help you achieve your freedom, so you can begin your life again to the full instead of just existing from day-to-day in here."

His eyes settled on her hand covering his. "How will I cope on the outside? Knowing that the love of my life is now dead? I might as well end it all now. What do I have to live for?"

Sally squeezed his hand then released it. "Think of the children. Think of Molly."

He shook his head. "I see what you're doing, and it won't work. Molly has coped without me all these years. She'll be better off without me turning up and disrupting her life."

Sally inhaled and exhaled a large breath. "Look at me, Craig."

When he lifted his head, she saw the pain and misery within his watery eyes and knew she had to snap him out of it. "Talking that way won't help. Self-pity is destructive and seldom serves a purpose. You need to be strong. Once we start delving deep into the case, we'll need your help to try and solve it. You'll only be able to do that with a strong resolve and determination. Don't you want to help us find the real killer?"

His eyes narrowed as he searched her eyes for answers that had evaded him over the years. "I'd like nothing more than to get my hands on the bastard, but I'd probably end up back in here on another murder charge."

"I'm not asking you to get that involved, but we'll need you to fill in the gaps in Anne's day-to-day life. Do you think you'll be capable of doing that?" Sally hoped to give the man a purpose in life, something for him to concentrate on rather than wallowing in his self-pity should the day arrive that he be released from prison. It was all about having the mental strength to cope with the changes she hoped he would experience in the next few months. She was prepared to do anything she could to provide him with a new beginning with his children.

He nodded. "I'll do all I can to help, although I told the last inspector everything I knew, and it backfired on me big time. How else did I end up inside? When all I was guilty of is loving the very bones of my beautiful wife since we first met."

"If you're willing to help, that's all we can ask. Now, going back to the events that night or maybe the next day perhaps, when exactly did Falkirk find your jumper?"

He shook his head. "It's a bit blurry now, the timeframe in which everything took place. It might have been the next day. I believe he got a warrant to search the house and found the jumper at the bottom of the wardrobe."

"And where did the blood come from, Craig?"

"I told that fool of an inspector, but he refused to believe me. Anne suffered from nosebleeds. They would just descend upon her without warning. We were snuggled up on the sofa one night, my arm was around her shoulder, she had an itchy nose and wiped her face on my jumper. She was horrified to see the blood when she pulled away. We both were. I told her it didn't matter; the jumper was old anyway. We tried to wash the blood out of it by hand and machine, but the blood buried itself in the intricate cable and refused to budge. I flung it in the bottom of the wardrobe to use when I do DIY or decorate. Never once did I think that would be the key piece of evidence that moron would pin on me to say that I had killed my wife. What a prick he was. Sorry, excuse my language."

Sally smiled. "You're entitled to your opinion on that one. I take it you recounted that story to Falkirk?"

"Of course I did. He was having none of it. He saw me as the guilty party, and nothing I could say or do was going to dissuade him from thinking that."

"Okay, do you know if Anne visited the doctor about her nosebleeds?"

"I'm sure she did." The chains rattled as he ran a hand through his hair, agitated.

"Put your hand down," the prison officer snapped.

Sally glared at the officer, narrowing her gaze as her anger mounted. "Then that's where we'll begin our investigation, by going to see her doctor."

"If he's still around. I think Anne said Dr. Mountford was near retirement age. That would put him in his late seventies to early eighties now, right?" Craig added.

"Can you tell us what surgery it was?"

"You're testing my memory here. I only visited the place once or twice. Steered clear of doctors wherever possible. Something with a tree name, Oakfields, Oakwood, perhaps? Up on the estate where we lived, it was. Should be easy for you to find, I think."

"If it's still around, we'll track it down. We'll see if we can locate Anne's medical files. Good, that's a start. I have to ask if either you or Anne had received any bother from any of your neighbours or anyone you knew in the months leading up to Anne's disappearance."

He fell silent as he thought. "No, I can't think of anyone. We pretty much kept to ourselves, were easy-going as far as our neighbours were concerned, even when the guy next door started his motorbike up at five every morning to go off to work. You make allowances for things like that in this life, don't you? If you didn't, the annoyance would grind you down in the end. I really can't add anything. I'm sorry."

"Any old boyfriends—or girlfriends, in your case—that we should know about?"

"No, there were none. We met at school, and neither of us had dated anyone else before."

"Did you owe money to anyone? A loan shark, anyone like that?"

"No, never. We lived by the rule that if we couldn't afford something, we went without. We saved up for everything we owned, never had anything on lease or credit. The only money we owed was for the house, but even then, we had a relatively small mortgage, only about twenty grand at the time. Of course, the idiots took the house from us when I couldn't keep up the payments." His head slumped again. "That was the kids' inheritance. Now what can I leave them or offer them? Nothing, a big fat zero, all because an idiotic inspector refused to do his job properly."

"I agree and can't apologise enough for what you've been through the last fifteen years. Did either you or Anne see anyone hanging around your house in the weeks or months prior to that fateful evening?"

"I can't recall anyone. You think someone might have stalked Anne for a while?"

"It's possible. What about at work? Did Anne ever mention that someone was showing her more attention than they should have?"

"No. She had a great working relationship with everyone at the factory, both on the production line and in the canteen. Hang on a sec—I'm lying. I had to warn one of her colleagues off."

"Warn him off? Why?"

"I think he was a harmless enough chap, although very clingy. Used to ring the house all the time, kind of pissed me off in the end, so I put a stop to it, verbally."

"Can you remember his name?"

"Endecott, something like that, I believe."

"Brilliant, we'll visit the factory and see what we can find out. It's asking a lot. Probably most of the staff will have moved on by now, but we might strike lucky. It's certainly worth a try anyway. Is there anything else you can think of? You said you didn't socialise much, but did either of you belong to a club of any kind? That you attended either separately or together maybe? A gym, squash club, perhaps go swimming together as a family?"

"Yes, we used to go to the local swimming pool together, but we'd never experienced any problems, not in the slightest."

"Okay, is there any other route you think we should go down? Even if you think it would be silly to consider it, just tell us."

He shook his head firmly. "No, nothing else. I can't believe someone we knew could be capable of such brutality." His eyes filled up with tears yet again.

"I know how upsetting this is for you. Forgive me, I'm sorry to have to put you through it all again, but it's the only way we'll get to the bottom of what truly happened. One last thought… what about at school? When dropping the kids off to school, did either one of you have a run-in with one of the other parents?"

"Not that I can think of. It's unthinkable that someone deliberately targeted Anne."

"Maybe it was just a random attack. Do you recall either reading or hearing about any other attacks in your area around that time?"

"I can't recall anything like that. We lived in a respectable neighbourhood, where things like that never occurred. Which is why the community turned on me, I guess. Once the police started sniffing around, searching the house en masse and carted me off to the station for questioning, it was hard for our neighbours to see me in the same light as before. Who could blame them? I definitely can't. I'm sure I would feel exactly the same way if the boot was on the other foot."

"Maybe, maybe not. I'd like to draw this meeting to a close now, if that's all right with you, Craig. I'll leave you my card. You have access to a public telephone in here, am I right?"

Craig nodded.

"Then I urge you to use it and call me if anything comes to mind after we leave. I also want to reassure you for a final time that we'll do our very best to right the wrongs that have wrecked your life over the years."

"Thank you, both. I truly appreciate you coming to see me and taking on my case. I wish you luck going forward."

The prison officer approached and fiddled with the padlock to release Craig from the table, then he yanked the man to his feet.

"Do you have to treat him like an animal?" Sally pleaded, hating the way the officer was manhandling Craig, who winced in pain as the man's hands bit into his arms.

"Whatever, lady. You ain't got any jurisdiction in here."

"I'll be having a word with the governor, believe me."

The officer glared at Sally and gave a nonchalant shrug. "Do what you've got to do, lady. Get back to your cell, Gillan." He pushed Craig ahead of him. The poor man almost toppled over because he was unable to spread his legs apart sufficiently enough to keep his balance.

Sally grabbed the officer's arm. "I mean it. Either you treat him with respect, or I will make a formal complaint about you. Got that?"

The officer pulled his arm away and grunted as he and Gillan set off back up the corridor to the cell wing.

"Come on, Joanna. Let's get out of here."

They followed the two men part of the way then turned right as the officer and Craig turned left. Sally glanced towards the left then stopped dead. Her heart pounded violently, so hard she thought it was about to explode. Standing on the other side of the bars was Darryl, her ex-husband. He had his back to her, but his build and hair colour were unmistakable. He was speaking to another man, who nudged him. Darryl turned around to look her way in what seemed like mega-slow motion. Sally knew she should have turned and rushed towards the exit, but it was as if she were mesmerised seeing him behind bars.

Joanna stood in front of her, sensing that something was wrong. "Boss, we need to go. They're waiting to let us out."

Sally shook her head and looked at Joanna. "Okay, I'm coming. Sorry."

Darryl's warped laugh followed them to the end of the corridor. Once the officer had closed and locked the metal door with bars, Sally glanced back at her ex. A shudder rippled down her spine. It was hard to tear herself away from Darryl. Seeing him had conjured up all sorts of vile images of them together, the worst one being when he had pinned her down in their home and raped her. She felt a hand on her arm and flinched.

"Sorry, boss. We need to get out of here, now."

"Come on, ladies. I haven't got all day," the officer on reception shouted abruptly.

"You're right. We're coming." Sally glowered at Darryl, which only made him laugh louder.

Once outside in the warm fresh air, Sally tore off her jacket and leant against the bonnet of her car to compose herself before she got behind the steering wheel.

Joanna kicked at the dusty car park surface. "Was that him?" she asked hesitantly.

Sally swallowed, her emotions in turmoil once more. "Yes. I feel such a bloody fool. What the hell did I see in him? Just looking at him disgusts me. Makes my skin prickle with hatred. Even now, after all this time, that bastard shouldn't be able to affect me like this. When will the torment end? Will it ever end?"

Joanna rubbed her upper arm. "You've done well up until now, boss. Think of the life you have with Simon. You've moved on. You might think at this moment that you're letting Darryl still affect your life, but he really isn't. *You're* having the last laugh, not him."

Sally smiled at her colleague. "You always know when to say the right thing. I thank you for that, Joanna."

"Nonsense. All I'm doing is pointing out the positives in your life at present. Always focus on them, and you can't go wrong, as my old mum always says. You know what? Nine times out of ten, she's right about that. Are you okay to drive, or would you like me to?"

Sally shook out the tension in her arms and smiled. "Nope, I'm fine now. Thanks for the pep talk. I think we're going to get on really well. I apologise for my mini-meltdown."

"There's no need. We all have them, boss."

They arrived back at the station at almost five o'clock. Sally called the team together so that she and Joanna could relay the information they had gathered from Craig Gillan.

"That's where we stand," she finished. "My initial thoughts are that the man is totally innocent. However, we've been duped by other manipulative suspects over the years, so I'm still going to proceed with caution. I'd rather do that than end up with egg on my face." Just then, the phone in her office began to ring. She raced through the line of desks to answer it. "Hello. DI Sally Parker. Can I help?"

"Hello, Inspector. DCI Green here. As promised, I'm getting back to you concerning your partner."

"I see. Have you managed to find him a suitable post, sir?" Sally crossed her fingers, hoping he hadn't. She really didn't want to lose Jack at this stage.

"I have found him a position. Whether it's suitable remains to be seen. There aren't a lot of vacancies at present. I have one in the control room; do you think that would be acceptable to him?"

"I'm not sure, sir. It's hardly a challenging role for someone of his experience."

"Like I've already stated, vacancies are very thin on the ground at present. Let me know in the morning, and I'll make the necessary arrangements."

"Thank you, sir. I'll ring you first thing." Sally hung up and called for Jack to join her. "Take a seat, Jack. That was concerning you."

Jack slumped into the chair. "Uh-oh, am I in trouble?"

Sally laughed. "Don't be ridiculous. That was Green on the phone. He's got another post for you."

Jack crossed his arms. His bulging biceps tugged at the seams of his jacket. "Go on, surprise me."

Sally twisted her mouth and bit her lip before she responded. "Umm... it's in the control room."

Jack's head jutted forward, and the side of his mouth hitched up. "What? Is that it? How many detective sergeants do you know who resort to working in the control room? What a bloody smack in the face that is after the years of service I've given this department and Green."

"Calm down. There's always an alternative—you know that."

"Calm down? You're kidding me. How would you feel, Sally? It's a bloody downright insult. And what's the alternative? To stay here and work on old cases, some of which should never see the light of day again? Bloody hell, what a choice."

"I can see how mad you are about this, partner, and that's totally understandable. Why don't you discuss it with Donna overnight and let me have your decision first thing? That's when I have to report back to Green."

He unfolded his arms and stood up. "And why don't I pick up the evening paper on the way home and search through the vacancies' page?"

"Come on, Jack. You know the team and I would be lost without you. Seriously consider what you want before you think about ditching the force altogether."

"Oh, I will. All right if I take off now? Looks like I'm going to have a busy evening ahead of me."

"Sure. Give my love to Donna and the kids."

As a disconcerted Jack left her office, Sally picked up the phone and called her mother. She was in desperate need of hearing a cheerful voice to chase away the angst she felt after seeing Darryl earlier. "Hi, Mum, how are things going?"

"Sally, oh, it's lovely to hear from you, darling. We're doing great. Dex is missing you of course. He spends his day sitting by the front door, waiting for you to come home."

"Aw... don't make me feel worse than I do already, Mum. It's not practical for me to have him during the working week. He'd soon get bored if he was left alone all day. How's Dad?"

"Loving his new role. It's wonderful to see his zest for life at the moment. We can't thank Simon enough for showing faith in him."

"It's a two-way street, Mum. Simon is grateful for all of Dad's expertise. They're going to make a great team. Umm... I need a quick chat with you."

"Sounds serious, dear. Is everything all right between you and Simon? He's such a caring man. I can't believe anything would be wrong there," her mother said, asking and answering her own question.

"No, everything is perfect between Simon and me. He's one in a million."

"And how's the new job going, dear?"

"It's okay, Mum, has its ups and downs at the moment. Teething problems I suppose the experts would call it."

"Okay. Then why am I sensing there is something wrong?"

"I'm delighted with the new role, Mum…" Sally sighed heavily. "It's just that I had to visit the prison today."

Her mother gasped.

"And yes, I saw Darryl. I froze, Mum. I really didn't want to show him how much he'd affected me, but I just stood there like a block of ice, unable to move."

"Oh, darling. How dreadful for you. He didn't get near, did he?"

"No, there were bars and a hallway between us. But he laughed at me, a vile, condescending laugh that creeped me out."

"I'm so sorry you had to go through that, Sally, but why did you go to the prison to see him?"

"Sorry to mislead you. My thoughts raced ahead of me. I didn't go to see him. I went to see another prisoner whom I believe to be innocent. As Joanna and I were leaving the prison, that's when I saw Darryl. God, why on earth did I marry *that*? I can't believe what an absolute fool I was, Mum."

"We all make mistakes in this life, love. It's what moulds us for the future. All you need to do now is concentrate on the life you have with Simon. He's the total opposite to the other scallywag. Move on and learn from your mistakes. That's all any of us can do. You have a wonderful man by your side now who loves and treats you like a princess. Those types of men only come along once in a blue moon. I should know. Forget all about Darryl and move on."

"Thanks, Mum. That's just the kind of reassurance I was hoping to hear. Why don't you and your Prince Charming come and share Sunday lunch with me and my Prince Charming?"

Sally's mother laughed. "That's a date. I think your father said that he would be ringing Simon tonight, regarding a new property he has in mind for renovation. What time should your father ring?"

"Around eightish, Mum. That gives us the chance to cook dinner and get the clearing up done before he rings."

"Perfect. Have a good evening, love. Don't even give that other waste of space another thought. You hear me?"

"I hear you. Love you, Mum. See you on Sunday, around one, okay?"

"Looking forward to it. Love you, too, dear."

Sally hung up, feeling at peace with the world again. Her mother's voice and the common sense she always spouted never failed to help put things into perspective. She unhooked her jacket from the back of the chair and walked into the outer office. After dismissing the team for the evening, she stopped off at the off-licence to purchase three bottles of wine: one to share with Simon that evening and two for when her parents visited at the weekend.

CHAPTER SIX

Simon called to say he was running half an hour late, so Sally decided she would use the time to knock up his favourite meal, lasagne. She was just sprinkling the cheese on top and slicing the tomatoes for the decoration when she heard his key in the front door. She reached into the cupboard above her and withdrew a glass. After pouring the wine, she awaited his arrival with the filled glass in her outstretched hand.

He wandered into the kitchen, his face lighting up as soon as he set eyes on her. He accepted the glass, wrapped an arm around her waist, then kissed her lightly on the lips. Sipping the cool wine as though it were nectar from the gods, he let out a satisfied sigh. "It's good to be home, finally. How was your day?"

"Mixed. And yours?"

"Full of dead bodies and lots of unanswered questions. How is the case going?"

"It's going." Sally pulled out of his grasp and bent down to get the frozen peas out of the freezer. She tipped two portions in a pot and filled it with water before she spoke again. When she glanced at Simon, he was wearing a look of concern. "What's that look for?"

"I know you well enough to know when you're keeping something from me. Do you need me to torture you, to tickle you, to make you share what it is?"

Sally picked up her glass of wine and led him to the table. They sat opposite each other, their hands still clasped firmly. "I came face-to-face with Darryl today."

"What? Where? When? How?"

Sally smirked. "I had to visit the man convicted of Anne Gillan's murder, her husband. Sorry, I went all around the houses to get to that. Once I'd finished interviewing him, I was waiting in the hallway with Joanna, and who should be standing at the end of that hallway but Darryl. God, it was terrifying to see him behind bars like that. It brought it all flooding back to me. If Joanna hadn't snapped me out of it, I have no idea what would have happened to me. As I walked away, he let out a deranged laugh, taunting me."

Simon's other hand caressed her cheek, and she tilted her head, trapping his hand against her shoulder. "You're safe now. You're with me. Even when he gets out, I will never let him lay another hand on you, sweetheart."

"I know, and I'm so grateful to have you in my life." She shook her head. "I'm so bloody angry at myself for reacting the way I did. I always promised that if ever our paths crossed, I would show how strong I'd become. I failed big time."

"There's no need to blame yourself, Sal. He's a twisted individual through and through. None of what you had to endure was ever your fault. You know what they say about men like that. They can bully women, but when it comes to having it out with a man, they crawl back into their shells like the pathetic creatures they are. There's no need to fear him now."

"I know, but he'll be getting out of there in a few years. I know he'll come after me."

"After all the crap he's dished out recently to your car and to Dex, there's no way he'll be given parole. Between us, we'll ensure that doesn't happen. Please don't let him go on ruining your life. He's not worth it, love. We have such a lot to look forward to. The wedding is just around the corner and, hey... you do still want to marry me, don't you?"

Sally left her seat, darted around the table, and fell into his lap. She ran her hand through his greying hair. "More than ever. I'm sorry for letting him affect me this way. I promise he will never do anything that will come between us, though, all right?"

"I should jolly well hope not. We're soulmates, Sally. Just remember that if you ever see him again. I'm going to make it my life's work to make you deliriously happy from this day forward. Life really is too short to reflect on the bad things that have devastated your life in the past. From now on, we're going to concentrate only on positive things. Deal?"

They wrapped their little finger around each other's and both said, "Pinkie deal."

Sally leaned forward, and they shared a long kiss. Pulling away, she said, "I love you, Simon Bracknall."

"I love you, too. About my name, please tell me you've decided once and for all that you'll be changing yours now?"

"That's a definite. I can't wait to get rid of Parker. It'll be my final tie to him."

"Good, I know it's a mouthful, Bracknall, but you'll soon get used to it. Now, how's that dinner coming along? I'm starving."

Sally hopped off his lap and crossed the kitchen to peer through the glass oven door. "It should be ready in five minutes—oops, I better put the peas on."

"I'll just go and get freshened up, if that's okay?"

"Of course."

Every evening, without fail, Simon showered as soon as he got home to get rid of any lingering smells of death either attached to his clothes or trapped within his pores.

Sally continued with the dinner, set the table, and was just plating up the lasagne when he entered the room again, wearing his jeans and a clean T-shirt. Her heart skipped a beat, the way it always did when he walked into a room in casual clothes. She was so proud to be his fiancée and was looking forward to becoming his wife in a couple of months, and nothing was going to stand in the way of that.

After the meal was finished and the kitchen cleaned up, they had just settled down in the lounge with their wine when the house phone rang. "Sorry, that'll probably be Dad. Mum said he was going to ring you tonight."

Simon kissed her forehead and went in search of the phone. "It's fine, honestly." He answered it. "Hello, Chris, how's it all going down at the sites?"

As Sally watched Simon speaking with her dad, she couldn't help her heart swelling with pride. She was delighted he and her parents got on well together, although they had also thought highly of Darryl until the news of his abuse had come out.

"Penny for them?" Simon asked, snuggling up alongside her on the couch once more after he'd ended his call.

"I'm just sitting here, wondering how lucky I am to have you in my life."

"*I'm* the lucky one. I can't believe how far we've come in the last few months. I thought you hated me the first time you laid eyes on me. Do you remember the case we were both working on back then?"

"Are you kidding me? As if I'm likely to forget the most gruesome scene I've ever witnessed during my career." She shuddered as she recalled the head sitting on a stake. Its eyes had been plucked out by the birds, and the man's body lay scattered around his head. The killer had taken a chainsaw to him, chopped him into tiny bits, and placed the body at regular intervals signifying the numbers on a clock. The man's head had been placed so that a shadow would be cast telling people what time it was—a sundial of the grisliest kind.

"Yeah, I thought you'd lose your stomach that day, although I was hoping you'd lose your heart to me."

Sally sat upright and looked him in the eye. "Crikey, you fancied me back then? That was over five years ago, right?"

"Yep. But I knew you were married, so I backed off. Had you been single at the time, I wouldn't have given up so easily."

"You're adorable. I had no idea. Anyway, we're making up for lost time now. What did Dad say?"

He grinned. "Swift change of subject there. We've arranged to meet at lunchtime tomorrow. He thinks we should be looking at our next investment as the other two jobs are almost finished. He's arranged for a couple of estate agents to value the homes for market. They've both said they think the houses should sell reasonably quickly. I'm happy to take his word on that, after seeing the quality of his work at the weekend. He really knows his stuff."

"Phew! I'm so glad things are working out well. So, what's the new project he has lined up?"

"An old Victorian semi in need of complete renovation. He's going over there again tomorrow to look at the roof. If it can be patched, he thinks we should go for it. However, if it needs a new roof, he says he's going to reluctantly say goodbye to the project. I'm happy to go along with his decision. I've agreed to meet him at the location at one o'clock."

"What if you're in the middle of a PM?"

"I'll delay starting a PM until the afternoon. I'm really eager to see this one. Your father says it's huge."

"You're both so funny. You have the enthusiasm of a five-year-old playing with his first car at Christmas."

His face creased up then straightened again quickly. "I love it when you smile."

"You're so sweet. *You* make me smile. I've never had true happiness in my life before. I'm grateful to you for that, Simon."

"How grateful?" he said, a twinkle sparkling in his eye.

They stood up and took their wine up to bed with them.

~ ~ ~

Sally was grinning broadly when she got out of her car the following morning in the station's car park.

"Well, it's good to see someone happy." Looking miserable, Jack joined her on the walk to the entrance.

"Hi, Jack. How did your evening go with Donna? Did you guys come to any conclusion?"

"Yes and no. Why does life have to be so damn hard at times? Why is it always the decisions we make as adults that steer our lives in a certain direction?"

Sally shrugged. "Life is what it is, full of decisions. Come on, don't keep me in suspense. What have you decided?"

He pushed open the heavy door for her and followed her into the reception area before he responded. His chin fell onto his chest.

Sally's stomach constricted. "Bloody hell, Jack, get on with it."

His head rose again and there was a broad smile pulling his lips apart.

"You bloody wind-up merchant. You're staying with us?"

"I am. I couldn't leave you in the lurch. You need my expertise."

"Don't flatter yourself, love, and don't give me such bullshit. It was the thought of sitting in a control room with headphones slapped on your ears all day that swayed your decision, right?"

"You're too smart for your own good sometimes, Inspector."

She dug him in the ribs. "Glad to have you back, Jack. Crap, now I have to inform Green that you're turning down the position. You certainly know how to make my life difficult, don't you?"

"Oops, sorry, boss. Do you want *me* to tell him instead?"

They ascended the stairs. "No, I'll take the brunt of his anger. Bloody hell, the things I do for you guys, just to keep you all happy. Maybe someone will do the same for me one day."

"Get outta here. You know you're appreciated by the team and that we've always got your back."

Sally smiled. "I know. Right, I'll leave you to tell the rest of them while I ring Green from my office. I need a coffee first. That's your cue to say you'll buy me one."

"Oh, right. Sorry, of course I will. It's the least I can do with a possible onslaught coming your way."

Sally wandered into her office, glanced out the window at the open landscape surrounding the station, then settled herself into her chair behind her desk.

Jack entered the room, placed two cups of coffee in front of her, and winked. "Thought a double dose would help."

"Creep." Jack closed the door, and Sally inhaled a large breath, preparing herself as she dialled Green's direct line. "Hello, sir, it's Sally Parker."

"Good morning, Inspector. Any news for me?"

"I'm ringing up about Jack Blackman… umm…"

"Get on with it, Inspector. It's not like you to be slow in coming forward. What's he decided?"

Sally chewed her lip for a second. "That he wants to remain with the team, sir. I'm sorry."

"Sorry? Why? I'm delighted that my little plan worked."

"You mean you offered him a lesser post intentionally?"

"Of course. How many officers do you know who are willing to take a substantial pay cut?" He laughed.

Sally joined in. "Well played, sir. I'm relieved that he'll be staying with us. Enjoy your day."

"You, too, Inspector. Don't forget to update me on the case when something significant comes to light."

"I'll do that, sir." Sally hung up and expelled a large breath. After dealing with the important post on her desk, she left the office to rejoin her team. "Okay, where are we now? I take it Jack has shared his news with you all?" Sally glanced around the group, and she received either a firm nod or a smile of affirmation from each of them.

"My theory is that he wanted to put himself in the limelight so decided to throw his rattle out of the pram."

Jack's face was a picture when the rest of the team laughed raucously. "I did not." He pouted, crossing his arms defiantly.

Sally smiled, happy and relieved that he would be alongside her on their new venture. "Right. Jack and I will be going out to visit the daughter, Molly Gillan, this morning. I'd like you all to continue digging through the files in our absence."

"Are we looking for anything in particular, boss?" Joanna asked.

Sally felt a guilty pang for ditching her as a partner so soon. "I need you to focus on the statements for me, Joanna. Also, can you check that everyone's address is current? Jack and I will work our way through them. Oh, and could you also try and find Dr. Mountford for me?"

"Of course." Joanna nodded and smiled broadly. Sally couldn't help but wonder if the smile was one of relief.

"With respect, boss, we'll be going over what we did yesterday. Is there anything else you need us to do, other than twiddle our thumbs?" Jordan asked quietly, as if voicing his opinion would get him into trouble.

"Hmm... this is all still a learning curve until all the pieces start to slot together. I think we'll spend a few days going over and over what we've been dealt. Okay, what if we look at trying to crack two cold-cases at the same time? After all, we have forty of them to go through, right?"

Jordan nodded. "I think that's a good idea, boss. Any particular one?"

"I'll leave that to you, Jordan. Why don't we leave Joanna to deal with the Gillan case, while you and Stuart sort through the files for another one. Nothing too taxing, though."

"Great. We'll get on it right away."

"Let me know which one you decide on when we return. I don't want you to start any leg work on it until I've cast my eyes over the case first, all right?"

"Of course. Thanks, boss." The enthusiastic DC crossed the room and began removing the files from the archive boxes.

"Are you ready, Jack?"

"Yep. Ready to rock and roll."

Sally and Jack left the station and drove for twenty minutes to Molly's address. Joanna had called the young woman the previous day to set up a possible rendezvous.

Molly was in her early twenties, very slim, and had long wavy brown hair.

Sally held out her ID for the young woman to see and introduced herself and Jack. Molly stepped aside and invited them into the hallway of her small terraced house.

"Come through. Sorry, I'm in the middle of decorating. I only moved in a few weeks ago. It seems to be never-ending at present. How can I help, Inspector?"

"You're aware that we're reinvestigating your father's case."

"Yes. My grandmother told me yesterday, and I'm thrilled. Overjoyed, to be truthful with you. I've fought so hard to get his case heard again. I've always known he was innocent. My mother's body showing up last week has only proved that."

"Well, I can't say for definite that we will be able to prove his innocence yet. It depends what evidence we uncover. What we do know is that the original investigating officer wasn't as thorough in his duties as he should have been. My team and I highlighted several discrepancies in another case we solved a few months back. We've been given the task of starting this case from scratch, but to do that, we need all the witnesses and people involved, like you and the other members of your family, to go over the events surrounding your mother's disappearance. I truly understand how uncomfortable this will be for you, but if you can be open and honest with us, that's all we can ask."

"Of course. Although you are aware that I was only eight at the time."

"Yes, we're aware of that. Nevertheless, you strike me as an astute young lady, Molly."

"Thank you. I had a wonderful relationship with both of my parents during my childhood, up until the age of eight, I should say. Then my whole world imploded. My mother vanished, and my father was put in prison within a few days. If it hadn't been for my grandparents stepping up to the plate, Jamie and I would have been shoved into the care system. I'll always be grateful to my grandparents for raising us."

"Not every grandparent would think of putting their life on hold in such circumstances. They seemed a very loving couple when we met them. Casting your mind back to the time your mother went missing, can you go over what happened that day?"

"It's imprinted in my mind. Dad had put us to bed that night around eight. Mum was on a late shift at work. I hated it when she had to fill in for holidays et cetera. Dad did his best, but his cooking wasn't up to scratch. Anyway, when we came down the next morning, we found Dad curled up on the sofa. He'd been sitting up all night, waiting for Mum to come home. He was a mess. I could tell he'd been crying. He gathered us together and told us that the police might be around for a few days. They were trying to help find Mum as she was missing.

"I was confused, so I climbed onto his lap and wrapped my arms around his neck, the way I always did when I needed him to explain something to me." Her eyes welled up, and she swallowed noisily. "I've missed out on so many cuddles over the years, not having him around."

"It must have been hard for you and your brother, confusing, too."

"It was. I don't think Jamie has ever recovered from that night. He was too young to understand, thought that Mum had run out on us, and then for Dad to be carted off to prison like that—he just thought our parents had deserted him. I did my best to try and reassure him over the years, but it's been pointless. He's such a lost soul now. He finds solace in the drugs he takes… I know I shouldn't tell you that, but it's the truth. I lost my brother the day my mother went missing. My once-happy family was destroyed that day. Not once have I ever thought my dad guilty of killing Mum. They loved each other too much. He worshipped her. Finding her body last week filled me with mixed emotions. Predominantly, my heart went out to my dad, for all the years he has suffered in that dreadful place. I was relieved that they'd finally found my mother. At least I can lay her to rest now, but that just leaves so many unanswered questions. Who would go out of their way to kill such a beautiful person? Why?"

"Well, that's where we come in. Hopefully, we'll have the answers to all your questions soon and be able to get your father out of prison and reunited with you and your brother."

"I hope so. I've visited him for years, and over the last couple of years, I've seen him deteriorate so much. I hate seeing the fight dwindle in his eyes. He doesn't belong in there—never has, Inspector. I truly can't believe he has lasted this long. I know I wouldn't have been able to if that had happened to me."

"I got the same impression when I visited him yesterday. Maybe it would be different if he didn't have you and your brother to come out to. He spoke of Jamie fondly. Is there no way of getting your brother to go and visit him?"

"No, Jamie's very confused. He has been for years. I try my best to be there for him, but the second I bring Dad into the conversation, he clams up and makes an excuse to leave. He promised me that he would help decorate this place. I even offered him my spare room, rent free, and he had agreed to move in, but all that changed when Mum's remains were identified. I met up with him in a café last week. I found it impossible to read exactly what he was going through. It was as if all the pain and anguish he felt as a five-year-old came flooding back. He's running scared. Scared of opening up, accepting that Dad is innocent, regretting the way he's treated our father over the years. I'm doing my best to talk him round, but he's becoming more and more reliant on those damn drugs, which is hampering my efforts."

"What about rehab? Is he under the doctor?"

"Rehab is for those who have the funds to send their loved ones to those places. I haven't got any spare money after buying this place. The mortgage is going to cripple me as it is. Buying this was my attempt at helping him out of his stupor. But I fear I might have failed. Maybe he's beyond saving after all these years. I don't know." She threw her arms up in despair. "As for the doctor, he's worse than useless. All he did was sit him down and tell him what a fool he was being, wasting his life being reliant on the drugs to see him through. Hardly what my brother wanted, or needed, to hear."

"Maybe you should seek another doctor's advice in that case. He obviously needs professional help. Can I ask when he started taking the drugs?"

"In his teens. I think he smoked his first joint when he was sixteen and got hooked straight away. No matter what I've said over the years, I've never been able to convince him what he's doing is wrong. He snapped at me once, told me that it eases his pain, and he was concerned about what would happen if he stopped taking them. Like I've said already, he's confused and a lost soul."

"Very sad. Would you like me to see what I can do about enrolling him in rehab? I can't guarantee that I'll find him a place, but if I did, do you think he'd be willing to go?"

"Honestly? I'm not sure. He says he would. However, I think he's just saying that to appease me. When it comes to the crunch, I think he would bolt, and I'd never hear from him again. I thought if he helped me get this place up to scratch, it would give him a purpose in life. As soon as I got the keys, he went into his shell."

"Do you have any other relatives who can help you reach out to him? Anyone he admired as a child? An aunt or uncle maybe? A teacher he was fond of at school or a football coach? Anyone along those lines?"

"No, I can't think of anyone. Hang on…" She placed her head in her hands as she thought then looked up with a pained expression. "Somewhere in my distant memory, I think I remember Dad had a brother. I'm not getting a clear picture of him and can't for the life of me remember his name."

"Not to worry, we can look into that at our end or ask your father the next time we see him. Anyone else?"

"I don't think so. We were quite a close-knit family when we were growing up, so I only remember both sets of grandparents visiting us when we were little."

"Don't worry, we'll find your uncle if he's still around. Can I ask for the address of the squat where your brother is staying?"

Molly stood and walked over to a notebook on the table. She jotted down the address and handed it to Sally. In return, Sally gave the young woman one of her business cards. "Thanks. Ring me if you need to chat about the case. I'll try and keep you up-to-date as we progress. Thank you for seeing us today. Will you be visiting your father soon?"

"Mum's funeral is tomorrow. I'm not sure if Dad is going to be there or not. The governor is still debating it."

"Well, maybe our visit to see your father will help sway the governor's decision. What time is the funeral and where? We'd like to pay our respects."

"At All Saints Church, just down the road, at eleven. You don't have to be there. You have enough to do as it is."

"I know. We'd like to attend, all the same. Is your brother going?" Sally asked as they walked towards the front door.

"He doesn't know about it. I don't have the courage to go to the squat by myself. I rang him last week, told him about Mum before he saw it on the news, but I haven't heard from him since. To be honest, I don't even know if my brother is still alive, Inspector."

Seeing how upset Molly was, Sally rubbed her upper arm. "Stay strong. We'll shoot over there now. If he's there, we'll bring him tomorrow, kicking and screaming if we have to," she said, trying to lighten the mood.

Molly smiled. "Now that I'd pay money to see. Send him my love and tell him I miss him and that there is a room waiting for him here if he ever cleans up his act."

"I'll look into the rehabilitation side of things when I get back to the station, too. It was lovely meeting you. I hope we can get your father out of prison soon."

"I hope so, too." Molly gently closed the door behind them.

"Next stop the squat, I take it," Jack said as they climbed back in the car.

"Wait, would you drive, Jack? I want to have a chat with Joanna, get things in place before we turn up at Jamie's, just in case."

"Sure. Although, I think you'll be wasting your time by the sounds of things."

"Maybe, maybe not. We'll see how he's taken the news when we get there."

They exchanged sides, and Jack rearranged the driver's seat to suit his long legs while Sally rang the station. "Joanna, we've just seen Molly Gillan. She's given us the address of a squat where her brother is staying. Do me a favour and run the address through the system." Sally gave her the address and waited.

"Boss, the place was raided last year. A large amount of drugs were found on the premises, and several druggies were banged up.

Nothing since then, although the house is still on the radar, kept under surveillance regularly."

"Excellent. Hopefully, we won't get any trouble when we arrive. I'll ring before we go in, and you can monitor the situation. If you don't hear from me again within ten minutes, send a backup team to join us, okay?"

"I'll organise a team to be on standby, boss."

"A couple more things before you go, Joanna. I promised Molly that we would look into trying to enrol her brother into drug rehab. I don't have a clue how such things work. Can you look into the criteria needed for someone to join up to one of these places? Also, Molly mentioned the only other living relative, apart from her grandparents, she thought she had was an uncle, her father's brother. I don't recall seeing him mentioned in the file. Can you delve into that for me? I'd like to question him if he's still around. Maybe he has an inkling about what happened to Anne back then."

"I'll get onto all that now, boss, and get back to you soon."

"You're a star. How are Jordan and Stuart getting on? Have they decided what case to tackle yet?"

"Yes, they're just going over it now. They'll fill you in when you return, if that's okay?"

"Of course. You carry on. Speak soon." Sally hung up and turned to Jack. "We need to be cautious going in, partner. We'll do the softly, softly approach in case anyone wants to kick off."

"Oh, joy, sounds like a bundle of laughs ahead of us."

"We can handle it. We're experts, right?"

Jack chortled. "If you say so."

They drove for another fifteen minutes then pulled up outside the squat. Sally rang the station again. "Hi, Joanna, we're just about to go inside. Put the backup team on standby. You know the rest. Do you have anything for me?"

"I was just going to ring you, boss. I have an opening in a rehab centre the other side of Norwich. They're prepared to keep the place open for a week. That's all I have at present. Nothing showing up on the uncle as yet. I'll get back to it. Stay safe, both of you."

"We've every intention of doing that, Joanna. Will ring you before the ten minutes are up, hopefully."

Jack and Sally exited the car and stepped into the litter-strewn front garden of the terraced house. There were no curtains at the window, just a blanket hanging down one side of each frame.

"I'm not looking forward to this," Jack mumbled once he rang the bell.

"Just keep focused on what we're here to do and ignore anything else you might see inside."

The door opened, and a sleepy-looking young woman stood behind the door, her hand raised to shield her eyes from the sun's glare.

"Beautiful morning." Sally pulled out her ID and suspended it in front of the girl's face. "Is Jamie Gillan in?"

Jack shoved his foot in the gap in case the girl slammed the door shut.

"Nah, he moved on ages ago."

"He did? How long?"

Chewing on a piece of gum, the girl replied, "About five weeks or so. Why? What's he done?"

Sally had an inkling the girl was lying. "Nothing. We just need a chat with him about his parents."

The girl hesitated then disappeared inside the house, leaving the door open. Sally and Jack glanced at each other and shrugged.

"Is that an invitation for us to enter?"

Jack smiled. "You know what, boss? I think it is. I'll go first."

"My hero," Sally jested, following her partner through the hallway, the walls of which were full of obscene graffiti.

Jack stopped at the first door he came to and opened it. Sticking his head inside the room, he called out, "Jamie Gillan? Police. We'd like to speak with you." He gagged when he closed the door. "There must be ten people in there, sleeping bags everywhere. I can't even begin to describe the stench."

"Appalling... we need to check every room, Jack. I'll ring Joanna and extend our time to twenty minutes."

As she quickly placed the call, Jack moved up the hallway and barged into the next room, his huge frame filling the doorway. He shook his head when he left the room. "Same as the first room. A few groans from them, but nothing else. Do you think he'll admit to being here, using these tactics?"

"Shame we never thought to get a picture of him from his sister. What do you suggest?"

He tapped his nose and winked. "Leave it to me." They walked through the house and discovered the only other room downstairs was a kitchen filled with takeaway containers, empty cans and plastic milk cartons. The stench made Sally heave.

They decided to retrace their steps and see what was going on upstairs. Jack took the lead once more and thumped on the first door they came to. "I've got a package for Jamie Gillan. Is he here?"

"Not here. Try the next room, mate," a muffled voice replied from beneath the covers.

Sally gave her partner the thumbs-up. He went through the same routine in the next room, where a young man shot up and ran to the door. He was deathly pale, wearing a filthy pair of orange boxer shorts and nothing else. Sally had seen more fat on a lab rat. She was sickened by his appearance.

"I'm Jamie. I've been expecting you."

"Get some clothes on," Jack ordered harshly.

The young man ran a hand through his long, dirty-blonde hair and looked at Jack as if he'd just dropped out of the sky. "Who the fuck are you to tell me what to do, man? Give me the package and do one."

Jack tapped at the youngster's forehead. "Anybody in there? Wake up and smell the roses, mate. We're the police. We want to have a chat with you, outside, away from this stench, preferably."

"Police? I ain't done nothing wrong."

"Not saying you have. Get some trousers on, or if you're that incapable of dressing yourself, I'll do it for you."

"Wait a sec." He closed the door and joined them again a few seconds later. He eyed them both warily. "Come on then, I ain't got all day." He marched down the stairs in his bare feet.

Jack and Sally met up with him just inside the front door.

"I ain't going out there. It's too cold. Say what you've got to say and get lost."

"First of all, it's a beautiful June day out there, and secondly, cut the shitty attitude." Sally eyed him with disdain, her sympathy for the young man dwindling faster than a receding tide.

"Stop ordering me around, lady, and tell me what you want."

Jack took a step forward, but Sally tugged on his arm. "He's not worth it, Jack. I'm Detective Inspector Parker, and this is my partner, Detective Sergeant Blackman. We've just paid your sister a visit. She gave us your address; she's concerned about you."

He focused on a patch of wall to the side of Sally, refusing to make eye contact with her. "Why? I'm all right by myself. Don't need my older sister bossing me about. I live my life how I want to live it."

"In a shithole like this, drugged out of your mind most of the time. What kind of existence is that, Jamie?"

"My kind. Who are you to stand there and judge me? Just tell me what you want and leave me in peace."

"Okay, we're here concerning your mother."

His face screwed up. "What about her? Molly said they fished her body out of the river," he stated as if he didn't give two hoots about her. Sally knew differently, though.

"How do you feel about her being found?"

He shrugged. "How do you expect me to feel?"

"I don't know. That's why I'm asking."

"Did *he* put her there?"

"Who? Your father?"

"Who the hell do you think I'm talking about?"

"Honestly, no. I don't think your father did it."

He looked at her, his eyes narrowing in suspicion. "Is that right?"

"After speaking with him yesterday, my gut feeling is that he didn't have anything to do with it. We're trying our best to find the evidence to prove his innocence. We can't do that without the help of the people who were involved."

He ran a hand over the patchy beard growing on his gaunt face. "Not sure what I can do. With no body, I got the impression that she might have run off, what with her just disappearing like that. I didn't have a clue." Tears glistened in his eyes, and his voice softened when he referred to his mother. Then he said something that caused Sally to gasp. "The day she left, she took my heart with her."

"I'm sorry. She didn't run off; she was murdered. Look, I believe all your father is guilty of is loving you too much. He's devastated that you've refused to have any contact with him over the years. In my experience, at times like this, families usually dig deep into their resolve and fight for each other. Fight to find out the truth of what went on. If, as Molly says, your parents had a good life together and never argued, then that's all the more reason for you to believe your father and to stand alongside him in his hour of need, not to ditch him and make the situation a thousand times worse."

He pushed away from the wall and stepped forward, but Sally stood firm. "Hey, lady, I don't need no lecture from the likes of you. You don't know what goes on up here." He pointed to his temple then his heart. "Or in here. How do you know it's not guilt I'm dealing with? Don't look at me like that. I don't mean I killed her. Guilt for treating my father so badly when I should have supported him, but it was too late for that."

Sally laid a hand on his arm. "It's never too late to start again. To repair the damage. Your father would love nothing more, I promise you, Jamie."

"It's too late for me. He, no they, wouldn't want a drug-taking wastrel around them now. They're better off without me. I'm hooked on the stuff with no way of getting off it. I never know from one day to the next if I'll survive another day. No one is more surprised when I wake up in the morning, having made it through yet another drug-induced sleep."

"If you really want to make amends with Molly and your father, I can help with that."

"How?"

"I have a bed lined up for you in a drug rehabilitation centre. If you're willing to get clean, that is."

He scratched the side of his head with his dirty fingernails. "Let me think about it. Wait, why would you want to help me?"

"For your father's sake. If we get him off the charges and out of prison, he'll want to be reunited with his children. He's missed you. He made a point of telling me that when I visited him. Don't give up on your dad, Jamie."

"I'll think about it. *If* you get him off, when will he be set free?"

"How long is that piece of proverbial string? Let's just say my team and I are working hard to make it happen. Hopefully, it won't be too long before he breathes fresher air again." She handed him a business card. "Ring me once you've thought things over. Don't waste your life away, Jamie. Don't waste the opportunity you've been given to better yourself. Not everyone is offered the opportunity to clean up their act like you've been given. If you want it enough, it's there for you. Just ring me once you've decided."

"Thanks… I mean it. I've got a lot of thinking to do about everything before I agree to taking that place in rehab, but thanks for giving me the chance."

"You're welcome. We'll go now. One last thing… do me a favour."

"What's that?"

"Give your sister a call. She's worried about you. Plus, she could do with your help decorating her new place."

"Damn, I've let her down again. I'll give her a ring today."

Sally patted his arm and smiled. "That's all I can ask of you, for now. Think everything through seriously, Jamie. I hope you find the answers you're seeking soon. By the way, your mother's funeral is tomorrow morning. I'm sure Molly would love you to be by her side during the service."

"I'm not sure I'm ready for that. I'll discuss it with Molly."

"It's at eleven. If you need a lift, give me a call." Sally smiled. Then she opened the front door and walked out onto the street, with Jack close behind her. She heard Jamie thank them quietly before he closed the front door.

"Think he'll go down the rehab route?" Jack asked when they reached the car.

"Who knows? I'm not sure he knows the answer to that himself yet. Molly was right. He does seem to be a very confused young man. He's only got to get his hands on some of the good stuff, and all his doubts will drift away. He'll be suckered into thinking that the drugs are the only answer to his questions. Sad, really. Glad I've never had the inclination to try the bloody stuff." She shuddered and lowered herself into the passenger seat, keen to let Jack drive back to the station.

"Never seen the point in taking drugs. Saw a video once on one of those science programmes, showing how many brain cells drugs kill off. That was enough for me. Doesn't appeal to me in the slightest," Jack agreed.

"I better ring Joanna to call off the backup team." Before she had a chance to place the call, her mobile rang. She smiled when she saw Simon's name displayed on the screen. "I'll take this outside. Can you ring Joanna for me?"

"Sure."

"Hello, you. How are things at the house? Is it a goer?"

"Sally, I have some bad news. It's your dad."

"Dad? What the hell is wrong with him?"

"I've just got here. I was searching the outside of the property, trying to find him, thought he hadn't turned up. Anyway, I went around the back of the house and found him lying on the ground, unconscious."

"My God, is he all right? Did he pass out, have a heart attack, what?"

"Don't go getting worked up. By the looks of things, he took a fall from the scaffolding. I know he mentioned going up to check the roof."

"What? He fell off the roof? Is that possible? Was there anyone else on site?"

"No, he was here alone. I called the ambulance, and they're on their way. I can't bring him round. I really don't want to move him in case he's damaged his spine or neck."

"Jesus, now you're scaring me. Does it look as though he's badly injured? Are his limbs facing the wrong direction?"

"No, not that I can tell. I'm used to dealing with dead bodies. I haven't got a clue how to assess a live patient. I'll keep trying to rouse him. I just thought you should know right away."

"Okay, what's the address?"

"It's Five, Orchard Road, Thetford."

"Gosh, we're miles away. It'll take us at least thirty minutes to get there."

"The ambulance should be here any minute. Let me ring you back with their prognosis, okay?"

"Thanks, Simon. Look after him for me."

"I will." Simon disconnected the phone.

Dazed, Sally opened the passenger door and slid into her seat. "I don't believe it."

"Whoa! What's wrong? You look as though you've seen a ghost, Sal."

"It's my dad. Simon thinks he's fallen from the scaffolding. He found him unconscious at the house they're interested in buying."

"Crap. Want me to take you there?"

She shook her head. "There's no point. The ambulance is on its way. Let them deal with the situation. Simon's going to ring me back. Damn, why did the old fool go up there without anyone else being present?"

Jack placed a hand on her knee. "Let's see what the paramedics say first and where they take him. Shall I head back to the station?"

"Yes. God, I hope Dad is going to be all right." An image of her Dad's funeral flashed through her mind, along with the devastation that would cause to her and her mother. She shook the maudlin pictures from her mind. *Be strong, Dad. You'll be in safe hands soon.*

CHAPTER SEVEN

The drive back to the station seemed endless as Sally waited to hear more news from Simon. He finally called her as she and Jack pulled into the station's car park. "Simon, how is he?"

"Right, first of all, I apologise for the delay. Your dad has regained consciousness. Sally, it's good and bad news."

"Just tell me!" she snapped.

"Sorry. Okay, I read the situation wrong when I arrived. Your dad didn't fall off the scaffolding."

"Christ, that's a relief. Was it his heart? Has he had a heart attack?"

"No, nothing like that. Sal, he was attacked!"

"What? How? By whom?"

"He's not sure. His head is still muzzy. He said he walked through the back gate to find two men waiting there. When he challenged them, they started laying into him. He doesn't have a clue why. One of them struck him with a metal scaffolding pole and knocked him out."

"Why? Is there anything to steal at the property? Were they robbing the place, Simon?"

"No, the place is a shell. Not unless they were intending to steal the windows or something along those lines."

"Why would anyone want to do that? Is he going to hospital?"

"Yes, they're just loading him into the ambulance now. He's going to West Suffolk Hospital in Bury St Edmunds to get checked out. They think he has concussion."

"Blimey, that's miles away. Okay, I'll see if I can take the rest of the day off and come down there."

"You don't have to do that. I've rung the lab, told them not to expect me back today. I'll stay with him while the docs check him out and bring him home when he's discharged. The paramedics thought it's likely he'd be released today."

"Are you sure?"

"Of course. It's all organised. Can you ring your mum, tell her what's happened?"

"I'll do it now. What would I do without you, Simon? You're a rock. I can't thank you enough."

"Nonsense, that's what fiancés are for. You'd do the same for me."

"I know I would, but you're an extremely busy man."

"Hey, my patients aren't going anywhere. They're not likely to walk out if I don't turn up for an op."

Sally chuckled. "You have a valid point. Okay, keep me informed, if you will. Send Dad my love. I love you."

"I will. Love you, too. Speak later."

Sally wanted to compose herself properly before she contemplated ringing her mother, so she decided to call her from her office instead of using her mobile. Coffee in hand, she settled behind her desk and picked up the phone. "Hi, Mum, how are you?"

"Hello, love. I'm all right, running around like a lunatic, making the most of my time alone with your father out and about. Have you heard how the house visit is going? All very exciting, isn't it? He was chuffed to bits when he left here this morning. Had a real spring in his step, he did."

Sally closed her eyes and listened to her mother chuntering on enthusiastically. "Mum, can you take a breath and sit down please?"

"I'm sitting. This sounds serious, love. Anything wrong?"

"It's Dad. He's had an accident."

"What? In the car? He said there was something not quite right with the car. I told him to take it to the garage the other day. Is he all right?"

"Mum, listen, for goodness' sake. He was at the new house when the accident occurred. Simon found him lying unconscious and thought he'd fallen off the scaffolding, but Dad woke up and said that two men attacked him."

"No! Why? Your father has never harmed anyone in his life. Why would anyone want to hurt him?"

Sally hesitated before she answered. *Yes, why would anyone hurt him, unless... Darryl! I wouldn't put it past him to do something like this. It wouldn't be the first time he's disrupted our lives from inside.* "I don't know, Mum, not at this stage. I just wanted to make you aware of what's going on. Simon has taken the rest of the day off and accompanied Dad to the hospital in Bury St Edmunds. The paramedics said that taking him to hospital was just a precaution and that he should be home by the end of the day. He's got a concussion."

"Oh my, poor Christopher. How lucky we are to have Simon in our lives and for him to have found your father when he did. A blessing in disguise, for sure. I'll just wait to hear from either you or Simon then. Please, keep me in the loop, Sally."

"Of course, Mum. Try not to worry too much. He's in the best hands now."

"I'll try. Goodbye, dear."

Sally sighed and hung up. She looked up to see a concerned Jack standing in the doorway. "Is your mum all right?"

"Scared shitless, but apart from that, yes, she's fine. Sit down, Jack."

"What's up? Apart from the obvious? You look serious."

Sally ran a hand over her face and tucked her hair behind her ear on one side. "I had a thought when I was relaying what had gone on with Dad to Mum. What if Darryl was involved in this?"

Jack shook his head in disbelief. "How? You're clutching at straws. Think logically about this. How would he know that your father was going to that address?"

Sally picked up a pen and threw it across the desk. "I know that logic should be telling me how foolish I am, but I can't shake this feeling that he's behind this. You've got to admit the coincidence can't be ignored. I see him at the prison one day, and the next, my father is knocked unconscious by two thugs. You know he has form regarding this, Jack."

"I know. And if this had occurred outside your father's house, I'd be inclined to agree with you, but it didn't. How would Darryl know that your dad was going to be at that house in Thetford today at that specific time?"

She rested her chin on her hands and stared at him. "I know what you're saying, but I still have more than a niggling doubt that he's behind this."

"He can't be. Believe me, no one would want to point the finger at him more than me. It just isn't plausible, Sally."

"I hear you. I was wondering if you'd do me a favour."

Jack frowned. "If I can—you know that. What do you need?"

"I need you to go and see Darryl, warn him off."

Jack shook his head. "If it's truly what you want me to do, I will, but you're barking up the wrong tree."

Sally slumped back in her chair. "But it would make me feel so much better."

"Think it over for half an hour, weigh up the pros and cons of me storming in there and accusing him. If you still feel the same way, then, yes, I'll shoot over there. My guess is that you'll think it's a daft decision."

"All right, smartarse, I trust your instincts on this one. Let me just ring Simon and then we'll go over things with the team."

Jack smiled and left the room.

Sally rang Simon's mobile.

He answered on the first ring. "Hi, I'm just moving to somewhere more private, two ticks."

"How is he?" she asked impatiently.

"He's doing okay. I was just going to ring you, in fact. His memory is less hazy now. He said he turned up at the property, was about to inspect the roof when two men approached him. They had a nasty streak, told him to get off the site. When he refused, they struck him with a bar and laid into him."

"Did they just walk in off the street? Were they the owners of the house, or the previous owners? It doesn't make any sense, Simon."

"I know. My take on it is that they were a couple of developers keen to get their hands on the property."

"What? Why?" Sally blushed, ashamed that she'd almost sent Jack on a wild-goose chase to warn Darryl off.

"I suppose this property-developing lark is becoming a cut-throat business. The property your dad and I were interested in could be a real money spinner. We could be talking about making a profit of around a hundred thousand pounds, just on this one house. There are going to be others out there who are also interested in making that sum of money."

"Bloody unscrupulous bastards. Why don't they thrash it out in the auction room like normal people? Why did they have to put Dad in hospital? What if they had killed him? They could have struck him in the wrong place with that pole and killed him. Would it really be worth these men facing a murder charge just for a profit on a house?"

"I hear you. Hey, I really and truly believe this is a one-off. Your father is adamant he wants to pursue our venture. He's willing to also try and identify the men. If word gets around that we're not scared of thugs like these, then they'll soon back off, love."

"Gosh, I hope you're right. In my experience, these types tend to dig their heels in."

"We'll see if your dad has a change of heart once he's out of hospital. I think he's as stubborn as you, though, and not likely to back down to these monsters."

"If he can identify them, that'll make our job much easier. Okay, you better go. Thanks for the update and for taking time off to be with him. I'll ring you later, love you."

"Ditto. Speak soon."

Sally pushed away from the desk and left the office. Needing to refocus her mind on work, she approached Jordan. "Do you want to run through what case you've chosen to explore?"

"Stuart and I thought we would look into the case of Paula Thompson from Norwich. She was convicted eight years ago of murdering her husband, Don."

Sally tilted her head, intrigued that her colleagues had chosen to delve into a woman's case and not another male's. "How?"

"Poison. They found the evidence sitting in the bathroom cabinet."

"How strange. So she didn't even try to hide the evidence? Doesn't sound very killer-like behaviour to me."

"Which is what struck us as weird and drew us to the case. All right if we plod on with it, boss?"

"Of course. Good luck. Run things past me as they appear, all right?"

Sally stood in between Jack's and Joanna's desks. "That leaves the three of us to deal with the Gillan case. What else have you managed to gather while Jack and I were out, Joanna?"

"I found out that the family doctor died of cancer last year."

"How sad. Okay, what else?"

"I went through the file again, focusing on the friends and family members. Managed to track down most of them, boss. The only one I haven't found yet is Craig Gillan's brother, Kenny."

"Hmm… keep trying, the more relatives we speak to the better"

"I will. Here are the details you need about the work colleagues who were questioned at the time of Anne's death. I can't believe they all still work there after all this time—that's remarkable in itself. Makes it easier for you to question them, I suppose."

"Great news. Maybe the firm is a good employer and the staff know where they're better off. A stable job is hard to come by today," Sally replied, scanning the list.

"When do you want to start questioning them?" Jack asked.

"Well, the funeral is happening tomorrow. We need to attend that first before we can contemplate going to the factory. Maybe some, or most, of these people will be at the church."

"It would be good to monitor them at the scene, especially when emotions will be running high. Do we know if Craig is going to be there?"

"I'll ring the governor after our meeting. It would be a shame if he wasn't. It might shock the other attendees, though." Sally ran a hand over her face. "Not sure myself if he should go, to be honest with you, but then if Anne's parents have no objection to Craig being there, I don't see why anyone else should kick up a stink. If he turns out to be innocent, then he has every right to be there. My worry is that if we ultimately find him guilty of killing her, we're going to suffer a massive backlash for allowing him to attend the funeral for one last gloat."

"It's a tough call," Jack agreed. "But then his human rights are going to come into play on this one, aren't they? He was married to her for over ten years, after all."

"I've not experienced anything like this before. I'll see what the governor has to say about it when I ring him. Anything else, Joanna?"

"Nothing as yet, boss."

"Okay, keep digging for Kenny's whereabouts. I'll be in my office, making some calls." Sally rushed back to her office and rang the prison. "Hello, Governor Wilkinson, this is DI Sally Parker. We met the other day."

"Ah, yes, I remember, Inspector. What can I do for you on this bright June day?"

His jovial banter caused her to falter for a second or two. "Umm… I'm ringing up to check if Craig Gillan will be allowed to attend his wife's funeral tomorrow."

There was a long pause before the governor responded. "Do you think he should? I told his daughter that I was mulling the decision over. It's not just Craig's feelings we have to take into consideration here, Inspector. I don't have to remind you at this moment in time the man is serving time for his wife's murder. Can you imagine the uproar that is going to create if he shows up?"

"I appreciate that—I truly do, sir—however, there is every indication that Craig is innocent of this crime. Could you live with yourself knowing that you denied him his human rights to be at the burial of his wife when we prove his innocence a few weeks down the line?"

"It's a quandary that I've been contemplating for days, Inspector. There's no easy answer either way, is there?"

"I don't envy your decision. Have you come across this scenario before?"

"Once or twice, but never in such a complex case. The other cases were to do with convicts attending their siblings' funerals. We allowed Craig to attend both his parents' funerals, don't forget."

"I heard. I do appreciate the predicament you're in, believe me."

He sighed heavily. "I'll need to run it past my superiors and get back to you."

"I can't ask for more than that. Will you let me know before the day is out, Governor?"

"I'll do my best. You know how evasive our senior officers can be."

Sally laughed. "That, I do. Okay, I'll wait to hear back from you then. Goodbye for now." She couldn't help but feel disappointed and let down that the governor didn't have the balls to make the decision himself. After all, he had daily dealings with the prisoner; his superior officers didn't. She would just have to sit and wait for them to hopefully come to the right conclusion.

A full three hours later, the governor confirmed that Gillan would be allowed to attend his wife's funeral. That was when Sally's stomach really tied itself into knots. *What if Anne's friends object to him being there? Maybe it would be worth having a police presence there in case things kick off.* She called the desk sergeant and asked if that would be possible for eleven o'clock the next day. He told her he could supply two uniformed officers for the occasion. That was good enough for Sally, and she quickly accepted the offer.

The end of the day loomed. Between them, she and her colleagues had made good progress on the two cases. She dismissed the team for the evening and rang Simon. "Hi, are you still at the hospital?"

"Yes, they've just told me that they're keeping your dad in overnight as a precaution. I'm just setting off home now."

"I want to see him. Will he be up to having a visitor?"

"Honestly, he looks done in. I'd leave it for tonight, love. I've been here all day and I think he's looking forward to some peace and quiet this evening."

"Okay, you win. Tell him I love him and that Mum and I are thinking of him and I look forward to seeing him tomorrow."

"I will. I'll duck out of giving him a peck on the cheek, if that's okay, though." Simon sniggered.

"Idiot. I'll ring Mum and let her know. She'll be worried out of her mind." Sally hung up and immediately dialled her mother's number. The phone was answered before it had completed the first ring. "Hi, Mum, it's me. No need to panic. Dad is fine. They're keeping him in overnight as a precautionary measure. Simon has been with him all day. He says dad is tired now and eager to have a rest."

"Oh, thank heavens. I thought you were about to give me more bad news. Are you going to visit him? I should be there with him."

"He's in safe hands, Mum. I offered to go, but Simon insisted that I shouldn't as Dad is exhausted. I feel bad about it, however, if that's what Dad wants, I guess we'll have to abide by his wishes. How are you?"

"A nervous wreck. It's awful sitting here staring at the phone, waiting for it to ring. I'll be better this evening, knowing that he's okay and having a good rest."

"Do you want me to drop by?"

"No, you look after Simon this evening. Please tell him how much I appreciate what he's done for your father today. Lord knows how things would have panned out if he hadn't been around to save the day."

"I know. I'll pass that on. Hey, look after yourself tonight, make sure you eat a proper meal. Dad will be home tomorrow. I'll drop by after work to see him, okay?"

"Yes, I've been busy baking. I've made myself a small casserole. Don't worry about me, dear. See you tomorrow."

"Ring me if you need me. Love you lots."

"Thank you, dear. Love you, too."

Sally hung up, collected her handbag and coat from the coat stand, and headed back out to meet the rest of her team. "Are we all set?"

They descended the stairs together and went their separate ways in the car park. Jack walked Sally to her car. "Is your dad all right?"

"Yeah, he'll be home tomorrow. I'll drop by and see him then. He's resting now. Simon has been a godsend today. Not sure what I would have done without him."

"Let's hope your dad can identify the men who did this to him. The sooner they're off the street, the better. Bastards. Fancy doing that to an old man... er, sorry, no offence."

Sally laughed. "None taken. I totally agree. Dad's not a spring chicken. They could have easily dealt a fatal blow, morons. Let's get the funeral out of the way tomorrow, and then I'll see if Dad can come in and go through the mugshots with us. Don't forget to dress appropriately in the morning."

"Crap, good job you reminded me. I would have turned up in my jester's suit, otherwise." Jack smirked.

Sally punched his upper arm. "Prat. Goodnight, Jack. Glad you're still with us, even though you give me a mountain of grief at times." She opened her car door and shot inside before he could retaliate. She saw his lips moving as he said something, but she pretended not to hear him.

In the end, he waved his hand at her in frustration and turned his back. She drove away with a smile on her face. The smile turned into an angry frown once she got caught up in the traffic, though, and she started to reflect on what her father had been subjected to. *If I catch you guys, I'm going to string you up by the knackers!*

CHAPTER EIGHT

The weather turned nasty on the morning of the funeral. Sally and Jack, dressed in black suits, joined a few of the mourners as they waited in the entrance to the church for the hearse to arrive. The people surrounding them were telling anecdotes of Anne's life, and Sally strained her ear to hear what was being said, seeing if she could glean any gossip or facts about what type of character Anne was, and if she had any secrets they should be aware of. What she did overhear were a few names mentioned that Joanna had highlighted for them to interview.

As the hearse pulled up outside the church and the pallbearers assembled, the group fell silent out of respect for the deceased woman. The mourners stepped inside the church and took their seats before the coffin was brought in and placed at the front of the church. Sally and Jack sat in the last row, surveying the mourners. As the pallbearers stood back from the coffin, Sally heard a shuffling noise at the entrance. She dug Jack in the ribs when she saw Craig standing there, a prison officer on either side of him. She was appalled to see that he was cuffed and still had the chains attached to his ankles. Sally shot out of her seat and approached the officers. She produced her ID. "Morning, gents. I'm DI Sally Parker. I'm the officer in charge of reinvestigating Mr. Gillan's case. Is there really any need for him to be trussed up like this? He's hardly going to run off, is he?"

The older of the two officers bristled and pulled back his shoulders. "I suggest you do your job, Inspector, and let us get on with ours."

"Has Governor Wilkinson told you to treat your prisoner in this way?" Sally asked quietly, trying hard not to grind her teeth out of annoyance.

"We're doing as instructed. Accompanying the prisoner to a funeral."

"His *wife's* funeral."

The older man leaned in with a menacing look in his eye. "You mean the woman he killed in the first place?"

Sally smiled calmly. "We've reopened the case after discovering grave inconsistencies in the original investigation. Please consider taking the leg chains off, at least. This might be an innocent man, officer."

"Either you get back to your seat, Inspector, or we take the prisoner back to the van and return to the prison. The choice is yours." His eyebrow hitched, and he gave her a toothy grin.

With a curt nod, Sally withdrew her notebook and jotted down the numbers on each man's lapel so she could make a formal complaint to the governor later.

Sally took a few steps and stood in front of Craig. The man's head had dropped onto his chest. A blank expression was etched on his face. She placed a finger under his chin, forcing him to look at her. "I know how difficult all of this is for you, Craig. Stay strong. Jack and I will make sure nothing happens. Sorry you're being treated so harshly."

"Dad, it's so good to see you." Molly rushed through the entrance of the church and flung her arms around her father.

Tears filled Craig's eyes as he kissed his daughter's cheek and looked over her shoulder at the figure of his son standing in the doorway of the church.

"Jamie came. I can't believe he came." Craig's voice was strained.

One of the officers stepped forward and pressed between Molly and Craig. "Step away from the prisoner, Miss."

"Give them a break! They're not doing any harm," Sally hissed at the officer.

"Just doing my duty, Inspector. Maybe you can make this young lady aware that she needs to keep her distance from the prisoner."

Sally tugged on Molly's arm. "Sorry, love. You better do as he says. Why are you so late?"

Molly looked over at her brother. "I had a struggle to get him to come. He's here now."

"I'm glad. We'll talk after the service, Craig." She left the group and made her way over to the entrance.

Jamie, who'd been leaning against the stone wall of the church, stood upright as she approached him, giving Sally the impression he was about to bolt.

Smiling, she said, "Jamie, how wonderful to see you. So glad you decided to come after all." She linked her arm through his and guided him down the aisle to sit beside Molly, who had taken her seat at the front of the church, next to her mother's coffin. Jamie hesitated for a moment beside the casket, under the gaze of the other mourners assembled, before he finally sat down alongside his sister. Sally returned to her seat and watched over her shoulder as the officers deposited Craig Gillan at the end of the last pew in the church, amidst mourners murmuring their dissatisfaction at having him attend their dear friend's funeral.

Sally's heart went out to the man, who looked to be emotionally overwrought by the proceedings as well as his own son's behaviour. The officers stood behind Craig, each with a hand on one of his shoulders as if he were about to abscond at any moment. Sally felt sickened by the officers' conduct and was already contemplating the vitriol she was going to let loose on the governor once the service had ended.

Jack nudged her elbow. "I know what you're thinking, but they're just doing their job. Have you any idea how many prisoners use the excuse of attending a funeral as a means of escape? Give the guys a break, eh?"

Sally sighed and reluctantly nodded. She gave herself a reality check. She needed to see things for what they were: Craig had been found guilty of killing the woman they were about to bury. It was hardly time to break out the celebratory banners.

The priest began the service, then a few of Anne's colleagues, who had been chosen to represent the firm, read their eulogies. Most of the emotional eulogies involved light-hearted incidents that had the other mourners chuckling and, in some cases, wiping away happy tears. Sally glanced over her shoulder at Craig, who seemed to be wrapped up in his own solitude, a dark shroud of guilt burdening his shoulders.

Sally observed the mourners and their individual reactions, jotting down the odd note when something irked her: an out-of-place smile or frown, anything that might aid her interviews with the workmates over the coming few days.

~ ~ ~

After the service ended, the mourners followed the pallbearers to the recently dug plot in the graveyard. Craig and his accompanying officers were the last to arrive. Sally felt sorry for the man as the guards forced him to remain at the back of the group and wouldn't allow him to stand alongside his wife's coffin as it was lowered into the ground.

That poor man. He doesn't deserve to be treated like this. I'll be having a serious word with the governor when I get back.

He glanced up at her now and again, and she offered him a reassuring smile, but Craig always looked away swiftly, as if embarrassed that she'd caught him looking at her. She could tell that the effects of prison life had been devastating on the man. He was unable to look anyone in the eye for long, in case they judged him. He was a severely broken man.

After the coffin was lowered, Molly took a few steps forward and threw a white rose into the hole. "Rest in peace, mother dearest. I'll miss you every waking moment until we're reunited." She returned to stand alongside her brother and handed him a white rose. She nudged his elbow, urging him to follow her lead and to say a few words before throwing the rose in the grave.

He shrugged and shook his head. "I can't, sis. I can't do it. Mum left us years ago."

Molly held his hand. "I know that, Jamie. Do it for me, eh? It'll help the grieving process, allow you to get on with your life."

"Will it? Do you honestly think she'd be proud of me, of us? What we've become over the years?"

Sally listened to the young man's confusion with interest. The mourners began whispering to each other and looking daggers at Jamie for disrupting the service, but Sally understood Jamie's need to say what he was saying and his hesitation in carrying out his duties for the mother he had lost at such a young age.

Molly nodded and removed the rose from his hand. "I will never force you to do anything that you don't want to do. Mother would never have stood in judgement over what you've become, Jamie. Take my word on that. She was the most gentle, genuine person I've ever met. She would be proud of you no matter what you've had to endure in your life."

A tear seeped onto Jamie's cheek. He gently took the rose from his sister's hand and walked closer to the edge of the grave. "I didn't know you well, but I've never stopped loving and missing you. Until we meet again, Mum." He threw the rose onto the coffin and returned to his position alongside Molly. His sister placed a comforting arm around his waist and pulled him close. He smiled down at her as the heavens opened.

The priest speedily conducted the rest of the service, then the mourners dispersed, most of them running from the graveside for cover in their vehicles. Sally and Jack sought shelter under her umbrella and watched as the guards relented their hold on Craig and allowed him to approach the grave. He was silent for a long time, lost deep in thought. Molly had given him a rose before leaving the area to search for cover.

Sally and Jack shuffled forward to hear what Craig said to his deceased wife. "Our time together, our life together, was cut short the day you died. I've loved you and missed you every day since. I hope that justice will be served soon and that the police find your true killer. I've been tempted to join you over the years, but I had no way of knowing if you were dead or alive. That hope was extinguished when they found you last week." His voice faltered, then he continued. "I'm still tempted to join you, but it looks as if the children need me. I'll promise you that I will watch over them, if you'll only point the police in the right direction of where to find your killer, in the hope the authorities will recognise my innocence and set me free. It's been an unbearable existence without you by my side. Until we meet again, I love you, Anne."

Jack nudged Sally, and she wiped away the stream of tears that had flowed freely during his touching speech. "We should go now, boss."

"Yes, let's get back to the station. I need to speak to Craig first." She handed Jack the umbrella, dipped under the edge, and joined Craig in the pouring rain. "Craig. I want to assure you that I'm determined, more than ever, to find the culprit who has seen fit to punish your entire family for the past fifteen years."

"I have faith in you, Inspector. As you can see, my children need me. Jamie needs to have stability in his life after all he's been through. It was heart-breaking to see how little self-worth he has and what he's become in my absence. An absence that should never have occurred and will no doubt take an eternity to put right. If indeed it is fixable. I have severe doubts whether that will be achievable, to be honest with you. Some evil degenerate did this intentionally, killed Anne and ripped our family to shreds in the process. I'm not sure we'll ever be happy again, but when I'm set free, I'll make sure my kids know how much they mean to me and how much their mother idolised them before she was robbed of her final breath."

"Take care, Craig. We are doing our best to secure your release."

"I have to believe you'll do that, Inspector, because I have very little else to cling on to."

Sally placed her hand on his arm. "Have faith. We'll talk soon." She rushed back under the cover of the umbrella and returned to the car with Jack. From inside the vehicle, they observed the stray mourners and watched them heckle Craig as the prison officers secured him in the back of the van and drove off. "Looks like these few are refusing to believe he's innocent. I think tomorrow is going to be a very interesting day when we start questioning them at the factory."

"How long do you think that's likely to last?"

"What? The questioning?" Jack nodded. "All day and the next. Who knows? Maybe a whole week. Let's just say that today's observations have definitely highlighted some characters that I'm eager to speak to."

"I know that look. If I were them, I'd be wary about how they treat you during the questioning."

Sally turned to face him and laughed. "So, you think I should go in there and prove what an ogre I am?"

He chuckled. "Just be your normal self, and they'll get the message loud and clear in no time at all."

She punched him hard in the thigh and started the car.

They stopped off at the baker's and bought the team baguettes and doughnuts for lunch. They would need sustenance for what lay ahead of them. Sally was determined to turn up at the factory the following day, armed to the hilt with everything she had.

~ ~ ~

Feeling mentally exhausted, Sally bid her team farewell at five thirty that evening and drove directly to her parents' house. Dex greeted her the second she stepped through the front door as if he hadn't seen her in months. She missed her golden Labrador and longed to spend more time with him, but she realised how selfish it would be to have her furry friend live with her on a full-time basis. At least with Dex spending part of the week with her parents, she knew he wasn't sitting in the house alone, feeling either depressed or neglected. This way, he had the best of both worlds and company all day long.

"Hi, Mum. Is Dad home yet?" she called out above the noise of Dex's appreciative welcome.

Her mother appeared in the hallway, looking flushed and wiping her hands on a multicoloured tea towel. "Hello, dear. Not yet. He's due any moment. Are you and Simon going to stay for dinner tonight? I've made enough to feed an army. Nothing fancy, only a fish pie."

Sally walked towards her mother and kissed her cheek. "That would be lovely, Mum. I better ring Simon, see if it's okay with him."

"There's no need, love. I rang him earlier. This is my way of saying thank you to you both. Lord knows what would have happened to your father if Simon hadn't turned up at that house."

"There's no need to thank us, Mum. Simon was just as devastated about it as we all were. If anything, he's blaming himself for what those brutes did to Dad."

"That's nonsense. He shouldn't blame himself. Those morons had an agenda. If it hadn't been your father, they would have attacked someone else who was interested in the house. Any idea what the outcome of that was, love? Have you caught the men yet?"

"Not yet, Mum. We're waiting on Dad identifying the men through mugshots. Otherwise, we're screwed. When is the property due to go under the hammer?"

"Next week I believe, dear. Your father will tell you when he comes home."

Hearing the beep of a car horn, Sally shooed Dex back into the kitchen and opened the front door to find an ambulance parked next to her car on the drive. "He's home, Mum," she called over her shoulder.

"Oh my, I look a mess. I must run a comb through my hair and tidy myself up."

Sally laughed. "Don't be daft. You look the same as usual. Come on, we'll go out and meet him."

Her mother closed the door to the kitchen to prevent Dex from shooting out into the road then joined Sally. She smoothed down the apron she was wearing and fluffed up her hair at the sides. "I'm so nervous."

Sally crushed her mother to her and kissed her forehead. "It's not even forty-eight hours since you last saw him."

"I know, but it feels like a lifetime."

Sally was suddenly riddled with guilt when she thought how Craig Gillan must have felt being locked up for the past fifteen years for a crime he hadn't committed. She shook her head. *That's work. This is your personal life you're dealing with now.* She left her mother standing on the doorstep and approached the back of the ambulance. Her father beamed at her from the wheelchair the paramedics had just lowered him into. "Hello, Dad. How are you feeling?"

"Sore, but eager to be home."

Sally backed away, giving the paramedics room to manoeuvre the chair into position before they wheeled her father up the drive and into the house.

"We're going to settle him in the house, Miss, if that's all right. Sorry, we can't leave the wheelchair here. Blame it on the cuts we're experiencing at present."

"No problem. If he needs one, then I'll hire one."

"I don't need one. That's the end of it. Boy, it's good to be home." Sally's father let out a huge sigh as he crossed the threshold.

Sally kissed her father on the forehead, avoiding the large white patch above his right eye. "Looks painful, Dad. Is it?"

"No. I'm a little woozy still, but nothing compared to what I've been experiencing in the hospital. I was desperate to come home." He smiled broadly at his wife. "Hello, dear, how are you?" He tried to get out of the wheelchair, but one of the paramedics clamped a hand on his shoulder.

"Just be patient for another few minutes, sir, then we'll be out of your hair."

Sally's mother hugged him then stood back. "Good to have you home, love. I've missed you."

Sally jumped ahead of the wheelchair and showed the paramedics into the lounge. "Dad likes to sit here."

"And you can pack that in, young lady. I will not be forced to sit in here and neglect my share of the chores around the house. Don't you think your mother has enough on her plate as it is?"

Sally wagged her finger at him as the paramedics helped him onto the sofa. "Now don't start getting shirty with me, Dad. All we're asking is that you take it easy for the next twenty-four hours, okay?"

The older of the two paramedics smiled and winked at her as if to wish her luck.

"Hello, anyone home?"

Sally's heart fluttered when she recognised Simon's voice. She rushed out into the hallway to greet him. "Come in. We're just settling Dad in. Have you had a good day?" She leaned in and kissed him.

"Fair to middling. Yourself? How did the funeral go?"

Sally looked over her shoulder; the paramedics squeezed past with the wheelchair.

"We'll be off then. Have a good evening, folks," one of them called out.

"Thank you for all your help. Goodbye." Sally closed the door and wrapped her arms around Simon's neck. "It was heart-breaking, not something I relish repeating anytime soon. I'll tell you about it later. I suppose I better see how the invalid is doing. I have a feeling he's going to be trouble this evening. Stubborn old fool."

"So that's where you get your stubborn streak from," Simon teased.

Sally's mouth gaped open and she punched him playfully in the arm. "I'll get you for that later."

"Promises, promises," Simon's reply followed her up the hallway.

"Right. Dad, you're going to listen good to me. I know you want to get up and start rushing around doing things, but I'm going to put my foot down. You can stare at me all you like, but Mum and I have discussed this. Just for today, please take it easy. Give your body a chance to recover. Simon is here, you can chat to him—no business talk, though—while Mum and I get on with the dinner."

Her father mock-scowled at her. "Very well. If I don't adhere to what you and your mother have organised, I know my life won't be worth living in the long run. Simon, where are you?"

Simon popped his head into the lounge and smiled. "Did the nurses kick you out, Chris?"

Sally's father flushed and beamed, then beckoned Simon to sit beside him on the sofa.

Sally shook her head, knowing it was pointless telling them not to discuss the properties they were involved in. "I'll bring those mugshot books by for you to look through tomorrow, Dad."

"No news regarding the brutes, I take it then?" her father asked, his hand hovering over the patch on his face.

"We haven't even begun the search yet, Dad. We'll need your input first. Come on, Mum, let's leave them to it."

Sally helped her mother put the finishing touches to the dinner, one ear trained on the conversation and the laughter coming from the lounge. It was good to see her dad in such good spirits. She made a mental note to get a uniformed officer to call round with the mugshot books in the morning.

Simon helped Sally's father to the table, then they enjoyed a pleasant meal after which Sally helped her mother settle her father into bed. He looked exhausted by seven that evening. Bidding her parents farewell, she followed Simon back to their home.

They collapsed onto the sofa with a much-needed glass of wine and each reflected on how the day had panned out.

"Your father is determined to go ahead with that house, you know?"

Sally sat upright and looked at Simon. "What? Why?"

He shrugged. "He said he refused to let the bastards win. I'm inclined to agree with him but wanted to see how you felt about things first."

"I'm appalled you two are even considering it. What if these goons take things further next time?"

"They won't. I'm sure."

"You're unbelievable. How can you say that, Simon?" Sally was gobsmacked by Simon's blasé attitude despite her father just spending twenty-four hours in a hospital bed.

"Okay, think of it this way: I'll make sure I'm with your dad at the auction house. These guys are bound to be there, as well. That's when your lot can swoop in and arrest them."

Sally relaxed into his chest again. "I should have known you'd be up to something. You have it all worked out in that complex mind of yours."

"Seems the logical course of action. If they're as desperate to get hold of the house as we suspect they are, they're not going to think twice about turning up and putting a bid in for a property they're eager to add to their portfolio. It's a no-brainer, right?"

"Clever dick! You're not just a handsome, superstar of a pathologist, after all."

He laughed. "I'll take that as a compliment, thanks. Let's hope we can ensnare the menaces. The auction is set for next week, on Thursday, I believe."

"I'll have a word with the desk sergeant at the station, see if we can make arrangements for a team of officers to do the necessary on the day. I'll still ask someone to visit Dad with the mugshots in the morning, just to follow protocol."

CHAPTER NINE

Sally drove into work fifteen minutes earlier than usual.

Pat Sullivan, the desk sergeant, had a twinkle in his eye that she hadn't noticed before. "I like that idea," he said of her plan concerning the auction. "Hope it's not putting your father in more jeopardy, though, Inspector."

Frowning, she asked, "How, Pat?"

"I'm just thinking there's a week to go between now and the auction. What if these guys hear that your father has been released from hospital and think he's likely to turn up at the auction to make a bid for that property? They'll want to ensure that doesn't happen before the auction, wouldn't they?"

"Good point. Can you get one of your guys to take the mugshots around to my dad this morning? If he identifies anyone, maybe we should pull them in early and not wait until the auction next week."

"I can organise that, Inspector. I'd be more inclined to get the nuisances off the street at the earliest opportunity, just in case."

"That's sorted then, thanks, Pat. I really appreciate it."

"No problem. Glad your dad is doing better now."

Sally continued through the reception area and up the stairs to her office. She was surprised to see Jack already stationed at his desk. "Blooming heck, I didn't even look for your car in the car park. Didn't realise you were already here, Jack. Everything all right?"

"Don't ask. I came in early for some peace and quiet."

Tutting, she nodded. "I want to get out to the factory by about ten this morning. Is that okay with you?" She popped a fifty-pence coin in the vending machine and selected a decaf coffee. "Want one?"

"Please, white with one sugar."

Sally returned to his desk with the coffees. "You want to talk about anything?"

"Nah, it's just the usual. No need for you to be bothered with my domestic *unbliss*… is there such a word?"

Sally laughed. "There is now. All I can offer is words of sympathy, mate, no solutions."

"We'll work it out. Want me to gather all the background information together?"

"Yep, everything. Let's hope the boss of the factory offers no objections when we get there."

"Do you think we should ring ahead?"

"Nope, let's surprise them. I'm actually glad this is happening after Anne's funeral. It's good to strike while she is still in her workmates' thoughts."

"I thought that also. Fingers crossed something comes up from the interviews today. Craig looked dreadful yesterday. Even my hard heart was bleeding for his situation. To have your kid cut you off like that… it doesn't bear thinking about."

"Yeah, we all think we lead tough lives, but do we really? When you hear of someone being banged up for nearly half their life over a crime they possibly didn't commit. To be frank with you, Jack, I think I would have found a way of ending my life had I been dealt such a low blow."

Jack chewed the inside of his mouth and nodded. "I hear you and wholeheartedly agree. Despicable miscarriage of justice if it turns out he's innocent. How does one ever come back from that? Where would he begin in rebuilding his life? His existence?"

"If we manage to get him off the charges, then that's where the hard work really begins. He'll need years of counselling. I'll bloody make sure he gets any compensation due to him—mark my words on that one. Right, dreaded paperwork time. Be ready to leave at nine forty-five, matey, okay?"

"Good luck. I'll be ready."

~ ~ ~

The car park was full when they arrived. Jack managed to squeeze his car into a tight gap close to some trees. "Wow, this place is huge. How many people did the original investigation interview?"

"Four. How bloody ludicrous is that?"

Sally sighed heavily. "Crap, crap, crap. I wish I could go over to Falkirk's house and give him a piece of my mind, but what would be the point? What a bloody tosser he is."

Jack followed her through the parked cars towards the entrance. "I truly don't know how he can sleep at night. So glad his pension was stripped from him."

"Quite right, Jack. Okay, let's push that to one side for now. If the manager is willing to give us the go-ahead to speak to more staff, then I think we should do it."

"We could be here the rest of the damn week if he allows us that privilege," Jack grumbled.

"And next week. Still, if that's what it takes, then so be it. Let's shake off all those negative thoughts and go in there with a positive attitude."

A brunette behind the reception desk peered over her half-rimmed glasses as Sally and Jack entered. "Are you the reps from Cartwrights?" she asked, no hint of a welcoming smile.

Sally produced her ID and introduced them. "DI Sally Parker and DS Jack Blackman. We'd like to speak to the person in charge, if it's convenient."

"I see. May I ask what this is relating to?" Her lips pulled tight into a line, and her eyes blinked rapidly.

"We'll tell that to the person in charge when they come to see us."

"Very well. Take a seat. I'll place a call. I can't promise anything, though."

Sally and Jack turned their back on the officious woman and sat down in the reception area. The woman stared at Sally the whole time she was on the phone to her superior, her voice hushed. After hanging up the phone, she called out, "Mr. Hammond will be with you shortly."

Sally smiled appreciatively and twiddled her thumbs around each other while they waited.

"I wish he'd get a move on," Jack complained, the way he always did when someone kept them waiting.

When the door at the end of the corridor opened, a smartly dressed man with slicked-back greying hair and a face full of rage approached them. "Hello. What's the meaning of this?"

Sally stood up and showed him her ID. "Hello, Mr. Hammond. I'm DI Sally Parker and this is my partner, DS Jack Blackman."

"Yes, yes, that much I got from my receptionist. What do you want? Have I done something illegal?"

"Not to our knowledge, sir. Would you mind if we spoke in your office?"

"Not until you tell me what this is about," he insisted, folding his arms stubbornly and tapping his foot.

Sally could feel the temperature of her blood rising. "Mrs. Anne Gillan."

His foot stopped and his brow furrowed. "What about her?"

Exasperated, Sally replied, "In your office would be preferable, sir."

The man relented and led them through to a large cluttered office. "Excuse the mess. My new office is being decorated at present. Take a seat. I'm aware of the name but unsure how I can help you with your enquiries, Inspector."

Sally and Jack sat down. Jack withdrew his notebook from his pocket, ready for action.

"Anne's case has been reopened. My team have been instructed to go over the case and to interview all the witnesses again. Several members of your workforce were interviewed at the time of her disappearance fifteen years ago."

"I see. Why here?" His tone turned sour once more. "Why not after hours at their homes?"

"It would be easier if we interviewed them here one after the other rather than go to four or five different addresses, Mr. Hammond."

He sighed heavily. "And if I refuse?"

Sally stared at him, holding his gaze, for a long time. "Then I would plead to your good nature to rethink your actions. How do you think your employees' families will feel when coppers show up at their homes?"

"If you're reinvestigating, does that mean Anne's husband might be innocent? But why was he considered to be guilty of her murder if there was no body found around that time? And yes, I watch a lot of programmes about forensics."

"You regard yourself as an amateur sleuth, in other words," Sally said, amused.

"I suppose I do. I didn't think a person could be charged without a body being found."

"There was a large amount of blood found close to Mr. Gillan's house that helped to convict him."

"Fifteen years, you say? Shameful if the man was innocent. That was before my time, though. I took over running this factory around ten years ago, but I've often heard Anne's name mentioned amongst the staff."

Sally's ears pricked up. "May I ask in what context?"

"Just the odd mention. The staff really liked her. I've never heard anything derogatory, if that's what you're implying."

"I wasn't. Will you grant us permission, sir?"

He picked up his pen and wound it through his fingers as he thought. "Maybe I should ring my contact in the police to see if I'm within my rights to deny your request. The last thing I need right now is my workforce to be disrupted. We have a huge order deadline to meet by the end of the week."

"If you need to verify who we are, then by all means do that." Sally smiled, hoping to appeal to his more human side.

"Maybe you're aware of my friend, Inspector. Chief Constable Stockard?" Hammond said, looking smug.

Sally nodded. "Very aware. Actually, he's the person who initiated reopening the case. He's instructed me and my team to deal with several cases apart from this one."

The man discarded his pen and sat forward eagerly. "Really? How interesting. Okay, you've persuaded me. Who is it you need to speak to? Are you sure these people are still working here?"

Sally motioned for Jack to read out the names from his notebook.

"Yes, I believe they are all still here. I can't give you a specific room to use because of the renovations going on in the nearby offices. Would a table in the canteen suit your requirements?"

"Perfect. Thank you very much for allowing us to speak to these people today." Sally felt buoyed by the opportunity to conduct the interviews in public. She hoped that would put pressure on some of the interviewees and perhaps cause someone to slip up during the interview.

"Give me ten minutes to make the necessary arrangements and to clear it with the section heads in charge of these people. If you'd like to take a seat back out in the waiting room, I'll ask a member of staff to show you to the canteen."

"That's very kind of you. We'll try not to keep them too long or disrupt things too much."

"Thank you. I appreciate that." He picked up the phone, and Sally and Jack returned to the waiting area.

Within ten minutes, a young man wearing stark white trousers and a matching top came to collect them. He greeted them with a curt nod and thumbed the direction he expected them to follow him. Moments later, they were settled at a table at the back of the canteen, where Anne used to work, awaiting their first interviewee.

"This is kind of spooky, considering this is the area where Anne worked," Jack observed under his breath.

"I think it's very apt. If she's watching over us, maybe she'll guide the interview process."

Jack's face screwed up in distaste. "Don't start believing all that mumbo jumbo."

Sally laughed. "I'm not. Just making an innocent observation, partner. Looks like this is our first interviewee. She seems pretty nervous."

The woman was wearing a red apron over her white overall dress. "Hello. I've been asked to come and talk to you. I'm Meryl Clegg."

Sally motioned for the woman to sit down. "Hello, Meryl, thank you for joining us. I'm DI Sally Parker, and this is my partner, DS Jack Blackman. There's no need for you to be nervous. You haven't done anything wrong."

She placed a hand on her chest and eased back into her chair. "Phew, that's a relief. May I ask why you want to see me then?"

"It's about Anne Gillan."

The woman bounced forward and clicked her fingers. "You were at her funeral yesterday."

"That's right, and I recall seeing you there."

"I had to go. She was my best friend. We worked together for years." Her gaze fell to the table. "I always hoped that she would come back. A few of us just thought she'd taken off."

"Can I ask why you thought she would take off like that? Was her marriage in trouble?"

"No, nothing like that. When someone goes missing, I suppose you try to think of the positives instead of going down the negative route. Presuming she was missing as opposed to her being dead… well, it's what I chose to believe. It was a bloody shock to hear she had been discovered in the river last week. Her poor kids. Molly seemed okay yesterday, but her son… he simply seemed lost to me."

"He is. He's struggled over the years, never once gone to visit his father in prison."

Meryl snorted. "And who could blame him? I've had my doubts about him over the years. Why shouldn't he have been locked up the way he was? Even if she'd merely gone missing, would she have done that if everything was all right at home?"

"But you've just told me their marriage was okay. Are you now telling me that it wasn't?"

"No. Anne always told me that she loved her husband, but when I thought she was missing, I couldn't help wondering if she had been hiding the truth. It's not uncommon for folks to do that, is it, Inspector?"

"That's true, I suppose. Especially where domestic abuse is concerned. Did you ever see any evidence of that, Meryl?"

She gasped. "My God. No, nothing like that at all. I never even suspected it. No, I think they were a solid couple."

"Glad we've sorted that out. If she was a good friend of yours, did she ever confide in you about anything out of the ordinary, something that caused doubts to run through your mind?"

Meryl thought over the question for a moment or two before she shook her head. "I can't recall anything. Such as what?"

"Someone making advances towards her, perhaps. Maybe a male work colleague had shown an interest in her, causing her to feel uncomfortable?"

Meryl chewed her lip, first one side then the other. "I can't remember anything like that, I'm sorry. Working in the canteen, we're subjected to the odd verbal abuse, more like friendly banter, but we tend to shrug it off. It's how colleagues react, isn't it? My hubby is a proper tease. Never knows where to draw the line that one. He's not alone, either."

"Did your husband tease Anne?"

"Of course he did. He teased all the ladies—still does. No one has ever taken him seriously. He's just an idiot, a court jester. The girls around here know that he means nothing by it. Hey, do you really think I'd put up with him making a nuisance of himself? I'd cut his balls off and serve them up to our German shepherd if he ever stepped out of line like that."

"Your husband still works here then?" Sally asked, not recalling seeing another Clegg on the list of people they had earmarked to interview.

"Yes, he works on the factory floor, stays out of my way most of the day. I couldn't put up with having him under my feet all day long, grant me with some sense." She laughed as a few members of staff entered the canteen and immediately looked in their direction the second they queued up at the counter to be served. "Oh my, looks like the masses will be descending soon. My supervisor will need me to help out with the rush. Gina rang in sick this morning, leaving us short staffed."

"One more thing before you leave us. Apart from your husband, are there any other members of staff who like to tease the womenfolk here?"

"Crikey, you'll need a bigger notebook than that, I'm afraid. Like I told you, it's factory banter. You accept it in the workplace. Have you ever worked on a production line? It's bloody mind-numbing, and some of these guys have worked here for the past thirty years. The wages are crap, too. They go out of their way to tease the women to brighten their day, and to be fair, the women give as good as they get."

Sally nodded. She would hate to work in such an environment. There were days when the solitude of her office gave her time away from her colleagues and space where she did some of her best thinking. Even then, the banter that went on at the station was mild in comparison to what the women working in the factory were subjected to. *Maybe someone went a little too far with their cheekiness?*

"Thanks for talking to us. Maybe we can chat later if you think of anything else we should know."

Meryl pushed back her chair and stood up just as a man bellowed, "Come on, Meryl, get your arse into gear. Some of us are starving over here."

Meryl's eyes rolled up to the ceiling. "That loudmouth is Alec, my husband. I better go. Sorry I couldn't be more help."

"Maybe we'll have a chat with your husband for a minute or two."

"I wouldn't get in the way of him feeding his face if I were you." She laughed and walked away.

"You thinking someone overstepped the mark with their banter?" Jack asked, finishing off the notes he was making.

"Don't you? What's that old saying? Many a true word spoken in jest. I'm all for having a laugh and a joke, but I know from my own experience that saying something jovial can disguise what a person is thinking or what their true meaning is."

"Yeah, I guess. I suppose it's a form of mental abuse, messing with someone's head."

Sally smiled. "You've hit the nail on the head, partner. That's exactly what it is. But in some cases, people's interpretations can be totally different. I'd feel desperately uncomfortable working in these surroundings, but then, that might just be because of what I've experienced."

"Meaning you're ultrasensitive nowadays?"

"Exactly. Anyway, I think we should add Meryl's husband to our list."

"Want me to have a word with him?"

Sally looked over at the man who was staring back at her. "I think Meryl's already done that, by the look of things."

Alec Clegg picked up his tray and headed in their direction, veering off at the last minute. Sally left her seat and approached his table. She extended her hand. "Alec Clegg? I'm DI Sally Parker. We'd like a chat with you after you've eaten, if it's convenient?"

"So I hear. I ain't done nothing wrong."

"I'm not saying you have. It's just an informal chat. Want me to contact your supervisor?"

His gaze drifted over to the queue that had grown substantially in the last few seconds. "No need. Phil is over there. I'll have a word with him. He usually joins me anyway. I'll get back to you when I've polished this lot off," he said, gesturing to the plate in front of him piled high with an English breakfast.

"Wonderful. We'll see you in a moment then." Sally returned to her seat, where she observed the interactions between the men and women in the queue. To her, it did appear to be just friendly banter, but she couldn't help wondering how far that banter went after hours. How many of these people were having affairs or dealing with unwanted advances?

She hoped the quandary wouldn't cloud her judgement when it came to questioning the men on the list. Sally considered handing the reins over to Jack for the next few hours, but he'd always left the interviews up to her, and she couldn't see him appreciating the sudden change. She swallowed her bout of anxiety and waited for Alec Clegg's manager to join him. She smiled when the man she presumed was Phil glanced in her direction after speaking to Clegg. He nodded and bared his teeth in a taut smile.

After ten minutes of waiting while the two men finished eating, Jack nudged Sally's elbow and nodded in the men's direction. She looked up to see Phil coming towards them.

He stood alongside her. "Hi, the boss rang me. Told me that you want to speak to some of my team, and now Alec says you want to have a quick chat with him, too."

"That's right. We'll be as quick as we can. We're aware of the tight schedule you're under at the moment."

The man grunted. "That's an understatement. We could do without this shit. I'll give you ten minutes maximum with each of the men on your list and five minutes with Alec. Got that?"

Sally could sense Jack bristle beside her and bashed him with her knee under the table. "That's very kind of you. Would you like to take a seat and get your interview out of the way now?"

He shrugged. "Makes no odds to me. I can't tell you anything." He slumped into the chair opposite them and crossed his arms across his slim torso.

Sally kept a smile on her face, hoping to break down the barrier that had suddenly formed between them for some unknown reason.

The supervisor appeared to be in his early forties, and he had a toned physique that most men half his age would have been happy to possess. "It was good of you to turn up at Anne's funeral yesterday. I did see you there, didn't I?"

"Yeah, I wanted to pay my respects. We all wanted to go, but only a few of us were allowed to attend because of this huge order we have to get out."

"I see, hence you only willing to give us a limited time to speak to these men."

"That's right. If the order is late, our bonuses go out the window. I've yet to miss out on a bonus and have no intention of this being the first time, either."

"We'll do our best not to disrupt your team much. I promise. What can you tell me about Anne Gillan? What type of person was she?"

He sighed a little. "She was a lovely person, never said a bad word about anyone. Everyone here loved her. We were all devastated when we heard she was missing, even organised our own mini search party."

"You did? I wasn't aware of that."

"You lot weren't interested back then. I tried to organise something with the copper in charge of the case, but he was having none of it. Told me to keep out of his way and to stop interfering in police business."

"That's awful and should never have happened. I'm sorry for the way the SIO spoke to you. That was uncalled for if all you were trying to do was help."

"Yeah, to say I was miffed would be an understatement. If that copper had allowed us to work alongside him, I reckon we would have found Anne at the time. Instead, she turns up sodding fifteen years later. That was bloody ludicrous. Why would any copper turn down the offer of help like that? Would you?"

"I have to say no, but things were different back then," Sally replied, trying to make excuses for Falkirk's cock-up.

"Yeah, right. I believe you, Inspector."

"Did Anne ever confide in you, Phil?"

His brow wrinkled. "Confide? About what?"

"Anything? Was anyone showing her attention that made her feel uncomfortable perhaps?"

His gaze dropped to the table, and he fidgeted in his chair. Jack's knee bashed hers, and she nudged him back, letting him know that she had noticed.

Finally, Phil replied, "Sorry, I was trying to think back; a little difficult when we're talking fifteen years ago. I don't remember anyone... oh, wait a sec. Steve Endecott. He used to be infatuated with Anne."

Craig mentioned the same name! "He did? Did you mention this to the investigating officer at the time?" Sally tried to recall what the original file had said about Endecott.

"Yeah, I mentioned it. The idiot—sorry, the inspector just brushed it off. Said he had an inkling who was at fault and was happy to proceed down that route."

Sally's eyes widened. "He actually said that?"

Phil raised his hands. "Hey, don't quote me. It's been a long time, and I can't tell you word for word if that was correct, but it was something along those lines."

"Does Steve Endecott still work here today?"

"Yep, half the time, he's in a world of his own." Phil surveyed the queue of men lining up for their breakfast and pointed to a smaller man at the end of the line. "That's him there, the short one. I seem to remember that Craig had to warn him off once. I believe he kept badgering her at home." He placed a finger on his temple and twisted it. "He's not all there."

"Meaning what exactly?"

"He's simple. Keeps himself to himself most of the time."

"Mentally incapacitated? Does he work here under a special scheme?"

"Not that I'm aware of. You'd need to have a word with the boss about that."

"We'll ask Mr. Hammond what the situation is after we've had a word with him. Can you think of anyone else?"

"Let me think. At the time, I mentioned Colin Slater's name to the—what did you call it? SOI?"

"SIO. Senior Investigating Officer. Mr. Slater's down on our list to see also. May I ask what your problem with him was?"

"I wouldn't necessarily call it a problem. The SIO at the time wanted me to tell him who I thought was friendly with Anne. I suggested Colin because the two were always caught having secretive chats. He'll be able to fill you in more about that."

"Thanks, we'll be sure to ask him. Anyone else? Did the SIO question all the staff here? There must be hundreds."

"Three hundred and fifty, to be precise. Back then, I suppose it was around the two-hundred mark. No, the SIO was only interested in talking to people who knew Anne well."

"The four names on the list?"

"Yep, that sums it up. Then he only spoke to them for five minutes, one after the other. At the end, he said he'd concluded his case and the right person would be charged later on that day and thanked me for my help. That night it was breaking news on TV that the police had charged the husband for her murder. The next day, everyone was in total shock at the news. How could your lot charge Craig with murder when her body hadn't even been found? Can you do that?"

"Sometimes, if the evidence leads us to suggest that a person is capable of doing such a thing."

He shook his head. "And you think he did it or not? Not, I guess. Otherwise, you wouldn't be investigating the case again, right?"

"At this moment in time, I'm inclined to think that Craig is innocent. We won't be able to right that wrong unless we find the person who was responsible for Anne's murder. The thing is, we won't be able to do that alone. I know what an inconvenience it is having us here, but it's the only way we'll find the person, by going over the case from scratch."

"I appreciate that. I'll make sure the guys give you all the information you need. If Craig isn't the one who killed Anne, that means there has been a killer walking the streets for the past fifteen years. That doesn't sit well with me, and I'm sure it won't with my work colleagues either."

"That's good to know. Okay, I think we're done here. Would you mind if we had a word with Alec now?"

Deadly Encounter

Phil looked over at Alec and grinned. "Yeah, I think he's finally finished stuffing his face."

CHAPTER TEN

After Phil left the table, Sally focussed on Steve Endecott, who had departed the queue and was sitting all alone at a table in the opposite corner. His gaze met hers once before he dipped his head and began to eat a bowl of cereal. "He does seem an odd one. I'm going to enjoy questioning him. Maybe we should ask Hammond if he's got any medical problems first?"

"I'll go back and see him if you like, while you question Clegg."

"Makes sense to me." She flashed her partner a smile. "The queue might have died down by then. You could grab us a couple of coffees when you get back."

"I knew that was coming," he mumbled and rose to his feet.

Seconds later, Alec Clegg sat down opposite her. "You still want a word with me even though your sidekick has run out on you?"

"Of course. He's nipped to the little boys' room." Sally pulled Jack's notebook in front of her and picked up the pen. "There's no need to look so nervous, Alec. We're just conducting a few enquiries and would be grateful if you would cast your mind back to when Anne Gillan was alive. Did you have much to do with her?"

His face visibly softened. "She was a lovely lass. Best friends with my wife, so yes, I had a lot to do with her. Saddest day for both of us when your lot turned up and announced she was missing. Devastated, Meryl and I was when we heard the news last week. How could anyone tie her up and throw her in the river like that? Her poor kids."

"Did you have much to do with Craig Gillan?"

"Not really. We used to go out on a few work outings a year back in those days. Chatted with him a few times at them but never really socialised with the couple after work. They always gave me the impression they liked each other's company. I think Anne dragged him along on the outings just to appease the management.

They expected the staff to go out of their way and show up if the management could be bothered laying on these events. You know what it's like. If you say no, then they'll start asking the question if you really want to work for the firm or not. Daft really, but they can be antsy about things like that."

"Work politics at play then." Sally smiled, glad she'd never been forced into attending any of the police functions over the years, especially when she was married to her ex. Her colleagues would probably have seen right through Darryl the instant they laid eyes on him, where she had been blinkered about his true character, blinded by love.

"Yeah, best to stay on their good side if you want to keep hold of your job. Mind you, Phil and me go back a long way. He'd always back me up if any likely crap came my way."

"Was Phil close to Anne, too?"

His gaze met hers, and he nodded. "We were all really close back then, at work anyway. When we went on the work's outings, Phil's missus was a surly cow, though." He looked over his shoulder, making sure Phil wasn't within earshot before he continued, "His wife was always accusing him of dipping his wick, if you get my drift."

Sally raised an eyebrow. "He liked the ladies then?"

"Ladies, teenagers, anything in a skirt back then. Seems to have grown out of it now, though."

"And his wife was aware of his affairs?"

"Now I never said he had affairs. I just said he considered himself a bit of a ladies' man. Catrina always put her three kids first. In the end, she told him to mend his ways or she'd kick him out and refuse him access to the kids. So he did."

"And when did his wife tell him this?"

His lips twisted as he thought. "I don't know, maybe fourteen or fifteen years ago."

"Hmm... around the time Anne went missing then?"

"Maybe. I think a lot of people took stock of their lives back then. I guess Catrina's threat forced Phil to tidy up his act. He loves his kids. The thought of never seeing them again made him keep it in his pants."

"I thought you said he didn't have affairs?"

"He told me he didn't, but like Meryl told me at the time, 'there's no smoke without fire'."

"Meryl's right—there rarely is. Can you remember how Phil reacted to the news that Anne was missing?"

"Like all of us. We were all dumbfounded. Tried to form a search party immediately, but that tosser—sorry for swearing—that idiot of an inspector running the case refused our help, said we'd get in the bloody way. Have you ever heard such crap? I wish we'd gone against his wishes now, but you just didn't do that sort of thing back then. Most people were scared of the rozzers. It's all different nowadays. Have you heard the lip some of these bloody yobs give your lot today? Disgusting. There's no respect for authority now with the youngsters."

"I truly can't say I've noticed that, Alec."

"Maybe you don't get out on the streets much."

Sally chuckled. "I do my fair share. I'm not one of those inspectors who enjoy being tied to their desk all day long."

"Hence you coming out to question us here."

"Exactly. Going back to the time Anne was pronounced missing, can you think of any of your workmates who took the news worse than others?"

He drummed his fingers on the table as he mulled over the question. Sally looked over at the queue and noticed that Jack had joined the end of it. She was relieved, as her mouth was on the verge of drying up.

"Well," he leaned in close and whispered. "There were Steve Endecott and Colin Slater."

"And they're the only two?" Sally thought it was strange that both Alec and Phil had named the same two men. "Is Colin working today?"

"Yes, I believe so. I seem to remember Anne and him being very, very close at one time."

"Are you suggesting they were having an affair?"

He bounced back in his chair and laughed. "Good God, no. But I always saw them having secretive conversations in between shifts."

"Do you know if they met up after work?"

"I wouldn't have a clue about that. You'll have to ask him that one."

"What else can you tell me about Colin? Or Steve?" Sally asked as Jack sat down beside her and handed her a mug of coffee. "Thanks, I need this."

Alec fell quiet for a moment or two. "I can't really answer that. I suppose I don't tend to mingle with those two much."

"Is there a reason why?"

"I have my own group of friends. Is there a law that has to say I have to speak to everyone I work with?" He smiled; his words weren't laced with sarcasm in the slightest.

"I guess not. We'll have a chat with them both, see what we can glean from that. If you can't think of anything else we should know, then you're free to go back to work."

"Thanks. I have another five minutes before I'm due back. Might as well grab another cuppa before I go. I hope you find what you're looking for and that Anne gets the justice she truly deserves. Do you think her husband is likely to get off?"

"That's hard to say at present. Depends how the rest of the questions pan out. Thank you very much for your time. I really appreciate you giving up part of your break to speak with me."

"I'd do anything for Anne, whether she's still with us or not. Such a sweet lady. We all miss her deeply."

"Let's hope we can uncover what really happened to her soon. One last thing before you go. Can you tell me how I get hold of this Colin Slater?"

"He should be in with the next shift. Steve's over there if you need him. Always been a bit of a loner, that one." He thumbed over to the left, in Steve's direction.

"Thanks, if you see Colin, would you mind telling him we need a quiet word?"

"Of course." He stood and rushed over to the queue, calling out, "Another coffee for me, Meryl, when you've got a tick. I need to neck it quickly. Talking to the fuzz took longer than expected."

Jack chuckled. "I ain't been called the fuzz for a long time. How did it go with him?"

"He seems genuine enough. He did, however, divulge that Phil Stephens had a penchant for the ladies, which declined rapidly after Anne went missing."

Jack took a swig of his drink then tilted his head. "Is that right? Well, that seems a tad suspicious."

"Exactly what I was thinking. I want to do an in-depth check into his past when we get back. Maybe Hammond can tell us if there are any incidences along those lines noted down on his work record. Did Hammond have anything to say about Steve Endecott?"

"Apparently, he's on medication for being bipolar. He's allowed to work here under the strict understanding that he doesn't use any of the machinery unsupervised."

"Interesting. I'd really like to leave him until last, but I fear his break will be over soon."

Just then a stocky, well-built, balding man approached the table. "Hello, I'm told you want a word with me. I'm Colin, Colin Slater."

"Ah, yes." Sally extended her hand and gestured for him to take a seat. "I'm DI Sally Parker, and this is my partner, DS Jack Blackman. We'll try not to take up too much of your time. We're making enquiries about Anne Gillan's death. You gave a statement when she originally went missing, and we'd just like to go over that statement and see if there is anything else you'd like to add to it."

"Ah yes, I saw you at the funeral yesterday. I was so upset—still am. Anne was one of my best friends." His eyes brimmed with tears.

"I'm sorry for your loss. How close were you?"

He smiled. "We weren't having an affair, if that's what you're getting at. Most people can't comprehend males having females as best friends unless they are sleeping with them. I loved Anne as if she were my sister. I've missed her dearly since the day she went missing. We had no idea that she'd been murdered until last week, really. The investigating officer on the case was a bloody dipshit. How he managed to secure a sentence against Craig is totally beyond me. They loved and cared for each other deeply—any bloody idiot could see that."

"Who would *you* have put in the frame for Anne's murder?"

"I haven't got a clue. Why are you questioning her co-workers again? Do you think it was one of us?"

"Not necessarily. Anne was walking home from work the night she went missing. We're hoping to perhaps jog someone's memory. Maybe someone saw her being followed that night, for instance."

"You're asking a lot for people to remember that far back, Inspector. I know folks will do their hardest to try and help. Everyone and their dog loved Anne."

"Did you have a special bond with her?"

"Yes, no one on this earth could wish for a truer friend than her. Since she went missing, there has been a gaping wound in my heart. She was the only one here who knew…" His head dipped.

Sally eyed Jack with wide eyes. She reached across the table and placed her hand over Colin's. "Knew what, Colin? You can tell us."

He swallowed hard and wiped tears from his cheeks. "That I'm gay."

Sally smiled. *So that's what was behind all the secretive conversations in the hallway.* "So, she was your confidante as you were coming out, is that it?"

"Yes, of course. Everyone knows I'm gay now. Back then, they just assumed we were having an affair. We laughed about the gossip. Even played up to it at times, just to wind folks up. Honestly, I will never have another friend as dear or as close as Anne."

"I'm glad she was there for you. Maybe she confided in you in return?"

"Yes, all the time."

"Did she mention if anyone was making a nuisance of themselves perhaps?"

His head came up, and his gaze drifted over to Steve Endecott. "Apart from that nutter over there, you mean?"

"He bothered Anne? Can you tell me in what way?"

"He used to ring her at home all the time. Kind of latched on to her. She showed him a morsel of kindness, and he pounced on it, expected far more than what she was willing to give him." His eyes narrowed in anger.

"And Craig was aware of this?"

"Only at the end. Anne said he overheard a phone call she had with Steve and put two and two together and came up with five. The following day, I was there when she tore Steve off a strip for causing her grief at home. She warned him to leave her alone, not to ring her anymore after work, that kind of thing."

"How did he take that?"

"He sulked for days. Avoided the canteen every time she was on duty. Anne was riddled with bloody guilt then. She wasn't the type to be mean to people. I tried to reassure her that she hadn't been mean to him. If Steve calling her at home was stirring up trouble between her and Craig, then she did the right thing by trying to put an end to it."

"Did things settle down for Anne at home with Craig? Or was there a permanent wedge driven between them?"

"No, they were very much in love. Anne dealt with the situation swiftly. Craig was happy about that. They went on with their lives after that, until… she went missing."

"How soon after the incident was that?"

He shook his head. "A week, maybe two." He gasped and whispered, "My God, you don't think it was him, do you?"

Sally withdrew her hand from his. "There's no point jumping the gun here. We'll have a chat with him and see what conclusions we come to. Are you aware of his illness?"

"Yes, everyone is. Phew, you just think he's mixed up and confused then?"

"Maybe. It might be why Anne felt sorry for him. Maybe she tried to help where she felt others had failed him, like the doctors, perhaps."

"I don't know about that. All I know is that I always try and keep my distance from the guy. It's the way he looks at you sometimes, as if he doesn't trust you. I have no idea why. I've not intentionally done anything bad to him over the years."

"Maybe he objected to your close relationship with Anne. Have you thought about that?"

He ran a hand over his clean-shaven chin. "Wow, you're right. I never even considered that."

"I don't recall seeing him at the funeral yesterday, or did I miss him?"

"No. He didn't go. Quite right too, if you ask me. Only her close friends went. It was heart-breaking for me to say goodbye. I'm glad that Anne was finally laid to rest after all these years of not knowing what had happened to her."

"Did Anne ever acquire interest from anyone else, shall we say?"

He looked over his shoulder and leaned in again. "Between you and me, I always thought that Phil liked her more than he was willing to let on. Let's just say, if she'd given him the green light, there would have been no stopping him."

"Interesting. And yet he was friends with Anne and her husband?"

He shrugged. "I doubt Craig's feelings would have got a look in, if you ask me."

"But nothing happened between them in the end?"

"No. Anne would have told me. We had no secrets."

"Thanks very much, Colin…" Sally broke off speaking because she felt Jack's knee pressing against hers, and she glanced his way. He was looking behind her and motioned with his head. She swivelled in her seat to see Steve Endecott, his head down, rushing out of the canteen. "Hmm… he knows we want to speak to him. Wonder where he's off to in a hurry. Let's get after him, Jack." She patted Colin on the hand and smiled. "Thanks again."

"Hey, no worries. I hope you find who is bloody responsible. They need stringing up for what they did to both Anne and Craig," Colin called out as she and Jack chased after Steve.

"Which way did he go?" Sally asked, craning her neck in every direction in the hallway with many doors.

Jack's arms flew out to the side. "I haven't got a bloody clue. Where do we start looking?"

"I don't know, but hanging around here discussing it isn't going to help us find him. He works on the factory floor, right?"

"I think so, although not with the heavy machinery."

Another worker left the canteen and squeezed past Sally. She grabbed his arm. "Hi, we're looking for Steve Endecott. Can you tell us what section he works in please?"

"That nutter! He works in packing. Couldn't be trusted to work anywhere else in the building, although he has in the past."

"And where is that?"

The man pointed at the door at the end of the hall. "Through there."

"Thanks for your help." Sally and Jack raced towards the door, but halfway there, Jack stopped outside a door that was ajar. He placed a finger to his lips and eased the door open to find a stairwell.

"My guess is he's gone this way. Maybe he was trying to put us off his scent. Knew we would go to his workstation if he disappeared."

Sally nodded. "You could be right. Maybe we should split up?"

"I think that would be a mistake. Just trust me on this one, boss." Jack tilted his head, listening for the slightest noise coming from the stairwell. "I think I can hear footsteps, but I could be wrong."

"Go on, we'll chance it. After you. Quietly, though, okay?"

They rushed up the stairs, their backs against the wall. As they reached the door to each level Sally dipped her head out to survey the area. Nothing. After the fourth flight of stairs, Jack placed his finger to his lips again and pointed up above. "I can hear distant footsteps, as if someone is pacing near the top."

Sally strained her ear to hear. The unmistakable noise of a door opening was followed by an alarm going off. "Crap! Go, Jack! Let's get up there quick." Fearing the urgency of what lay ahead of them, she chose to forge ahead with her partner rather than calling for backup. They could revisit their choices once they knew exactly what Steve was planning, although she had a rough idea what the young man had in mind.

The climb up the stairs grew more exhausting with every step. Jack was a long way ahead of her only because of the heels Sally was wearing. Panting, she was relieved when she reached the final step. The door to the outside was open, and she could hear Jack talking to someone on the roof.

"Shit! Just what we frigging need." Sally fished her phone out of her pocket and called the station. Breathlessly, she relayed what was going on to Joanna, shouting above the din. "Ring the appropriate services. I'm going to try and talk him out of it, Joanna, but he's on medication. I have no idea how stable he is. Just call for help." She ended the call, inhaled and exhaled a few large breaths, and went through the door with the alarm still ringing in her ears.

What she found struck fear into her heart and posed yet more questions about Steve Endecott. He was standing on the edge of the building, looking as though he would jump if either she or Jack got any closer to him. Sally had never found herself in such a situation before. "Jack, come back. Don't get close to him," she demanded in a hushed voice, not wishing to distract Steve.

She swallowed the bile that had seeped into her throat, waited for Jack to join her, then placed a hand across his torso. "Leave this to me. I've rung the station. Joanna has put everything into action. All I have to do now is try and keep him talking until help arrives."

"Good luck with that. One word out of place, boss, and I think he'll jump," Jack replied, his mouth twisting with apprehension.

Sally tentatively walked a few paces then stopped. "Hi, Steve. Do you mind if we have a chat?"

The slightly built, short man began placing one foot in front of the other until he was teetering on the edge then retreated again. He remained silent.

Sally tried to communicate with him again, but the confounded noise of the alarm still going off hindered her attempt. She thought she heard sirens in the distance as well. *I wish they would shut that damn thing off.* She turned and mouthed to Jack, "Get them to cut the alarm."

Jack shook his head. "Sorry, boss, I ain't moving from here."

Sally rolled her eyes then returned her attention to Steve. "Please, Steve, come with me. All we want to do is have a chat with you."

Again, her plea was met with silence.

"Steve, whatever has driven you to this can be overcome. Nothing is worth this. Please, listen to me. All we want to do is have a chat. You're not in any trouble. I promise you."

His head slowly twisted her way. He looked at her through narrowed eyes, a look of pure hatred resonating in their depths. He opened his mouth to speak but failed to form any words.

"Steve, you can talk to me. I mean you no harm. Let's discuss things properly, away from the edge. What do you say?"

In slow motion, his head turned away and down. Sally took a few steps nearer. She felt a waft of breeze on her arm as Jack attempted to grab her. She looked over her shoulder and smiled, letting him know that she knew what she was doing and to trust her. Her voice softened. "Steve, why won't you talk to me? Did you do something to Anne?"

Silence, except for the alarm constantly bombarding her ears.

"Steve. Speak to me, tell me what you did to Anne."

"Nothing," he finally replied. "I loved her. Cared for her."

"Then that's a good thing. Come away from the edge, and we'll discuss what's going on, get you the help you need to get through this."

"I wanted to be there for her. I had a right to be there. I loved her."

A lump formed in Sally's throat. "At the funeral, you mean?"

"Yes, they said I wouldn't be welcome. All I am guilty of is loving her."

"That's a shame. I'm sure that must have been hard for you to take. Maybe we could go to her grave together and pay our respects. How about that?"

"I went already. I sat with her all last night. Felt close to her for the first time in years. Why? Why did she have to leave me? Deny contact with me when I needed her most? Why? I loved her. I've never loved anyone like Anne before, or since."

"I'm sorry about that, Steve. Did Anne know how you felt about her?"

He turned to face her slightly and nodded. "Yes, she was aware. Why did he do that to her?"

"Who?"

"Craig. He could never love her the way I loved her. She had never felt true love, not with him. He was only interested in her body. I wanted to delve deep into her mind. Was desperate to know her inner thoughts and desires. I would have done anything to be given the chance to love her properly, instead of from a distance."

"That's a shame, Steve. Come with me, tell me how you would have treated Anne if she had consented to be with you."

He turned away again and Sally took another few steps towards him. She was only six feet from him, aware that she should be much closer if she was going to save him. She softened her voice further. "Talk to me, Steve."

"I'm finished. Done with talking. Explaining my inner thoughts to incompetent psychiatrists who just can't comprehend what is going on in my head."

"I promise to find you someone willing to listen to you, Steve. Please give me the chance to do that."

"I'm done. Done with everything. I thought last week was bad, when I heard on the news that they had discovered Anne's bones…

but not being allowed to show up to pay my respects at her funeral was the last straw. I have nothing. Where I once clung to the hope that she may return to me, now I have nothing. My whole life is a waste. Why should I go on pretending that I am appreciated by these people?"

"These people? Do you mean here at the factory?"

He nodded. "They constantly ridicule me behind my back. They think I don't hear their sniggers when they pass me in the hall or stare at me in the canteen, but I do. How heartless can some people be? I've never hurt anyone in my life before. I choose not to mix with them; why does that make me strange? I prefer my own company. No, that's wrong. I preferred Anne's company, but she was stolen from me. Now all I want is to be with her. Do you think she'll be waiting for me?"

"I'm sure Anne wouldn't want you to do anything silly, Steve. Please, step away from the edge and talk to me properly. I'm willing to listen, to make sure you get the help you need to go on in this life."

"I'm done. Finished. My life ended the day Anne's bones were found. How could anyone destroy such beauty? She was beautiful inside and out. My one regret is that she turned her back on me and never explained why. I didn't deserve to be treated that way. However, I forgave her years ago. I know who was behind her hateful words on the phone that night. It was him."

"Who? Craig? Her husband?"

"Yes, he was riddled with jealousy. Insecurity was evident in his eyes every time we met. He knew that I could take her away from him at a moment's notice, had I really wanted to. I just needed her to love me as much as I loved her."

"And did she?"

He shook his head. "No. Too many outside influences. We needed to spend time together for her to appreciate what I could do for her. I would have worshipped her had she let me. Do you think she'll let me now?"

Sally stepped forward, to within three feet of him. She could see over the edge of the building. Below, a mass of people stared up at them, shielding their eyes from the blazing sun. The sirens had faded a few minutes ago. She counted two fire engines and an ambulance near the entrance. Several firemen were securing the area, forming a barrier with their bodies and outstretched arms. "Steve. This isn't what Anne would have wanted. She's still around us now, watching over you. She would be devastated if you ended your life in the hope that you would be reunited in the afterlife. There's a natural progression in this world. Who knows where the body ends up if that path is interfered with? Does any of us truly know what happens to a soul when it is torn from our body too soon? Our path is set in stone. It's not your time to go yet, Steve. Please, please reconsider your actions." Sally tested her reach to see if she could grab him. He was three inches out of her grasp.

"Why should I? No one wants me? I'd be better off dead. I know Anne will be waiting for me. Nothing you can say can alter what I think. Nothing."

"I'm sorry. I didn't mean to be so negative. But if you believe in God, do you really think He will be happy that you've ended your life? Tampered with the plans He had in place for you?"

"Who cares? All I care about is finally being with Anne. I'm coming, Anne. You will love me, and together, we'll be eternally happy."

Before Sally could grab his overalls or his arm, Steve toppled off the edge of the building. Sally screamed and ran forward. Jack pulled her back, twisted her in his arms, and smoothed a hand over her hair. "You did your best, Sal. He was determined. Nothing you could have said or done would have changed his mind."

"I failed him, Jack. Just like dozens before who had failed him. May God accept his troubled spirit."

CHAPTER ELEVEN

Sally and Jack composed themselves then rushed back down the stairs and out the front entrance. Sally glanced sideways, relieved to see that the paramedics had covered Steve's body. She gulped when she noticed Mr. Hammond marching towards them, his face the colour of a ripe tomato.

"This is the thanks I get for letting you question my staff? How bloody dare you! I'm going back to my office now to report you to Stockard. You're not fit to be an inspector if you allow this sort of thing to happen."

"I'm sorry. I tried my very best to talk him around."

His hand swept behind him. "Ha! Sorry? You think a simple apology like that is going to help these people forget what they've just seen?"

Jack took two steps forward. "Hey, this isn't the inspector's fault. You should have kept the staff inside, stopped them from gawping at Endecott. You knew he was on medication and likely to jump—don't put the onus on the inspector. Maybe if you guys had treated him better over the years, this could've been avoided. I've never seen someone so determined to end their life as he was. Even in the canteen, before he got up on the roof, he seemed withdrawn and isolated by the other members of staff. So I suggest you take a good look at yourselves before slinging any blame our way."

"Thanks, Jack." Sally placed her arm on his to calm him then said to Hammond, "He's right. I feel bad enough as it is that I was unable to prevent him from jumping but then, we've only known him ten minutes. Where were you guys when he needed help over the years?"

A fireman shouted, "Come on, guys, the show is over. I suggest you get back to work now."

The staff began shuffling past the covered body and into the building, giving Sally and Jack mixed looks as they passed. Some were downright disgusted, while others appeared to reflect their own guilt at the situation.

Before Hammond followed the last member of staff through the front door, he stopped and pointed at Jack. "For your information, Sergeant, there was little I could do to prevent the staff from observing what Endecott did. The fire alarm was going off, in case you'd forgotten. Our assembly point is right here. Maybe that was at the back of Endecott's mind when he carried out his plan. You haven't heard the last of this, either of you. You're not welcome here ever again—do you hear me?"

Sally and Jack just stared at him and nodded. The man was out of order, and Sally felt that the recriminations were going to be felt for months, if not years, to come, adding to her guilt. They were just about to leave when Meryl snuck out the front door to talk to them.

"He finally done it then?"

"Who, Steve?" Sally asked.

"Yes. That's why he used to contact Anne. She told me in confidence that he threatened to commit suicide half a dozen times or more. In the end, Craig told her to tell him to get lost, more for her sake than his. She felt guilty for turning her back on him, but I think it was the right thing to do. You can't help someone who isn't prepared to help themselves. To my knowledge, he'd tried to end his life twice before. Please don't feel guilty. He got what he wanted in the end."

"Thanks for sharing that, Meryl. He told us that he wanted to be with her, and there was nothing I could do to stop him. I still feel really bad, but your words have lessened the guilt a little."

"No need to feel guilty over someone like that, love. His type spend their entire lives blaming others. He was wired differently to us. Dozens of doctors have had him under their care in the past and failed him, so there's no need for you to carry all that weight on your shoulders. I better get back now." She rubbed Sally's upper arm a few times then disappeared through the front door again.

Sally walked over to the paramedics. "Take care of him, won't you?"

"We will. Sorry you had to witness it first-hand. There are some people we're unable to help in this world, and he was one of them.

Most people just threaten it. They say it's the coward's way out, but it takes guts to throw yourself off a building like that."

Sally nodded. "I'm inclined to agree. There was no reasoning with him. What's done is done. Will he be taken to the mortuary now?"

"Yes, we'll take him straight there. Did he have any relatives?"

"I'll check back at the station. I don't think so, though. He was a lonely soul in need of love."

"Sad," the paramedic agreed.

Jack nudged Sally's elbow. "Come on, you need a drink. We should get back to the station."

"Can you drive?" Her hand shook as she handed him her car keys, then they walked back to the car in silence.

At the station, Sally went straight to her desk, took out a half bottle of brandy she kept in the bottom drawer—for medicinal purposes during the winter months—and poured a small tot into her cup. She could hear Jack filling the team in on what had occurred. She closed her eyes, and all she could see was Steve Endecott preparing to jump. She knew that devastating image would haunt her for months to come.

Needing to hear a friendly voice, she rang Simon.

He answered on the second ring.

"Hi, love, it's me."

"Hello, stranger. Everything all right?"

"Not really. I just needed to hear your voice. You should have a new arrival coming in anytime soon."

"Sounds ominous. What's wrong, Sally? It's not Craig Gillan, is it?"

"No. Not Craig, but you're right—it is a suicide. I tried to talk him out of it, but he refused to listen and jumped…" She found it impossible to suppress the tears any longer.

"I'm sorry, darling. Please, you shouldn't blame yourself. If someone is determined enough, there is very little anyone else can do to stop them ending it all."

Between sobs, she replied, "I know… I tried… he was just a few inches beyond my grasp. It doesn't stop me feeling like shit. Nothing will."

"I wish I were there with you, to hold you. Do you want me to come over?"

Sally smiled as if he were there in the room with her. "I'll be fine. I just needed to tell you how much you mean to me. I love you, Simon Bracknall, through the good times and the bad that lie ahead of us. Please, always remember how deep our love is."

"I couldn't have said it better myself. Want me to pick up a takeaway on the way home this evening, save us cooking?"

"Why not? Sod the diet for a change. Thank you for being you."

"See you later. I love you, Sally Parker."

"I know, and I love you, too. See you in a few hours."

Feeling a little better, Sally downed the rest of her brandy. She wiped away any traces of mascara from her eyes with a tissue then left the office to face her team. "I'm okay. Save your sympathy for the victim. Where are we on things, Joanna?"

"I've been concentrating on trying to track down Craig's brother, Kenny, and I think I've finally managed to locate him. He's about twenty miles away in Suffolk." She handed Sally the address.

"No excuse for him not to attend Anne's funeral the other day, not unless he felt he wouldn't be welcome. Jack, you and I will venture out there to see him in the morning."

"Is there anything specific you're hoping he can answer?"

"I want to know why he didn't show up at the funeral, and maybe he can also give us an insight into Craig and Anne's marriage that the others can't."

"Never thought of that."

Sally winked at him. "That's why I'm the inspector around here."

He groaned. "Should have known you'd fling that one at me."

"Okay, I've had enough drama for the day. I'm sure you all have, too. I think we should wrap things up and start afresh in the morning. Jordan, perhaps you and Stuart can bring me up-to-date on how the other case is developing in the morning, before Jack and I set off."

"Will do, boss."

Sally spent the next half an hour sifting through paperwork until her mind had finally had enough and forced her to quit for the day. Jack walked her to her car.

"Are you sure you don't want me to give you a lift? I could even go out of my way and pick you up in the morning, if you like."

"That's sweet of you, partner. Honestly, I'll be fine. Enjoy your evening with Donna and the kids, oh, and your grandchild."

"Do you have to remind me that I'm a bloody grandfather every five minutes?" he replied grumpily.

"No, but it's fun." Sally jumped into her car before he could release a barrage of abusive words.

When she parked the car, Sally noticed something sitting on the doorstep outside Simon's home—she still had problems sometimes thinking of it as her home as well. The medium-sized package was addressed to her. There was no postmark on the brown paper. She took the parcel inside and opened it while the kettle was boiling.

Inside the brown paper was a plain cardboard box, no wording on the outside. Puzzled, Sally opened the box to find a small porcelain doll. She pulled it out and studied it. The similarity to herself was amazing. She approached the nearest mirror and held the doll up beside her. If she didn't know any better, she would have sworn the doll had been modelled on her.

"That's ridiculous," she said, sweeping a hand over the doll's blonde hair, which was even styled like hers.

She was still studying the doll when Simon arrived home about an hour later. The smell of the Indian takeaway caused her stomach to rumble. He kissed her on the cheek. "That's pretty. Wow, the resemblance is remarkable."

Sally's brow furrowed. "You said that as if this is the first time you've laid eyes on it."

He walked into the kitchen, collected the plates from the cupboard, and started to serve up the food. "What do you mean? It *is* the first time I've seen it. I didn't even know you possessed such a beautiful doll."

"I didn't… I don't. This was sitting on the doorstep when I came home. I presumed it was a gift from you."

He spooned the boiled rice onto two plates then looked up at her. "Me? It's not the sort of thing I would dream of sending you, love. Sorry to disappoint you."

"If not you, then who?" Sally gasped then tore into the lounge. She picked up the box and shook it. A slip of paper drifted to the carpeted floor. She grabbed it and read it aloud. "You'll always be my princess doll." Fear rippled through her veins.

Simon appeared in the doorway with two plates in his hands. "Sal, what the hell? What's wrong?" He rushed forward, placed the plates on the table, and gathered her in his arms. "Talk to me."

"If you didn't send it, then there's only one other person it could have been."

"What? Darryl? But how? How does he know where you live?"

Sally rested her head against his shoulder. "I don't know. He's dangerous, Simon. Even more so now that he's locked up in that place. It can't be a coincidence that this turns up just a few days after we came face-to-face in prison a few days ago. Why can't he just leave me alone to get on with my life?" I even had my suspicions that he was behind the attack on Dad, but Jack persuaded me it couldn't have been him as he wouldn't have known that Dad would be at the property at that specific time. Am I losing my mind? What if he has someone tailing Dad? Or you, come to that? Why? Why does he refuse to let me go?"

Simon sighed heavily and pulled her close to his chest again. "I don't have the answers, love, but I'll think of the solution, given time. Do you want this?" He reached down and grabbed the doll off the arm of the chair.

"What do you think? I want to tear its limbs out of its sockets, but how do I know it isn't some kind of voodoo doll? I wouldn't put it past him. He's sick. It's as if he has put an imaginary noose around my neck with the intention of yanking it, to tighten it now and again to keep me in line. I can't bear it, Simon."

"Look, as long as I'm around, there's no need for you to worry. We'll get in touch with the governor of the prison, make him aware of what Darryl is up to. He won't be allowed to harass you like this for much longer. Oh, and I'm inclined to agree with Jack. I doubt Darryl would have had anything to do with the incident with your father."

She shook her head. "I don't believe in coincidences, especially when my loved ones are at risk. He's punishing me for being happy. How the hell can we stop him from wrecking our lives? He clearly has help. That's not even his handwriting on the package. If it had been, I wouldn't have opened it."

"We'll do it. I promise you, love. He won't be allowed to get away with this. The doll should be set aside as evidence. I can take it in to see what fingerprints show up if you like. It might help arrest Darryl's co-conspirator on the outside."

"Thank you. But if we put away the man who sent the package, it won't end there. Darryl will just employ others to do his dirty work. For all we know, he might have a posse of men willing to carry out his dirty deeds for him. He was always the most underhanded person I knew."

Simon pushed her away again and rested his hands on her cheeks. "Whatever he throws at us, we will overcome, Sally. I promise you. Nothing—I repeat *nothing*—will prevent me from marrying you, if that's his intention." He kissed her.

"Damn, I forgot about the wedding. Do you think that's what is behind all of this?"

"At the moment, we're talking about a single doll. While it's upsetting, I don't think we should blow this out of proportion, love. You have my word that any foolish tricks he has up his sleeve leading up to the wedding will do nothing to sour my love for you. Now, let's forget about Darryl and the ridiculous gift he sent and enjoy our food. I'm starving."

"You're right. He's not worth the trouble. I'll have a word with my boss in the morning, see if he has any suggestions what to do about him."

"Apart from moving him to another area, I don't see that there is anything they can do about him. Let's put the thought aside for now and enjoy our evening. You've had a tough enough day as it is." He retrieved the plates from the table and waited for Sally to sit down before he handed her one. "Enjoy."

The plate was piled high with several different curries, rice and a garlic naan. She tried to enjoy her meal, but the day's events proved to be too traumatic for her, and she ended up leaving half her dinner. "I'm sorry. It was just too much in the end. Want a coffee?"

"I'll make it. You stay there and put your feet up. Why don't you ring your parents?"

Terror struck her. Why hadn't she thought to do that? "My God, you're right. I hope everything is all right." She grabbed her mobile.

Simon swooped to stop her dialling the number. "Hey, if you ring them in a state, they'll know something is up. My advice would be not to tell them anything until Darryl has been dealt with."

She kissed him on the cheek. "How come you always know the right thing to say?"

"I don't most of the time, just on this occasion. Trust me, your mum and dad have been through enough over the past few days themselves without this incident adding to their stress load."

Sally smiled and dialled her parents' number. She chatted to her Mum for the next ten minutes, asking after her father's welfare and that of her dog before she hung up.

"There, that wasn't so bad, was it?"

Simon sat on the sofa and pulled her into a cuddle. They remained that way for the rest of the evening, both content to be in each other's company. Although Sally's mind raced, trying to come up with ways in which to exact her revenge on her ex. Maybe moving him to a different prison might disrupt his intentions. Knowing Darryl, however, she feared nothing could have been farther from the truth. Once he had his mind set on something, he usually saw it through to its conclusion, whether he was behind bars or not. Getting one of his lackeys to deliver the parcel was proof of that.

CHAPTER TWELVE

Before joining her team, Sally made a slight detour to visit DCI Green to make him aware of the parcel Darryl had sent.

"But what proof do you have it was him?" Green asked, his brow furrowed as he sat behind his large desk.

"I just know it, sir. You don't think it's a bit suspect that I should receive a parcel, hand-delivered with no note or return address on the package, within a few days of running into him at the prison?" Sally enquired in disbelief.

"Call it a coincidence."

She folded her arms and tapped her foot slightly. "I'm sorry, but I can't—and I won't—accept that, sir. I thought I would have your backing on this, but obviously, I was mistaken. I'll ring the governor myself, make him aware of the situation, see if he can put a stop to my ex-husband harassing me."

He wagged a finger at her. "There's no need for that. I'll place a call and pass on your concerns. I think you'll find that the governor will see things from my point of view, Inspector. Without firm evidence, he's unlikely to reprimand your ex."

"So, what? He gets away with it?" she screeched.

"Calm down. Let me have a word and get back to you later today."

"Simon has taken the package away to test for fingerprints, but you know as well as I do what a conniving shit—excuse my French, sir—Darryl can be. He wouldn't have gone near the doll before it landed up on my doorstep."

"Again, if that's true, then there will be very little we can do about it, but we'll do our best. Now, how is the case coming along? Do you think this Craig Gillan is guilty of murdering his wife?"

Sally pushed her annoyance about her ex aside for a moment and updated the DCI on what had taken place the day before at the factory.

He bounced back in his chair. "What? I had no idea. Are you telling me that you think Gillan is innocent? If so, then who killed his wife? This suicide victim?"

"I genuinely don't believe so, sir."

"So, who?"

"At this point, your guess is as good as mine. I'm going to do some extra digging into a few of the people we interviewed yesterday and carry out some more background checks on the rest of the staff, but that alone could take days, if not weeks, to complete. I was hoping to wrap this case up within a few weeks."

"Your reason being?"

"Because I think Craig has suffered enough over the years. To have been imprisoned for something he didn't do and to then spend the next fifteen years in a six-foot cell is unthinkable in my book. I shudder to think how a member of my family would react to that situation. Not only that, to spend those years wondering what has happened to your spouse, while someone else is forced to raise your kids."

"Okay, I'm getting a clear picture. Do you have enough resources? Can I offer you a few bodies to add to your team?"

She shook her head, not willing to upset her team's working relationship. "No point, sir. I think we have everything covered in that respect. Two of my team members have even started on another case."

"Oh, and how is that progressing?"

"I'm going to check in with them the second I get back. Right, I just wanted to bring you up-to-date on things. I better get on now."

"Good. I'll ring the governor for you now."

"Thank you, sir."

She left his office and trudged back to the incident room. Jack was perched on his desk, drinking a cup of coffee, talking to Jordan. They both looked serious. "Morning, everyone. Everything all right, guys?"

"Morning. Jordan has a few queries about the Thompson case. Will we have time to go over it with him this morning?"

"Of course. Let me get things moving from where we left off at the factory first with Joanna, and I'll be right with you."

Jack stood up and headed for the vending machine. "After you've had a coffee, of course."

"You know me so well. Joanna, actually, this concerns all of us, so gather around, everyone. I want to fill you in on what occurred yesterday. I'm not sure Jack and I accomplished much by interviewing the people who gave their statements fifteen years ago. What we did glean is that all the persons we questioned thought highly of Anne Gillan. There may have been a few flirtatious moments between her and a few of the men. Whether that was perceived as being inappropriate by some people, it's hard to tell. The poor man who was besotted with Anne, Steve Endecott, obviously lived a tortured life. I think the fact that he was omitted from the group who attended Anne's funeral truly was the last straw for him. I don't think his suicide had anything to do with us wanting to question him. Not here anyway," she stated, pointing at her head. "Although, in my heart, I can't help feeling that I contributed to the man's death." She raised a hand to prevent Jack disputing such a daft claim. "No amount of reassuring words you offer will change my mind on this. We've all felt like that at some time or other in our careers, I'm sure. To have the man within my grasp and to not be able to react quickly enough to prevent him from jumping, will haunt me for the rest of my life." She sighed heavily.

Jack shook his head. "Boss, you're wrong to blame yourself. We could tell the minute we spotted him on the roof what his intentions were. There was nothing you could have said or done to prevent him taking his own life."

"Thanks, but it's still a burden that will live with me for a little while, Jack. Moving on, after I've had a chat with Jordan and Stuart about the other case, I need us all to concentrate on the Gillan case for today. There are a lot of employees at that factory. I'm not saying they all worked there at the time Anne went missing, but I do think the number is likely to be more than those we questioned yesterday. We're talking perhaps two to three hundred employees. I want us all checking into the backgrounds of these employees, see if any have previous records that should be highlighted."

"I can make a start on that first thing, boss," Joanna replied quickly.

"Brilliant, Joanna. I also want to fill you in on an incident that happened last night at home, too."

Jack cocked his head to one side. "Has your dad taken a turn for the worse? I thought he was improving."

"No, thankfully Dad is on the mend. When I got home last night, I found a parcel waiting for me. Simon has taken it in for analysis. I'm surmising that it was from Darryl. It was a porcelain doll, the spitting image of me, just creepy." She shuddered, emphasising her point. "Anyway, that's why I was a little late. I stopped by the chief's office this morning to see if he could deal with it for me."

"And is he? If not, I'll take a bloody visit out to the prison and sort him out for you, no problem."

"It's fine, Jack. He was a little apprehensive at first, but I managed to convince him that Darryl was behind the harassment. He's going to ring the governor today. Makes me sick that Darryl is still intent on causing grief, even from behind bars."

"He's a tosser. Needs bringing down a peg or two if you ask me. Do you think he knows about your wedding? Is that what this is all about?"

"Maybe. That's the conclusion Simon and I came to last night. It's unsettling either way. I have no idea what he's going to do next. I'm beginning to feel like a victim of the Kray Twins. They persecuted people on the outside from their cells, didn't they?"

"Yeah, well, it ain't going to happen to you. If the chief doesn't achieve anything I think you should take it higher. It's not right."

Sally rubbed his arm. "I appreciate your support, Jack. I'm determined not to let him get away with this. Between us, Simon and I have a fair few contacts of our own who we can count on to sort him out, if it comes to that." She sipped at her coffee. "I don't want to dwell on it, Jack. I just wanted to make you all aware of what's going on. Back to work. Let me do the necessary in the office, and I'll be back in a jiffy."

She entered the office and expelled a large breath, appreciative of her partner's gesture, however, at the same time aware that any intervention into Darryl's antics would cost her physically and mentally in the end. The post pile was negligible for a change, so she dealt with the two letters and returned to the team to find Joanna had pulled up a list of employees at the factory and shared them out amongst her colleagues.

"Before we get down to that, Jordan, what are your concerns with the Thompson case? Start from the beginning, if you will."

Jordan picked up his notebook and sat back in his chair as Sally pulled out a chair next to his. "Paula Thompson was found guilty of murdering her husband, Don, almost six years ago."

"He was poisoned, right?" Sally asked.

"Yep, the evidence was easy to locate too apparently, it was just sitting there in the bathroom cabinet, although Paula has always pleaded her innocence, but then, who doesn't?"

"Very few, I agree. Which is why our task is going to be pretty hard when we investigate these cold-cases. Sorry, go on."

"At the time of her sentencing, Paula had a four-year-old daughter. The case notes said that the daughter was in the house when her father died."

"Awkward. So, what's your dilemma? You want to know if it would be worth questioning the daughter?"

"Yes, boss."

"You know there are procedures put in place for that, right? As long as you follow those procedures, then there shouldn't be a problem, Jordan."

"Thanks, boss. That's not really the dilemma I have with this one, though. The girl has refused to speak to anyone since her father's death."

"Damn. The poor mite. I can understand your apprehension. Maybe a social worker or counsellor can offer you some advice. We need to tread carefully here, Jordan."

"I know, boss. The girl lives with her aunt, who has given me the authority to speak to the child. I just didn't want to go ahead and do that without you giving me the thumbs-up first."

"You're a smart guy, Jordan."

"I had a brief chat with a friend who works at Social Services who told me that it's not uncommon for kids who have experienced this kind of trauma to become introverted. Saying that, she told me that she's never dealt with a case where the child has stopped speaking altogether before."

"It's a tough one, Jordan. My advice would be to take a female with you when you try and question the girl, make sure the aunt is present at all times, and go from there. The girl probably writes things down, or has she learnt sign language? She must communicate with her aunt somehow."

"From what I can gather, they go through reams of paper every week."

"By the sounds of it, the girl hasn't gone completely into her shell, in that case. Just tread carefully, and you'll be fine. As a matter of interest, what's the aunt's take on Paula doing the crime? Is she Paula's sister or the husband's sister?"

"Paula's sister. She gives me the impression that she thinks her sister is guilty, but I haven't really spoken to her alone, without the niece being present in the room."

"Maybe do that before you start questioning the little girl."

"Thanks, boss. I'll give her a ring and arrange a meeting."

"Good. Let me know how you get on. I still need you and Stuart back on the Gillan case just for today."

"No problem. I've got a list of people to check out here." He waved the printout at her.

Sally smiled at the DC and stood up. "Jack, can you do me a favour and check through the backgrounds of the people we questioned yesterday, including Steve Endecott?"

"What's the point of looking into his background?"

"Just do it for me, Jack. I need to be prepared in case I get summoned to an internal investigation."

"You think that's likely to happen?"

"Who knows?" Sally sat next to Joanna's desk and held out her hand. "Do you have a sheet for me, Joanna?"

"Of course, boss. We can work together if you like. You shout out a name and I'll input it into the computer."

"Sounds like a good plan to me."

Halfway through the afternoon, Sally received two phone calls. One was from DCI Green to tell her that the governor intended to pull Darryl over the coals and to stop all his privileges for the next week. The second call was from Simon, and she took that call in her office.

"Hi, how are things going?" she asked, already feeling drained.

"Not too bad. I have a name for you."

She could hear the relief in his voice. "That's fantastic. Who?"

"William Gross. His fingerprints were all over the package. No one else's, unfortunately."

"I didn't expect there to be. Darryl probably instructed the bloke to go shopping on his behalf, armed with a photo of me."

"You're probably right. Want me to tell you what his rap sheet consists of, or do you want to look into that yourself?"

"If you have the info, that would save me time."

"Mostly petty stuff. A few burglaries, nothing major. So that's a relief."

"Bad enough if he was put inside. I'll get uniform to pick him up. Thanks, love."

"No problem, always glad to help. What did Green say about the package?"

"I've just heard from him. He contacted the governor who assured Green that Darryl's privileges have been stripped for a week. I suppose if he does anything else, they'll bang him up in solitary or lock him in his cell. Not sure how things work on the inside. I'm just pleased the governor was willing to accept my word on events."

"Good, that should do the trick. How are you feeling?"

"Tired. Still have the image of Endecott falling running through my head. That'll probably stick with me for days."

"I know it's easier said than done, but try and put it to one side."

"Yes, Doctor. I better get on. Thanks for letting me know about Gross. See you later."

"That's a date. Enjoy the rest of your day."

"You, too."

Sally hung up and rang the desk sergeant immediately. "Hi, Pat. It's Sally Parker. Do me a favour, will you please? Can you pick up a William Gross? He's got form for petty crimes. Can you pick him up and bring him in for questioning?"

"Of course. I'll need to know why, ma'am."

"He sent a strange parcel to my house, but I don't want that mentioned when you bring him in. Can you just tell him that you want him to help with your enquiries—you know, the usual fib? I'll get Jack to interview him."

Pat Sullivan laughed. "I get it. I'll ring Jack the second he steps in the door."

"You're a star. Thanks, Pat." Sally hung up and left the office.

"Jack, Simon has just identified the person who sent the package to my address. I've instructed the desk sergeant to get uniform to pick him up. Will you interview him for me? Not sure I can trust myself not to tear his knackers off."

Jack tried to keep a straight face, but he roared with laughter. "Yep, I'll do it."

"Right, let's crack on with going over these names. The quicker we get through the list, the earlier we can call it a day. If we highlight anyone of interest, Jack and I will visit them tomorrow."

Joanna cleared her throat and began hesitantly, "Sorry to mention it, boss. I know you've had a lot on your plate today, but I just wanted to remind you that you intended to go and see Craig's brother today."

Sally thumped the side of her head. "Damn, I knew there was something I had planned to do today. Dealing with Endecott's death has really thrown a spanner in the works. Don't be afraid to remind me if anything like that happens again, Joanna."

"Will do, boss. I know how eager you are to chat with him."

Sally looked up at the clock on the wall. It was almost four thirty. "It's too far for us to think about going tonight. Fancy going out there in the morning, Jack?"

"Why not? Maybe we can chase a few of the others up at the same time."

Joanna spoke again. "I've highlighted one person of interest so far. A Nigel Sommers. He's on the sex offenders list. Might turn out to be unconnected, as he's into fiddling with teenage girls."

Sally screwed her nose up. "I think you might be right. Still worth speaking with him. We'll do that tomorrow. Let's stick with it, guys."

Jack was called out of the office to interview Gross around thirty minutes later. He reported back to Sally that Darryl had paid the man two hundred pounds to buy the doll and to send it to her address.

"Sick shit! He must have a bloody tail on me, if he knows Simon's address. That's unnerving in itself."

"Yeah, might be worth moving if that's the case," Jack agreed.

Sally gasped. "I can't ask Simon to do that. He's lived in that beautiful house for years. There must be a way we can prevent Darryl from hounding us like this."

"Apart from getting him transferred to another prison, I'm not sure what else to suggest. Even then, I doubt it would stop him from employing more lowlifes to seek you out."

"Just what I wanted to hear, thanks, partner."

Jack's shoulders slumped. "Sorry, you know what I mean. Yes, we've dealt with Gross, but he'll probably be the first of many..."

Sally raised her hand and shook her head. "I get the picture, Jack. You're not helping me."

"Anyway, I arrested Gross for his part in harassing a police officer. He seemed shocked to hear that, had no idea you were a cop. He'll be regretting his actions in a cell overnight. Are we calling it a day? I promised Donna I'd take her out for a meal tonight. It's the anniversary of our first date."

Sally pulled a soppy face. "Aww... ain't that sweet of you to remember?"

Jack shrugged. "Hard to forget when Donna has it circled a dozen times on the calendar."

Sally and the rest of the team laughed as they made their way out of the station.

CHAPTER THIRTEEN

Sally drove into work feeling less anxious than she had the day before. Thankfully, the vile images of Steve Endecott ending his own life hadn't disrupted her sleep, unlike the previous night. She had a renewed determination in her step as she ran up the stairs to the incident room. "Morning, all."

Joanna and Jack raised their heads for a moment to reply then got straight back to work. Sally continued into her office and joined them ten minutes later. By then, the rest of the team had arrived. "Okay, what do we have?"

Joanna raised her hand. "I've now found two names listed on the sex offenders register: Nigel Sommers and a Robin Fleshman. I have the addresses to hand, but they'll probably be at work at the factory during the day."

"Good point. Okay, is that the list of employees exhausted now?"

Joanna nodded.

"Right, Jack and I will return to the factory. Not sure what kind of reception we're likely to receive, but that's fine by me. Then we'll head over to Kenny's address. Jordan, have you had any further thoughts on your case?"

"I've arranged to have a chat with the aunt today. Thought I'd kill two birds with one stone and speak to the girl afterwards, around fourish. Would it be okay to take Joanna with me? No offence, Stu." He grinned at his partner on the case, who shrugged his acceptance.

"Good idea. Joanna, are you up for a trip out later?"

"Always, boss."

"That's settled then. Stuart, you can man the office in case Jack and I are delayed."

"Like I have an option, boss."

Sally smiled then tapped Jack on the shoulder. "Are you ready to rock and roll, partner?"

"I was born ready," he replied in a dumb American accent.

"Don't give up the day job, for goodness' sake."

~ ~ ~

Sally had decided not to ring ahead to get the all-clear from Mr. Hammond, and he seemed more than a little surprised to see them when he came out of his office. Sally offered her hand, but he refused to shake it.

"What are you doing here, Inspector?"

"We need to interview another two members of your staff if you have no objections, sir."

"And if I have? After what happened the last time you spoke to one of my employees, I think I'm well within my rights to refuse you access to anyone else."

"That was an unfortunate incident. I assure you, it's one that I have no intention of repeating. Perhaps you could arrange for us to use an office this time round?"

"You don't ask for much, Inspector, do you? Okay, I have a meeting elsewhere in the building for the next half an hour. You can use my office if you like. Don't let me regret my decision, or I'll be straight on the phone to Chief Constable Stockard."

"You have my guarantee on that. Thank you for giving us a second chance."

Hammond nodded abruptly and walked over to the receptionist's desk. "Give the police officers what they need. I'll be back in thirty minutes."

"What do you need?" the receptionist asked tersely.

"We need to speak with Nigel Sommers and Robin Fleshman, thanks."

"Take a seat, and I'll arrange for them to come and see you."

The first man to arrive had long hair tied up in a ponytail. His face was gaunt, and he looked undernourished. "I'm Nigel Sommers. You want to see me about something?"

"Care to join us in your boss's office. I'm DI Sally Parker, and this is my partner, DS Jack Blackman." The man appeared confused but followed them into the office anyway.

Jack assembled three chairs around the desk.

"What's this about? I ain't done nothing for ages. I've gone straight."

"Well, we're reinvestigating the death of Anne Gillan, a former work colleague of yours, I believe. Does the name ring a bell?"

"Of course it does." He sniffed then wiped his nose on the back of his hand.

"How well did you know Anne?"

"Not very well. She used to serve me in the canteen. Didn't really speak to her except to order my grub."

"Did you have any contact with her after hours?"

"No, I've just told you that. Why? Am I a suspect?"

"Not really, we're merely making enquiries. Did you by any chance see Anne walking home that evening?"

"When? Fifteen years ago? Are you nuts? I didn't have anything to do with her death. Just because I've got a record, you think I'm guilty of all sorts. I was guilty of kissing an underage girl who swore blind that she was bloody eighteen. Then she called the cops on me. I ain't been near a friggin' woman since. You lot cry wolf too much for my liking. Not worth the effing risk."

"I'm sorry you had a bad experience. I have to ask everyone who came in contact with Anne. I'm sorry."

"That's bullshit, and you know it, lady. Otherwise, there'd be a queue of two hundred people outside this office. Everyone in this damn factory knew Anne. How come I've been singled out? Because I'm the one with a damn record. That bloody incident will haunt me my entire life now. Every time something happens in my neck of the woods and is reported on the news, the tongues wag and the fingers start to point in my direction. Bloody sick of it, I am. Yes, I've been tempted to move over the years, to start afresh somewhere else, but moving costs money, and I don't make a packet here, so I'm stuck with this shit."

"Would you mind toning your language down, buster?" Jack said.

"Sorry. I apologise. It just gets to me." Sommers hung his head in shame.

"I can understand that. Sorry if the questioning is uncomfortable for you, but I'm sure you can understand why we have to ask.

Okay, that's the interview over. Thanks for your time, Mr. Sommers." Sally dismissed the man, overwhelmed by her feelings of guilt as he walked out of the office. "It is harsh why we always come down on these guys," she admitted in a hushed voice.

"What can we do when the reoffending rate goes through the roof at times? Are you getting soft in your old age, Sal?"

She swiped the top of his arm just as the door opened. A ginger-haired man stuck his head round the door. "Robin Fleshman. You wanted to see me?"

"Come in, Mr. Fleshman. Take a seat. I'm DI Sally Parker, and this is DS Jack Blackman."

He sat in the chair and crossed his arms. "Why do you need to see me?"

"We're interviewing anyone who knew Anne Gillan. Did you know her?"

"Yes, but only to say hi to. I never really had a conversation with her. She used to serve me in the canteen. They're always rushed off their feet in there, so no time for general chit-chat. I was shocked to learn she'd gone missing, but even more upset to hear that her body had been discovered last week. She seemed a pretty decent woman."

"Ah, I see. Maybe you saw her leave work on the night she went missing?"

"If I did, I don't really remember. That was donkey's years ago."

"Worth a try. Maybe you overheard someone talking about Anne?"

"About what? Not that I can recall. She had a few people she hung around with, I seem to remember. I saw you in the canteen yesterday speaking to them. What about that nutjob Endecott? Did you ask him before he killed himself? He always seemed to hang on her every word. I saw them having a slight disagreement one time."

"That's interesting. No, I don't think he had anything to do with her death. I think all he was guilty of was carrying a torch for her."

"I kept my distance from him. He gave me the creeps."

Sally contemplated the irony behind his words, wondering how many people had said the same about him over the years once they learned about his record. "Okay, thank you for your time, Mr. Fleshman. You're free to go."

"Thanks. I hope you nail the evil shit who killed her."

"We hope so, too."

Fleshman left the office.

"Where do we go from here? Everywhere we turn, it's a dead end," Jack stated dejectedly.

"I desperately want to talk to Kenny now. That's our next stop. Maybe dropping by unannounced will be the only way of seeing him."

"It's a long shot, one that's going to take us out of our way."

Sally rose from her seat and headed towards the door. "It's necessary, Jack. Come on. I'll buy you lunch on the way. Will that put a smile on your face?"

"Might do."

As it was approaching twelve, Sally drove to a quaint village pub she knew close to the factory. The Four Feather's car park was already beginning to fill up when she parked the car. "Shall we just grab something light? I didn't realise it would be this busy."

Jack shrugged. "A sandwich or roll suits me."

They settled on two cheese-and-ham sandwiches washed down with orange juice before they set off again. Almost an hour later, they arrived at Kenny Gillan's address. Sally rang the bell to the little cottage that had a pretty garden at the front. There was no reply. Sally spotted a path that led around the side of the cottage and Jack followed her into the back garden. It was one of the prettiest gardens she'd ever seen. Either Kenny or his wife really cared for the plot. The lawn was cut very low as if someone had mown it within the last day or two. "Someone has been here recently. Otherwise, this would be a mess."

"Do we know where he works? Maybe we could drop by and see him there," Jack suggested.

"No, I don't have that information." Sally peeped through the kitchen window. It was immaculate, not a thing out of place and no dishes in the sink. "Okay, I've seen enough. I'll drop a card through the letterbox to let him know that we called and want to see him. We'll see if he responds to that within the next day or two. If not, we'll have to come back and try and track him down through his work." A strange feeling rippled through Sally. Something wasn't adding up.

"There's a garage out front. I'll take a look in there on the way past."

They walked around the side of the property again and stopped alongside the garage. "Crikey, I haven't seen one of those in years."

"What is it?" Sally asked, pulling Jack aside to peer through the window herself. Inside was a red Ford Capri. "Would you call that a vintage car nowadays?"

"I suppose it must be. Maybe he's starting a collection. I can't see it being his main car. If you look at the gravel driveway, there's evidence of another car being parked here."

"Get you, Sherlock. Why wouldn't those tracks belong to the Capri?" Sally challenged him.

"I could be wrong and talking utter nonsense of course."

Sally tutted. "I'm winding you up. I think you're right, Jack." She scribbled on the back of one of her business cards and popped it through the letterbox. "It's a waiting game now."

"Would it be worth having a chat with the neighbours while we're here?"

Sally nodded. "Let's split up. I'll go left." She knocked on the cottage next door, which was a little run-down compared to Kenny's immaculate abode. An old lady carrying a yapping Yorkshire terrier opened the door.

"Hush now, Tootsie."

The dog stopped barking.

"Hello, what can I do for you, dear?"

Sally flashed her warrant card. "Hello, I'm DI Sally Parker of the Norfolk Constabulary. I was looking for Kenny Gillan, your neighbour. Do you happen to know where he works?"

"Gosh, he did tell me once upon a time. I'll be damned if I can remember now. Is he in some kind of trouble? You know his brother is behind bars for murder, don't you?"

"Yes, I'm aware of that, and no, Kenny isn't in any trouble. I was merely hoping to have a chat with him."

The woman let out a long sigh. "That's a relief. You never know what goes on behind closed doors. The bloomin' newspaper is full of horror stories. Hark at me, you're in the police. You must see some horrendous sights in your job."

Sally nodded. "We do. But the bad cases are still few and far between in our area. Does Kenny live at the cottage alone?"

"No, he's got a wife and a little girl of about ten. They're a lovely family. Moved here not long after his brother was put in prison. I didn't have a clue who he was, but old Derek across the road—he's gone now, rest his soul—he was the one who told me about his brother. Dreadful business, of course. The discovery of his sister-in-law's body on the news last week was probably the last thing poor Kenny wanted to see."

Sally's curiosity spiked a little. "Oh, why's that?"

"You know what the gossip treadmill is like. We all know Kenny in this close, but those living in the nearby streets are a different matter."

"Has Kenny been verbally abused? Is that what you're telling me?"

"I wouldn't say that. I know there have been a few cars pulling up and people pointing at the house. Sad world we live in when that's how people choose to live their lives, seeking out others and making their lives a misery like that."

"It is. I'm sorry to hear that. Has Kenny spoken to you about how he feels about that?"

"No, dear, he doesn't have to. I can see how angry he is about it. I think his wife, Alison, is pretty peeved about the intrusion, though."

"May I ask how you know that? Has she spoken to you, voicing her concerns?"

"No. I don't speak to them much. I've heard her screaming at him in the back garden, not when the daughter is around of course. Heart-breaking it is to see a once-happy family going through a tough time."

"And this has only happened since the news was aired about the sister-in-law's body being discovered?"

"That and the intrusion into their privacy from the neighbours in the adjoining road."

"You've been most helpful. I've left a card for them to contact me upon their return. Thank you so much."

"I like to help the police when I can, dear. I hope you get to speak to him soon."

Sally waved at the woman as she shut her rickety wooden gate and joined up with Jack by the car. "Anything?"

"Not a sausage. No one in from what I can gather. What about you?"

"I'll tell you in the car. Still no further forward with regard to where he works."

On the journey back to the station, Sally relayed her conversation with the old lady and they speculated what it could mean. "Seems strange that folk should pull up outside his house, don't you think?"

"If you try to figure out the craziness going on in folks' minds in today's society, you'd soon end up going nuts. I blame all those gossip magazines myself. Everyone and their dog thinking they have a right to know what's going on in everyone else's life. It's sickening."

"I'm with you on that one. What if—I'm trying to think outside the box here, so bear with me—what if proof of Anne's death showing up last week has disrupted the marital home?"

Jack looked at her, and his nose wrinkled. "I can't see it myself. The wife would have known that Kenny's brother was in prison, wouldn't she?"

"I have no idea. What if Anne's death caused the wife to ask questions? Perhaps Kenny deliberately hid the truth about Craig Gillan being in prison, and when the story broke on the news, the wife demanded some answers."

"Possibly, and you think that's why the arguments have started up?"

Sally shrugged. "Who knows? Pure speculation until we can speak to either him or his wife. Let's see if they contact us and go from there. I'll leave it a few days. If they haven't got in touch by Tuesday, I might drop by in the evening and see him."

"Well, you ain't coming alone. I'll come with you."

Sally smiled. "I was hoping you'd say that. Do you have any plans for the weekend?"

"Not really. I suppose it depends on the weather, as usual. What about you?"

"Nothing planned as yet. Not sure if Simon has got anything in mind for us. I suppose I'll find out tomorrow—if he gets the day off, that is. Depends on his workload. He's trying to palm the weekends off on his junior assistant. Reckons he's put in enough years of working eighty-hour-a-week shifts."

"Nice that we'll get the weekends off now that we're tackling the cold-cases. Less urgency from above to get the cases solved, right?"

"Within reason. I'd feel happier if we could wrap up each case as swiftly as possible if we can."

"What if we run out of cases?"

"I don't think that will ever happen, Jack. At the moment, all we've been asked to do is delve into Falkirk's cases. There must be loads of bent coppers like him around. Maybe we'll be asked to look at other regions' cold-cases, providing we do a good job on the ones we've been asked to solve."

"What a dreadful thought. All those innocent people sitting behind bars because some tosser of a corrupt copper decided to bend the rules and stitch them up."

"Let's not think about it too much. Concentrate on the cases we're dealing with now and see where that leads us before we get ahead of ourselves."

Once they were back at the station, Sally immersed herself in paperwork while she waited for either Kenny or his wife to get in touch. At six o'clock, she'd finally had enough and drove to her parents' house to pick up her dog, Dex, for the weekend.

As usual, the golden Lab was super pleased to see her. She walked into the kitchen to find her parents sitting at the table, eating their evening meal. "Sorry, didn't mean to interrupt. How are you, Dad?"

"Better each day that passes, love. Any news on catching the culprits yet?"

"I checked with the desk sergeant before leaving, but they haven't managed to locate the thugs yet. They're probably lying low. Are you and Simon still intending to put in a bid for the house?"

"Last time we spoke, that was the plan. The auction is on Tuesday at eleven."

"Okay, I'll see if Jack and I can drop by on the day. Obviously, it depends how things progress with the case we're working, but I think we can spare an odd hour or so. It'll be interesting to see if the thugs turn up and bid for the house."

"That'll be great. It'll make your mother feel happier knowing that you'll be there. Simon's taking the morning off, I believe."

"I know. That's unheard of. He's such a workaholic, but he's really got the renovating bug. It wouldn't surprise me if he gave up being a pathologist altogether in the near future."

"Has he said that?" her father asked, placing his knife and fork down and relaxing back in his chair.

"Not in so many words. There's a certain sparkle in his eye that I think he'd be foolish to ignore. Saying that, he had to go through seven or eight years of training to become a pathologist. To give up that amount of dedication at the drop of a hat would be daft to me. I guess there's no telling what lies around the corner for either of us. If renovating houses gets his blood pumping, unlike his day job, then why shouldn't he persevere with it?"

"Makes sense to me. I think I need to start looking around for another builder who matches my high standards. Not sure how long I'll be able to keep up with the demand he expects from me if he has got the bug." Her father laughed.

"We'll see how things pan out. I'm going to take Dex, and love you and leave you, if that's all right? Do you want to join us for dinner on Sunday, or would you rather leave it for this week? You won't offend me if you say no."

Sally's mother placed her hand on her husband's and glanced up at Sally. "Can we leave it for this weekend, love? Let's get your father back to full health as soon as we can."

"No problem. If you change your mind, give me a ring." Sally kissed her mother and father on the cheek and collected Dex's leash. "I'll ring you over the weekend and bring Dex back on Sunday evening, as usual."

"Have a lovely weekend, dear," her mother said.

Her father smiled and waved. "See you on Sunday, when you bring the boy back."

CHAPTER FOURTEEN

After spending a restful weekend with Simon and Dex, Sally drove into work on Monday morning with a renewed vigour. They had spent most of Sunday strolling along the Circular Walk on the Norfolk Coast Path and delivered an exhausted Dex back home to her parents late Sunday evening. The two days of rest had done her father the world of good because he was back to his chirpy self and very much looking forward to attending the auction house on Tuesday.

The desk sergeant welcomed Sally with a subdued smile.

"Morning, Pat, anything wrong?"

He sighed heavily and nodded. "It's not good news, I'm afraid, ma'am. I've just left a note on your desk."

She frowned. "About what?"

"I had a call this morning from a friend of mine who is a nurse. She knows that someone at this station is investigating the case, and she told me that Craig Gillan had been taken to hospital."

"What? What's wrong with him?"

"Looks like he was roughed up by some fellow inmates."

One name planted itself in Sally's mind immediately: Darryl Parker. "That's terrible. Thanks, Pat. I'll ring the governor ASAP and find out how it was allowed to happen. That poor man has been through enough as it is over the years without having to contend with this shit."

"I agree."

Sally raced to the incident room, where Jack was already at his desk. "This is becoming a habit, you beating me into work, Jack. Everything all right?"

"Yeah, it's called 'me avoiding the breakfast mayhem'. Did you have a good weekend?"

"I did, but it's just been spoilt by the desk sergeant telling me that Craig is in hospital."

"What? Gillan? How?"

"I need to ring the prison to find out exactly what went on. Pat heard that he was attacked by fellow prisoners. I want to know why and how something like this is allowed to occur under the guards' noses."

"That's sick. I wonder why they picked on him, or was it some kind of riot?"

"I need to check the facts first, but I have my suspicions."

"No! Darryl? He wouldn't dare."

"Wouldn't he? I doubt it would have taken him long to figure out why I was at the prison last week. The governor has already stripped him of his privileges. This could be his way of getting back at me."

"I'd get all the facts before thinking along those lines. Not everything that happens inside can be attributed to him."

"You know I don't believe in coincidences, Jack," she snapped uncharacteristically, making Jack flinch. "I'm sorry. Ugh... I hate that man so much for what he's put me through. He still has control over my life, and I've had as much as I can take."

"No need to apologise. If he's behind this, then the prison authorities will have to deal with him. Maybe they'll buckle and contemplate moving him to another prison now or upping his sentence even. He's obviously still a considerable problem in spite of being banged up. By rights, they should throw the book at him. If he's guilty, that is."

"I reckon he is. But even if they relocated him to another prison, there's no guarantee he won't continue to send former inmates to harass me, or do even worse, come to that." She shuddered at the memories just thinking about her ex had stirred up.

Jack nodded. "Don't let him win, Sal. You've come a long way. You're a much stronger woman now. Maybe that's what is truly bugging him—the fact that you haven't crumbled."

"Thanks, Jack. I really needed to hear that." She held up her hand and clenched her fist. "I can beat him. I refuse to let that bastard get under my skin ever again. I'm going to ring the governor, see what the real story is."

"I'll bring a coffee into you."

She smiled her appreciation, thankful that her partner had decided to remain a part of the team. She walked into the office and sucked in a couple of deep breaths to calm her nerves before she placed the call.

Governor Wilkinson instantly accepted her call. "Sorry, Inspector, I had every intention of ringing you first thing. You know how it is once the paperwork consumes you."

"That's okay, and yes, I completely understand. So what happened?"

"Craig Gillan was on his way to have dinner yesterday when he was pulled into one of the cells. My men hadn't noticed he was missing until it was too late. We had no idea who was to blame at the time, but we have since learned on the grapevine that four men attacked him. He's in hospital with a couple of broken ribs, as well as a broken arm and a fractured skull. To be honest with you, I think it could have been a lot worse than it is."

Sally gasped. "That's horrendous. How on earth was it allowed to happen?"

"It's something I'm investigating. I will not let this drop, I can assure you."

"I have a name for you: Darryl Parker."

He sighed. "The same name crossed my mind also. As soon as I have proof that he was behind the assault, I'll lock him up in solitary confinement."

"Is there anyone else it could be, Governor? He has money. He could have easily paid the four men."

"No doubt. You know how it is, Inspector. Without proof, there is very little I or anyone else can do about it."

"I hope that doesn't turn out to be the case, Governor."

"Leave it with me. The second I find out, you'll be the first person I call. You have my word on that."

"Okay. Will it be all right if I visit Craig today? Just to lend him my support?"

"Please do. I'll contact the officer with him to let him know."

"Thank you. Goodbye, Governor."

"Goodbye, Inspector."

Sally hung up, looked at the post lying on her desk, and chose to ignore it. Concern for Craig far outweighed her need to deal with any urgent memos from head office.

She pushed away from her desk and left the office. "Come on, Jack. We're going to the hospital."

"We are?"

"I'll fill you in on the way. Joanna, no news on Kenny or his wife getting back to us yet?"

"No, boss. That's a tad strange. Giving them the benefit of the doubt, they might be away on holiday."

Sally thought back to the lawn being in tip-top shape at the cottage. "Maybe. I suppose they could have tidied up the garden before going away. Try and track down where the couple work while we're gone. I think that should be our priority now." She turned to Jordan. "Damn, I don't have time to listen to an update on your case. Did everything go okay when you interviewed the aunt and the girl on Friday?"

"Yes and no, boss. I'll fill you in when you get back. There's still an aspect of the case I need to look into this morning, something that doesn't sit right with me."

"Okay, we'll run through things the minute I get back. I promise."

Jack was already waiting at the door. Sally caught up with him, and they set off.

Thirty-five minutes later, they arrived at the hospital. After locating a parking space, they rushed through the corridor towards the reception desk. Sally showed her ID to the receptionist. "Hi, I'm DI Sally Parker. Can you possibly tell me what ward Craig Gillan is on please?"

"Just a second. Ah, here we are. He's on the men's ward, in a private room. Follow the green line on this level, and the room you're looking for is number twelve."

"Thanks very much."

They raced through the winding corridor and knocked on the door. The prison officer was sitting at the foot of Craig's bed. He jumped out of his seat and approached them.

"This room is off limits."

Sally flashed her ID. "I'm investigating Mr. Gillan's case. I rang the governor about an hour ago. He was going to call you."

"Yes, sorry, he did. Gillan is asleep at the moment."

Sally glanced at Craig. His face was covered in varying shades of bruises. His right arm was in plaster, and his head was bandaged.

Tears misted her eyes as she approached his bed.

He seemed to sense her presence and stirred.

"Hello, Craig, how are you feeling?"

His eyes fluttered open and shut intermittently. In a croaky voice, he replied, "Like four men jumped on me and beat the shit out of me."

She smiled down at him and placed a hand on top of his. "I'm sorry this happened to you. Do you have any idea who was involved?"

His eyes opened, revealing bloodshot eyeballs. "I've seen them around, but I have no idea of their names."

"Maybe you can give a description to a police artist, when you feel up to it of course."

"I'd rather not, Inspector. I appreciate that you're trying to help. I just think they'll do their utmost to finish the job next time."

"If you're sure."

Craig nodded and raised his head a little to look at the officer, then his gaze drifted back to her. "I'm sure."

Sally read Craig's meaning. "Can I ask you to step outside for a moment?" she asked the officer.

"I'm not supposed to leave the room."

"Under normal circumstances perhaps, but we're serving police officers. I'm sure you can bend the rules just for today."

His shoulders slumped in resignation. "I'll give you fifteen minutes. I'll grab a coffee in the canteen while you chat."

"I appreciate that."

After the officer left the room, Sally and Jack sat down beside Craig. "Do you think the guards allowed this to happen to you, Craig?"

"They knew. There was one of them standing on the landing, grinning as those guys dragged me into the room. Why? Why pick on me? I keep my head down in there, have done for the past fifteen years. Nothing like this has ever occurred before. Do you think it's because you've reopened my case?"

Not wishing to mention who she thought was behind the attack, she shrugged. "Maybe. I'm not sure how things work on the inside. I've heard some horror stories over the years but always about people who deserved the punishment. I wouldn't put you in that bracket. The governor has assured me he'll be looking into the incident."

"That's reassuring—not! One of his damn men was involved for Christ's sake. He ain't gonna do anything. You wait and see."

"I'll ensure that he does. I promise you. These men and the guard who did nothing to prevent the attack will be brought to justice."

"I wish I had as much confidence about that as you have." He sighed. "I haven't heard from you for a few days. Is everything going okay?"

"As well as can be expected. We spent a few days at the factory where Anne worked, talking to her friends and the people who knew her well."

"And? Do they all still think I killed her?"

"Surprisingly, no. Most of them have always thought you were innocent."

"Well, at least that's something. Did you talk to that weirdo Endecott?"

Sally glanced at Jack then turned back to speak to Craig. "I did. I don't think he was guilty of anything other than being infatuated with Anne."

"What gave you that impression? May I ask?"

"The events leading up to his death."

His eyes widened. "He's dead? How?"

"He ran onto the roof before we had a chance to interview him. I tried to talk him out of what he was planning but failed. His last words to me were that he was going to be with Anne finally. He jumped off the roof in front of all his work colleagues."

Craig's uninjured hand covered his face. "My God, how awful. I knew he was besotted with her. He used to ring Anne all the time at home, every time something went wrong in his life. It got to the point that he was ringing her four or five times a week. In the end, I blew my top. No one should have to put up with that crap at the end of the day. He was locked up a few times after attempting suicide. Anne felt guilty every time he was sectioned, felt that she had somehow let him down. I told her she was being silly, but that was her all over. She cared about people every day of her life. It broke her heart when she had to tell him to stop ringing her. But I couldn't put up with it a moment longer. We had a right to lead our own lives without feeling guilty because of that man. I'm sorry he's dead, but he's been threatening to kill himself for years."

"I'm sorry he put you and Anne through such torment. Sometimes a person's cry for help gets out of hand, and they try to involve other people to solve their anxieties. He was very confused at the end. I can't imagine what he must have been like when Anne was alive." Sally paused before mentioning his brother. "We've been trying to locate Kenny, without much luck. He's the only person we haven't interviewed who the original officer in charge took a statement from. Any idea where he works, Craig?"

"That's strange. Blimey, now you're asking. He used to work in the office at a steelworks before he moved area. I really can't tell you what he does now because I haven't spoken to him since I've been inside. Maybe Molly will know."

"Sorry he hasn't been in touch. Can you remember the name of the firm or where it was located perhaps? We could give them a ring. Failing that, I'll ask Molly if she knows."

"Something Steels... sorry my head is still a little fuzzy. On the outskirts of Norwich, it was. The company was named after his boss. I can't give you more than that."

"That will do, I hope. Can't see too many steelworks being located in the area. What about his wife? Can you tell me where she works?"

"Alison? No idea. I'm not much help, am I?"

"You're doing fine. It was wrong of me to question you when you're clearly not a hundred percent. We'll do some more digging when we get back to the station."

The door opened and the prison officer came into the room. "You about done in here?"

Sally and Jack rose from their chairs. "Yes, we're done. You take it easy. Hopefully, they'll allow you to stay here till you make a full recovery before they move you back to the prison. In the meantime, you have my assurance that we're doing everything we can to get you out of there."

"Thanks, Inspector. I hope you manage to track down Kenny. When you do, will you pass on a message that I would love to see him one day, if he has the time to visit me, that is?"

"I'll be sure to pass that on, if we ever track him down. Wishing you a speedy recovery, Craig."

They left the hospital and drove back to the station.

"What are you thinking, boss?"

"I'm wondering why Kenny still hasn't got in touch with us."

"Me, too. Can we put it down as suspicious behaviour, or do you think he's just forgotten, too busy to get in touch perhaps?"

Sally shrugged. "Maybe, even if he's choosing to ignore us for whatever reason, there's no excuse for his wife not to get in touch with us."

"Why should she?"

"I left a card the other day."

Jack turned to face her. "Maybe he got home first and hid the card. Perhaps she has no idea we're trying to track them down."

"Maybe. We'll see if we can find out where he works, make that the priority for today."

Moments later, they arrived at the station.

"Joanna, I need you to look up a business for me. The details are a little sketchy. I'm looking for a steelworks around the Norwich area. The business is named after the owner, if that helps."

"I think I know it," Stuart called out. "Grayson Steels. One of my uncles used to work there."

"Excellent. See what you can find out, Joanna. Kenny Gillan no longer works there, but they might know where he moved on to."

"Leave it with me, boss."

"Right, Jordan, shall we go over your case?"

Jordan sat forward in his chair and picked up his notepad. Sally drew up a chair and sat alongside him.

"Well, Joanna and I visited the aunt. After we spoke to her, Fiona came into the room. She was really scared, didn't say a word, just looked down at the ground the whole time during the interview. Joanna did her best to gain the girl's trust, but she was having none of it. So, we're no further forward there. However, I've spoken to the girl's counsellor today, and something she told me sparked something up here," he said, pointing to his forehead. "She told me that it's not uncommon for a child to become introverted, which backs up what my mate who works for Social Services told me. However, the counsellor also added that the child probably became introverted when she *witnessed* her father's death."

"Wow, that's interesting. Therefore, Falkirk could have been right on this case then. The mother probably did kill the father."

"Definitely looks like it to me. On the other hand, the counsellor also told me that Fiona might be in shock because she believes her mother to be innocent and that she's been taken away from her."

"Damn, why does there always have to be two sides to every story, especially with a case such as this? Okay, let's leave things as they are for a moment. Maybe you questioning the girl might jolt her memory a little and force her to get in touch with us. Stranger things have happened."

"I'll leave it for now then. Maybe ring the aunt in a few days, just to see how things are going? How about that?" Jordan replied thoughtfully.

"Sounds like a good idea to me. Well done, Jordan."

"Boss, I have something for you," Joanna shouted.

Sally rushed back to Joanna and perched her backside on the desk nearby. "What is it?"

"Fortunately, the receptionist has worked there for years. She remembered Kenny Gillan and agreed to look up his personnel file for me. There she noted that a reference had been requested from a builders' merchants in Suffolk, where Kenny had applied for a management position."

"Excellent news! At last we're getting somewhere. Can you look the name and number up for the company, and I'll give them a ring?"

Joanna smiled and handed her a Post-it note. Written on it were the name and telephone number of the firm. "Already done, boss."

"I do have the dream team working for me today. Thanks. I'll give them a discreet call, see if I can locate the elusive Kenny. Wish me luck." Sally sat down at her desk and let out a weary breath. It was only halfway through the working day, but she was already feeling exhausted. She picked up the phone and dialled the number. "Hello, is it possible to speak to the person in charge, the owner of the company perhaps?"

"Just a moment. Can I ask who's calling?"

"Sally Parker. Thanks very much."

There was a pause before a man's gruff voice filtered down the line. "Hello, this is Mark Thrower. What can I do for you, Ms. Parker?"

"Hello, Mr. Thrower. I'm an Inspector with the Norfolk Constabulary. I was wondering if you have a Kenny Gillan working for you?"

"I have. What's my old mucker done now?"

Sally detected a smile in the man's voice. "Nothing. I'm just trying to track him down. Is he at work today?"

"Yes, he is. Do you want me to pass you through to him?"

Sally's heart skipped a beat. "No, that's okay. What time does he usually leave the office?"

"Around six, give or take ten or fifteen minutes."

"That's brilliant. I'll catch him after work then. Can I ask you to keep this conversation to yourself, Mr. Thrower?"

"Of course, if you tell me what he's done wrong. Speeding fine? He's had a fair few of those in the past."

"No, nothing like that. We just need to have a chat with him. Nothing cloak and dagger about why we want to see him, I promise you."

"My lips are sealed then."

"I appreciate your time and the information. Thank you." Sally hung up and bellowed for Jack to join her.

Jack appeared in the doorway, a frown wrinkling his brow. "What's up?"

"Kenny Gillan is at work now. I've told the owner of the company that we'll swing by to see Gillan this evening as he leaves, but I'm thinking we should take a trip out there now. What say you?"

"I like your thinking. Can we grab a sandwich on the way? I'm starving."

Sally shook her head. "Why is it you men are always thinking about your stomachs?"

"I wasn't aware that I do. A body needs fuel for it to function properly, I'll have you know."

Sally pulled a face at him. "Learn that in the army, Bullet?"

"Common knowledge. When do you want to set off? I thought I'd treat the others to a sandwich before we leave."

"That's kind of you. Ham and cheese on a brown roll for me, if you're buying. We'll have lunch and then shoot off."

Jack left the office and returned with her lunch ten minutes later. They set off for Suffolk twenty minutes after that. After eating her roll, Sally had to admit, her partner knew his stuff. Her weariness disappeared, and she felt invigorated once again. Either that, or she had a good feeling that things were finally going her way with the case.

CHAPTER FIFTEEN

The builders' merchants was a hive of activity when they arrived at around two fifteen. Sally and Jack walked into the reception area and produced their IDs.

"DI Sally Parker and DS Jack Blackman. We'd like to speak with Kenny Gillan, please?"

"Ah, sorry, but he's left the office for the day."

Sally and Jack issued each other frustrated looks. Sally smiled at the woman on reception. "I spoke to Mr. Thrower earlier. Is *he* available for a quick chat?"

"I'll just check." The receptionist placed the call and nodded at Sally before hanging up. "He'll be with you shortly. Care to take a seat?"

"Thanks."

Sally and Jack stepped away from the counter and began pacing the floor until Thrower finally appeared. Sally couldn't help but notice how sheepish the man looked.

His face was flushed when he approached them. "Sorry, Inspector."

"For what? Betraying a confidence? I asked you not to tell Gillan, and you specifically went against that instruction. I could have you for obstructing a police investigation. Where is he?"

"I know, and I regret my actions. I was just winding him up, but he freaked out. Kenny ran out of my office and left the building. I asked Ginny where he had gone, and she said he'd received a call from home that there was some kind of emergency."

"He's at home then? How long has it been since he left?"

"About thirty minutes, I suppose. Me and my big mouth. If it's any consolation, I've been kicking myself ever since."

"What's done is done. If he contacts you, will you ring me right away? Here's my card."

"Of course. Once again, I'm sorry."

Sally and Jack rushed out of the building and sped away from the merchants, the tyres on the car churning up the gravel driveway.

"I'm not liking this guy's reaction to us wanting to chat with him, Jack."

"Mighty suspicious, I have to agree. Want me to call for backup?"

"No, I think we'll be able to deal with him ourselves. Let's hope we're not too late. His address should still be in the satnav under 'recent destinations'. Sort that out for me, will you?"

According to the satnav, they were eight minutes from Kenny's home. Sally found it impossible to push down the sinking feeling gnawing at her stomach. *I hope to Christ we haven't missed him.*

When they arrived at the address, it was obvious Kenny had gone. The question was for how long? Sally struck the steering wheel with the heel of her hand. "Get on to the station, Jack. We need to trace his car. The more this guy goes out of his way to avoid us, the more I'm inclined to think he has something grave to hide, like being Anne's murderer! That gives us the authority to order a search warrant for his address. Get Joanna on that. I'll stop your game, Kenny Gillan, if it's the last thing I ever do."

When they arrived back at the station, Joanna informed Sally that the warrant had been requested and should be through within the next twenty-four to forty-eight hours.

"Okay, well, there's not a lot we can do about that. Joanna, I need you to dig deep on Kenny. He's running for a reason—I want to know why."

"I thought you might say that, boss. I've already made a start."

"Found anything yet?"

"I think so. Can you leave it with me to do some research before I report back?"

"Of course. I'll be in my office if anyone wants me."

A little while later, when Sally was in the middle of filling out another mundane form about procedures from head office, Jordan poked his head around the door. "Do you have a second, boss?"

"Come in and sit down. What's wrong?"

"Hopefully, it's a good thing. Fiona's aunt has just rung me. She's asked me to call round there after Fiona has finished school. I was hoping you'd give me a bit of guidance how to proceed."

Sally smiled. "You don't need any guidance from me, Jordan. You've done a fantastic job on the case so far. How did the aunt sound?"

"Thanks for that. She sounded all right, a little hesitant when she asked for a meeting. Can I take Joanna with me? Or would you rather she stayed here and kept up the search for Gillan?"

With that, Joanna knocked on the door and entered the room.

"Why don't we ask her? Fancy a trip out to see Fiona with Jordan?"

Joanna slipped the piece of paper she was holding in front of Sally.

Sally read the note, and her gaze darted back up to Joanna. "You're kidding me? Why didn't this information show up before? More to the point—why didn't Craig bloody mention it?"

"Not sure why it wasn't highlighted before. That's probably my fault, boss. As far as Craig is concerned, perhaps he wasn't aware of it. The case was dismissed in court."

"The sixteen-year-old girl took it all the way to court and then admitted that she made up the rape charge. Does that seem likely to you? It doesn't to me. Sounds like he intimidated her before the jury could find him guilty. Crap!" Sally threw herself back in her chair. "He's looking more and more suspicious the deeper we look. Why the heck wasn't he questioned properly by Falkirk? When did the case go to court, Joanna?"

"That's the first thing I checked. It was a few months before Anne went missing."

"I wonder if he's been tempted since, or has marriage put paid to his temptations? So many questions and so few answers."

"Would it be worth putting the house under surveillance, boss?" Jordan suggested.

Sally nodded thoughtfully. "I was wondering the same thing. I'll run it past the DCI. I'm unsure what budget we're working to being a cold-case team now. Leave it with me, guys. Joanna, would you mind accompanying Jordan out to see Fiona again this afternoon?"

"Fine by me. What time, Jordan?"

"Set off in about fifteen minutes."

Sally smiled. "Excellent, that's sorted then. Tread carefully, as usual. Let's hope you return with some good news."

The second Jordan and Joanna left the office, Sally picked up the phone and rang DCI Green. She apprised him of the situation regarding Kenny Gillan. When she asked for permission to use a surveillance team, he hesitated.

"Sir? It's looking more likely that he's the killer."

"Okay, just until the warrant comes through. By the way, there's talk of the complaints team looking into that suicide case which occurred in your presence last week."

"What? Why? I did everything I could to talk the man out of jumping. He was determined to end his life, though. Jack witnessed the whole thing."

"I know. If Jack can back you up then there shouldn't be a problem. This shouldn't come as a surprise to you, Inspector. It's procedure, after all."

"I know, sir. It still sucks, though."

"Don't let it interfere with your work. They'll summon you for an interview, and that will be the end of it."

"I hope so, sir. I'll keep you informed about the case."

"Please do, Inspector. Chin up."

She put the phone down, miffed by what DCI Green had told her. She was aware of how these things went. That didn't stop her feeling ticked off by it, though. She shrugged. *C'est la vie!* Wearing a covering smile, she left the office and walked towards Jack and Stuart. "Hi, guys, how are you doing?"

Jack eyed her suspiciously. "What do you need?"

She stabbed an imaginary dagger in her heart. "I'm wounded, Jack."

"Yeah, right."

"I've been given the go-ahead to put surveillance on Gillan's cottage. Any takers?"

Both Sally and Jack looked in Stuart's direction.

"What?" he asked. "You think I haven't got a life outside this place? Okay, maybe you're right. I'm up for it, boss."

"Gee, thanks, Stuart. Do you want to go home for a few hours and then shoot over there? You've got the address, haven't you?"

"Yep, I have the address." He grabbed his jacket off the back of his chair and left.

Deadly Encounter

"Want me to check if an alert has gone out for Gillan's car?" Jack asked.

"If you would. I hate this—it's a bloody waiting game now until that warrant appears. By the way, don't forget we're going to the auction house tomorrow."

"I hadn't. I hope I don't get tempted to buy a house while I'm there. Donna would lynch me."

"I hear it's best to keep your hands in your pockets, just in case, and don't even think about scratching your nose." Sally laughed.

"Yikes, thanks for the warning. So, if these guys who attacked your dad show their faces, we're going to arrest them on the spot?"

"That's the plan. *If* they show up. That will depend on how much they want the property."

~ ~ ~

The following day, the team assembled back at the station and shared varying news. Jordan was the first person to bring the group up-to-date. "Looks like Fiona witnessed her mother giving the poison to her father."

"How? Bloody hell! I'm not surprised she's a confused young lady."

"That's not the worst part. Apparently, the mother was holding her daughter in front of her. She placed her arm around Fiona's neck and held a knife in her hand. She threatened the husband that if he didn't drink the poison, she would end their daughter's life."

"WTF? That's insane."

"Yep. The best part is that Fiona told us the news herself. It might have had something to do with me opening up to her about my uncle being poisoned by his brother."

"I didn't know that, Jordan. I'm sorry to hear that."

"It was years ago, boss. I've pushed it to the back of my mind. Anyway, she said she's lived with the trauma for long enough and was now eager to get on with her life. She felt guilty about her father's death, thought over the years that she was to blame for him taking the poison."

"That poor kid. We'll make sure she gets the best counselling around. No kid should go through life feeling used and abused like that, especially when the mental abuse was carried out by a parent. That's a wrap on that case then. Type up your report, and we'll pass it on to the parole board. That'll ensure the mother remains behind bars, away from her daughter. What a sick woman."

"I'll do it this morning," Jordan said, nodding.

"Anything at the cottage, Stuart?"

"Nothing, boss. No cars turned up, and no lights went on in the house."

"That's a shame. Sorry it was a waste of time for you, Stuart."

"No problem, boss."

"Okay, Jack and I have to disappear for a few hours mid-morning. We're hoping to catch the thugs who beat up my father last week. With any luck, when we return, we'll have some news on Kenny's warrant. Joanna, while we're otherwise occupied, maybe you can try and find out if Kenny or his wife own any other properties. A holiday home somewhere, perhaps. It's a long shot, but that's all I have at the moment."

"Leave it with me, boss."

"Right, give me an hour in my office, Jack, and then we'll set off."

~ ~ ~

An hour later, Sally drew the car to a halt outside the auction house. She spotted her dad's and Simon's cars on the way into the building. "They're both here. I'm just going to have a quick word with them first, and then we'll leave them to get on with it and find a discreet position to observe the proceedings."

"Hey, you two." She kissed her dad and Simon on the cheek. "Have you spotted them yet, Dad?"

"No. Do you think it's a good idea for you to be speaking to us?" her father replied nervously.

"We're generally chatting. No harm in that, Dad. I need you to give me the nod when you see them. Jack and I will stand on the opposite side of the room and watch for you to give us the signal, all right?"

Her father inhaled and let out the breath which puffed out his rosy cheeks. "Okay, love."

"You'll be fine, Chris. Sally has this covered."

"We'll get into position. Good luck, you two."

Sally surveyed the auction attendees who were a mixture of women, men in suits and quite a few tradesmen in work gear. She was surprised to see so many women there. Some were accompanied by men, others by themselves. Maybe it was a sign of the times that more and more women were becoming property developers. They certainly had a keener eye than men for interior design.

The auctioneer announced the first lot, and the people who were standing in the foyer filtered into the room. Sally watched her father's eyes scanning the room. They widened when he spotted a heavily built man standing by the door. His gaze drifted her way again, and he flicked his head in the man's direction. Sally nodded and nudged Jack in the ribs. "Okay, Dad's picked the bruiser out at the back. We need to drift over that way towards him during the auction."

"Shouldn't the uniformed officers be inside rather than sitting in the car park?"

"Scared, are you? Come on, Bullet, he'll be no match for you. We'll pounce on him before he notices we're there. Let's hold fire until he starts bidding on the same lot as Dad and Simon, though. You tackle him, and I'll slap the cuffs on." Sally kept one eye on the auctioneer and squeezed past people to get closer to the man, who appeared to be alone.

The first two lots went unsold as they didn't reach their reserve price. The third lot was the one Simon had his eye on. He raised his hand to start the bidding off at a hundred thousand. Sally used her peripheral vision to keep an eye on the man and saw him raise his hand. This was all the confirmation she needed. She tugged on Jack's arm, but he seemed engrossed in the auction. "We need to get closer, get around his back. I want to strike soon, Jack, in case he takes off."

"After you."

Sally weaved through the crowd and ducked down to pass the man, who was bidding. Jack joined her. Sally looked over to her father for further confirmation. He was nodding with widened eyes. Simon raised his hand at a hundred and eighty thousand. Before the man could respond, Jack grabbed his arms and forced them behind his back, while Sally slapped on the cuffs.

"What the hell is going on?" the man asked, his gaze darting between Sally and Jack.

"You're under arrest for grievous bodily harm," Sally stated.

"You're nuts. If I lose this house…"

"You'll what? Do the same to me as you did to my father last week at the house?"

The auctioneer's gavel went down, then Simon and Sally's father joined them in the foyer. The man was fuming, and he started kicking out at Jack until Jack stamped on his feet. "Behave, you bloody idiot."

"Is this the man, Dad?"

"That's one of them. Where's your mate, sonny?"

"I don't know what you're talking about, old man. I've never seen you before."

"I've heard enough. Put him in the car, Jack."

The man wriggled fiercely, but Jack managed to overpower the brute and pushed him through the entrance and into the car.

Sally kissed her father. "You did well, Dad. I'll get someone else to question him when we return to the station."

"Thanks, love. So glad we've got him. What about his mate?"

"He doesn't look the type not to tell tales, especially if there is a deal on the table. I think he'll spill the beans in a matter of hours. Let's hope so, anyway. I better get going." Sally pecked her father and Simon on the cheek and climbed in the car, where Jack was keeping the suspect company in the back seat.

"Great, now I'm gonna be subjected to a woman driver taking me to the nick," the thug grunted.

Sally grinned at him in her rear-view mirror. "It's just not your day, love, is it?"

Jack laughed. "Hey, at least you only get to put up with her driving once in your lifetime. I'm subjected to it every day."

Sally chuckled and inserted the key in the ignition. The backup panda car followed them back to the station, where Jack handed the thug, who was still refusing to divulge his name, over to the uniformed officers for the desk sergeant to deal with.

Feeling elated, Sally ran up the stairs and into the incident room.

Joanna smiled and waved a sheet of paper at her. "It's through, boss."

Sally rushed towards her and surveyed the warrant. "Bloody brilliant. Okay, Jordan, Stuart, Jack and I will shoot over to the house now while you man the phones, Joanna. I don't suppose there's any news on another address yet?"

"No such luck, boss. I thought I'd give Craig's daughter a call but wanted to run it past you first."

"Great idea. Get on to that now and call me if you come up with anything."

"I will. Good luck," Joanna called after them as the four rushed out of the room.

In the car park, Sally opened her car door. "We'll meet you there, boys."

Just under an hour later, Sally pulled the car to a halt outside Gillan's cottage. There were no cars in the drive. Jordan drew his car up alongside Sally's, then they all gathered at the front door. She knocked on the door, but it remained unanswered.

Turning to Jack, she ordered, "Do your thing, Bullet."

Jack shoulder-charged the front door, which gave way on the second attempt and banged against the wall in the hallway. He entered first, followed by the others.

At the base of the stairs, Sally said, "You two see what you can find upstairs." Then she followed Jack through the hallway to the back of the house. The characterful cottage had low beams everywhere, but the rooms were too claustrophobic for Sally's taste.

"Ouch, shit! That's the fourth frigging beam I've hit," Jack complained, rubbing the slight bump already developing on his forehead.

"Oops, maybe it would be better if you walked around on your knees," Sally joked.

"Ha bloody ha. Where do you want to start?"

"Well, every room has to be searched, so you choose which one you want, and we'll begin. Just a sec... I'll check on the boys first. Anything up there?" she called out from the bottom of the stairs.

"No one's up here, boss. Want us to start searching?" Jordan called down, standing at the top of the stairs.

"Yep, make sure you wear your gloves."

"Already on, boss. Are we looking for anything in particular?"

"Anything pertaining to either Anne or Craig Gillan for now, and then we'll go from there." Sally walked back through the house and started searching the kitchen, leaving Jack to search through the built-in storage cupboards in the lounge. That job, at least, he could carry out while down on his knees.

Sally started rifling through the drawers in the pine dresser in the kitchen. She hated the smell of old wood; it tickled the inside of her nostrils until she finally sneezed. Inside the first drawer was everything needed to lay a table: a nice set of cutlery and coasters with placemats, both everyday ones and a posher set she assumed the occupants preferred to use for dinner parties. Apart from that, she found very little else. A search of the second drawer produced the same result. Sally moved around the room, searching in the kitchen cupboards, both high and low, but it proved fruitless.

She walked into the dining room next door, where a long sideboard stood along one of the walls. It had three drawers and three large cupboards. When she opened the first cupboard, it was full of games such as Monopoly, Cluedo, Jenga and quite a few packs of cards. In the second cupboard, there were mainly kids' toys, and in the third were a bunch of archive files. On the spine of the first file was written *bank statements*. Sally extracted several statements and skimmed through them. No large sums, in or out, jumped out at her, except for Kenny's monthly salary. However, she discovered there were two separate mortgage payments coming out of the account.

Jack came into the room behind her. "What have you got?"

"His bank statements show signs of him having two properties. Two separate mortgage payments going out every month."

"Interesting. Must be where he's hiding out. Want me to contact the mortgage companies?"

"No, I need you to help me look through this lot. I'll ring Joanna, tell her to check the mortgage company."

She dialled the station. The ever-efficient Joanna answered the call on the first ring. Sally rolled off the information for her to trace then hung up. She then handed three of the files to Jack and placed the other three on the floor for herself to search.

"Bingo! Maybe that was a wasted call you just made, boss. I've found insurance policies for this address and an address in Cromer."

Sally grimaced. "Crap, that's about an hour and a half from here. Okay, well at least we have proof of another property. Let's see if we can find anything to do with either Craig or Anne amongst this lot. Let's put a time limit on this of ten minutes then shoot over to the Cromer address."

"I doubt that's going to happen. Would he really keep something like that on show, where his wife could stumble across it?"

Sally glanced at the picture of Kenny and his beautiful blonde wife, sitting in a gilt frame on top of the sideboard. "I wonder if she knows."

"I wouldn't have thought so, if he did the deed. We haven't found any proof of that yet, boss."

"I know, but I think it's only a matter of time before we do." They heard the footfalls of Jordan and Stuart coming down the stairs.

The two men appeared in the doorway. "Waste of time upstairs, boss," Jordan told her, his eyes rolling up to the low-beamed ceiling.

"It doesn't matter. We think we've found the proof we need in these files. We'll continue to search in here."

Jack clicked his fingers. "I'll be back in a sec." He stood up and immediately bashed his head on one of the beams. "Shit, damn and blast. You lot can stop laughing. It's lucky you're all short arses."

Jordan and Stuart punched him in the arm as he passed. "Shorter, not short," Stuart complained. "Hey, where are you going?"

"I'll be back soon."

"It's not like Jack to run out on me. Grab a box, you two. We might as well complete the search—who knows what we'll find next?"

"What then?" Stuart asked.

"We've located a second address. I've put a limit of ten minutes at this location, then I think we should shoot over to Cromer to see if Mr. and Mrs. Gillan are hiding out there."

They spent the next five minutes rifling through the Gillans' personal papers, unable to find anything else of significance, until Jack entered the room again, wearing the smuggest of grins. "I've called SOCO. They're on their way."

Sally's brow furrowed. "Why? What have you found?" She rose to her feet, shaking out the pins and needles in her legs.

"The car. Remember we spotted it in the garage the other day? I noticed an insurance document for it and found the key to the garage on a hook in the hallway. I opened it up and went inside to have a look. I doubt it's been used in years. Two of the tyres are flat. I found what looks like blood in the boot. I left the garage and rang SOCO straight away. Looks like we've found all the evidence we need to bang the weasel up, when we can get our hands on him."

Sally clapped her hands in glee. "Fantastic. Well done, you. Right, here's what I think we should do next. Jordan and Stuart, I want you two to stay here until SOCO have dealt with the car. They'll probably tow it away and search it back at the laboratory. I'll ring Simon, make him aware of what's going on and what we need from the examination. In the meantime, Jack and I will head over to the address in Cromer, see if we can track down the elusive Kenny. Give me two ticks, Jack. Maybe you could ring Joanna and fill her in?"

"It all makes sense to me," Jack replied, dipping in his jacket pocket for his mobile while Sally left the cottage to ring Simon.

He answered his mobile, out of breath.

"Sorry, were you busy?"

"Only just arrived back at work. Your dad and I decided to hang around at the auction house longer than anticipated."

Sally cringed. "Oh no, that sounds expensive."

"Don't worry, we didn't buy anything else. We wanted to experience the feel of the auction more, studied what the punters were doing, their discreet behaviour, looking for tips for the next time, I suppose you'd call it."

"Phew, that's a relief. Not sure Dad should be taking on too much work at the moment, not until he's fully recuperated."

"Don't worry, I have no intention of burying him under more pressure. He's got another builder lined up to come onboard with us."

"Fabulous news. Maybe Dad could become more of a site manager rather than get his hands dirty on future projects."

"My sentiments exactly. Anyway, what can I do for you? I take it this call is about business, considering we only parted company a few hours ago."

"It is. I think we've finally struck lucky. Jack has just contacted SOCO about a car we've found at Kenny Gillan's address."

"The warrant came through then?"

"Yes. I wondered if you could work your magic and get the tests hurried along for me."

"Of course, I will. Have you found anything suspicious inside the vehicle?"

"Jack thinks he's spotted some blood in the boot."

"If that's her blood in the boot of Kenny's car, then that should be enough to put him away. Blimey, fancy Craig's own brother doing the dirty on him like that and allowing him to take the blame for fifteen years. I wonder if they were having an affair."

"Anne and Kenny? I can't see that myself, but who can tell? It's definitely something I intend asking Kenny, once we catch up with him. Okay, I better go. I'll see you later. Oh, and congratulations again on adding to your property portfolio."

"See you later, darling. Oh, and Sally… it's *our* property portfolio, *not* mine."

"I love you, Simon Bracknall."

CHAPTER SIXTEEN

"Damn, that's all we need," Sally said angrily, watching large drops of rain bounce off the windscreen. "We're only five minutes away from the house now."

"A drop of rain has never hindered us before. I'm sure we'll cope," Jack replied, rubbing his palm against his thigh.

"Are you nervous?"

"Me? No. Anxious to catch the bastard after the run-around he's given us. How could he do that to his own brother?"

"I concur. Only it's not just his brother this has affected—it's Molly and Jamie, too. The whole situation is tasteless, and I can't wait to hear what his bloody reason is for robbing that poor family of such a lovely lady."

"What I want to know is how he's slept at night, knowing what pain he was causing."

"Let's just say I'm going to enjoy ripping him apart in the interview room. I wonder if his wife knows?"

"I doubt it. If he's managed to conceal the truth from his brother and the kids all these years, he's probably done the same to her."

A few minutes later, Sally drove past Kenny's address.

"Looks like his car is there. What now?" Jack asked.

"I'll park up in an adjoining road and we'll walk back, catch them unawares."

She found a parking place in the adjacent road, switched off the engine, and sucked in a large breath, then let it out through her teeth. "Let's do this, partner."

They left the car and dashed back to Gillan's road. Sally paused to survey the area. "I can't see an alleyway leading to the back. We're both going to have to take the front and hope he answers the door."

Jack nodded and they set off. The heavens had opened even more, and Sally's hair was already clinging to her face. They had just crossed the road a few metres from the house when the front door opened and a man stepped out.

"Shit, it's him." She called out, "Kenny Gillan?"

The man's eyes narrowed to see who was shouting his name, then he bolted towards his car. He jumped in the driver's side and started the vehicle. The engine roared. Sally hopped into the road and ran towards him. Jack stayed on the pavement but matched her pace.

Kenny put the car into gear and revved the engine. Sally remained defiant and strode towards him. Suddenly, the car accelerated and hurtled towards her, naught to fifty within a few seconds. Sally heard Jack shout, and the next thing she knew, they both struck the ground as the car flew past.

Jack let out a whistle. "Jesus, that was close."

"A sure sign of guilt. Quick, back to the car, Jack. We can't let him get away again."

Jack hauled her to her feet and Sally winced. She'd turned her ankle in the fall.

"Are you all right?"

"I'll be fine. Take the keys. Get in the car. I won't be far behind you."

Jack sprinted the couple of hundred metres to the car while Sally hobbled after him. She cursed her luck as she saw the tail end of Kenny's vehicle turn the corner of the long road. He already had an advantage on them because he knew the area. Sally shook off the negativity as Jack drew the car up alongside her and flung open the passenger door.

She jumped in the car. "Quick, after him. Don't worry about me, go, go, go."

Before she'd even closed the door, Jack slung the car into gear and the car lurched forward, slamming the passenger door shut as it sped after Gillan. "We're gonna need backup now, boss."

"I agree." Sally picked up the radio and requested the help of any nearby patrol cars. The control room responded within a minute or so to say four cars were in the area and on the case. "That's a relief."

"You'll need to keep control informed about our location, boss."

"Really? Is that how this works, Jack?" Her reply was laced with sarcasm. "I'm sorry, my ankle is bloody sore, making me a grouch."

"I didn't think anything of it. You sound the same as normal to me," Jack joked. His ribbing earned him a thump in the leg.

"Let's hope he hits traffic up ahead."

"Highly possible, given the time of day with the kids coming out of school."

Jack did well to catch up with the vehicle within minutes. They heard the sirens around them, indicating that backup wasn't far away.

Sally stared ahead as the road curved. "I hope the patrol vehicles can get ahead of him and cut him off. They're more likely to do it than we are."

"If not, I have no idea how we're going to stop the weasel."

"Stick with it, Jack. Lady Luck will have an answer for us soon."

Jack snorted. "Well she ain't been on our side so far, what with this rain and you doing your ankle in."

"Okay, fair point. We mustn't lose heart."

Gillan decided to slam the brakes on and take a shortcut. Jack was right behind him in the manoeuvre. Sally was impressed with his driving skills, considering it was her car he was driving. She relayed the car's whereabouts back to the control room.

At the end of the alley, Gillan took a left then a sharp right, then he was back onto the open road, heading towards the coast.

"At least he's heading out of town," Jack noted.

Sally let out a relieved sigh and radioed the information back to base. "Wonder what he's got in mind?"

"I reckon all will become apparent soon enough."

The chase continued, a convoy of police cars following Gillan. Sally urged the control room to set up some kind of roadblock and appealed for the patrol cars to organise a stinger operation. But she was disappointed when the operator told her that they had no other spare units available to head Gillan off. Frustration tied her stomach into knots. She feared Gillan was about to get away from them again and there wasn't a damn thing they could do about it, unless one of the patrol cars sped past them and intercepted Gillan's car.

"I recognise this route now. We're going towards the pier."

"Really? Would he be stupid enough to leave his car when he knows we're right on his tail?"

"I have no idea what his intentions are. I just know where he's heading."

Ten minutes later, Kenny Gillan slammed the brakes on and deserted his car. He ran for the pier, just as Jack had predicted.

"Go, keep up with him, Jack. I'll get the boys in blue to assist you."

Jack yanked the handbrake on and took off after Gillan. Sally hopped out of the car, literally, and instructed the uniformed officers to follow them. "Is anyone Taser-trained?"

"I am, ma'am," a middle-aged officer said, placing his hand on the Taser resting in his belt.

"Don't be afraid to use it. We believe the man murdered his sister-in-law fifteen years ago."

The man mock-saluted her, and the eight officers ran after Jack. Sally retrieved the keys from the car's ignition and locked the door before hobbling after the officers. She could see the men gathered around Gillan, who was shouting at them to stay back. He was on the very edge of the pier. Sally finally caught up with them and weaved her way through the officers to where Jack was standing only a few feet from Gillan. The memory of trying to coax Endecott away from the edge of the factory roof blazed through her mind. She shook the image free and spoke to Gillan. The officer with the Taser had it aimed at Gillan's chest.

"Don't do this, Kenny. Give yourself up. We can help you if you let us."

"I don't need help. I screwed up. I'm looking for a way out now."

Sally shuffled closer to the suspect, her mouth drying up. She swallowed and moistened her lips. "Why? Why now? Think about your wife and daughter—Tina, isn't it?"

He stared at her, the expression on his face changing as he contemplated her words. His gaze drifted to the sea beside him, and when he looked over his shoulder, Sally clicked her fingers for the officer holding the Taser to take the shot. Kenny Gillan instantly hit the ground as the volts surged through his slim body. Two of the officers approached him and yanked the man to his feet. Cuffs in place, the two officers walked Gillan towards Sally.

"You disgust me. The lives you've destroyed and continue to destroy—for what?"

The man's head slumped in shame, and he couldn't look at her.

"Take him away. I need him taken to Wymondham Station. Bang him up in a cell overnight, let him experience what he's put his brother through for the past sodding fifteen years."

His head rose and their gazes met. "I didn't mean to do it. It was an accident."

"Some accident. Accidents rarely end with someone's body being butchered."

She watched as the officers put the suspect in the back of their car.

"How's the leg?" Jack asked on the way back to the car.

"Like it never happened. Funny how a satisfying ending helps to relieve the pain. Let's get back to the station. I have an important call to make."

"To the prison?"

"Yep, only to make an appointment to see Craig. I want to share the good news with him myself."

Jack smiled. "He's probably still in hospital. Well, that's yet another case solved. We just need to find out why he killed her."

"We'll question him first thing in the morning. Let him stew in the cell overnight. Maybe it'll prick his conscience into telling us the truth tomorrow."

~ ~ ~

The next day, Sally and the team assembled in the incident room earlier than usual. Sally was determined to have all the facts at hand to hit Kenny with during the interview. Simon rang her at nine o'clock with the news that the blood inside the boot of Kenny's Capri, along with several hairs that SOCO found attached to the car's interior, belonged to Anne.

When she and Jack entered the interview room, Kenny was already sitting at the table, his head bowed. Alongside him was a female solicitor whom Sally had met a few times before.

"Hello, Miss Vaughan. Nice of you to join us."

"Hello again, Inspector."

Sally gave Jack the nod. He announced that the interview was about to be videoed and audio taped.

Sally cleared her throat and asked her first question, the most obvious question she could think of asking. "Why? Why kill Anne Gillan, Kenny?"

He sighed heavily a few times, his eyes fixed on his hands twisting together on the table in front of him. "I didn't mean to."

"So, you are openly admitting that you killed your sister-in-law?"

"Yes. But I never meant to kill her. I thought she loved me."

"What gave you that impression? Were you sleeping together?"

"No, not for the lack of trying on my part."

"Then why would you believe that she loved you? I'm finding that very hard to fathom."

He inhaled a shuddering breath. "She was all I ever wanted in a woman. Kind, compassionate…"

"Who belonged to someone else, your brother nonetheless. Are you delusional? Why would you think her kindness constituted that she loved you?"

"I don't know. I was confused at the time."

"At the time? You mean, when you confronted her in the street, late at night, wielding a large kitchen knife?"

"Yes. I had no intention of killing her. I wanted her to run away with me. To start afresh somewhere else. She didn't really love him. I knew deep down she had feelings for me that she suppressed in front of him. When we were alone, she was all over me."

"But you stated you hadn't slept together. How could she be all over you?"

"She listened to me. Hung on my every word. But whenever Craig was present, she pretended to be distant from me. I couldn't stand it any longer."

"So you killed her?"

Tears dripped onto his cheek, but Sally didn't have an ounce of sympathy for the man. "I released her from the torture she lived with every day she spent with that moron. He couldn't give her what I could give her."

"Love isn't always about the material things you can furnish a partner with, Kenny. During my investigation, it's been highlighted over and over again how much they meant to each other. You destroyed that happiness through envy and jealousy. Please don't try to deny it."

"I didn't mean to. I wanted her to come away with me. I could give her all the things that I used to listen to her crave for with him."

"And in your delusional state, Kenny, did you ever consider Molly and Jamie?"

"I would have cared for them, if only she'd said yes and come away with me. We could have become a proper family."

"You're unbelievable. Your needs, no one else's, tore that contented family apart. So much so that Jamie can't even bear to look at his father in the eye, let alone speak to him. But you didn't stick around to see the damage you had caused, did you? You cut those kids out of your life. Is that how you should treat someone you care about? Mind you, you're swearing blind that you loved Anne, and yet you ended up taking her life. What a callous and twisted individual you truly are."

"I'm sorry. I let the kids down. I couldn't bear to look at them knowing that I had killed their mother. Looking at their features every day would have reminded me of what I had lost."

"You didn't lose her, Kenny. She was never yours in the first place. I've heard enough. We'll see what a judge and jury think of your confession. I hope they lock you up for life. You deserve to lose everything, just like your brother has over the years."

Sally left Jack to end the interview process and departed the room. She leant against the wall outside, her heart pounding, and waited for her partner to join her.

Jack left the interview room, and together, they climbed the stairs. "Why? It was such an easy confession. Why couldn't he have confessed years ago?"

Jack sighed. "Maybe he hadn't anticipated her body showing up like that."

"It's sad. To put Craig through all that torment over the years. Others blaming him for killing the one person he loved more than life itself. I can't wait to tell him the truth. I have a surprise for him too."

"What's that?"

She tapped her nose and continued to climb the stairs. "You'll see. We have to be at the hospital at eleven thirty. Time for a coffee and a celebratory cake, I think."

Jack turned around and began descending the stairs. "I know a hint when I hear one."

Sally laughed and called after him, "I fancy a celebratory chocolate éclair if you're buying, matey."

"Huh, you'll have what you're given."

EPILOGUE

Sally felt the emotion stir within her as she and Jack wound their way through the hospital corridors to Craig's room. She rapped her knuckles on the door and pushed it open. She was surprised to see Governor Wilkinson sitting beside Craig's bed and the prison officer standing at the end of his bed.

The governor stood and walked towards Sally with his hand outstretched. "Good to see you again, Inspector. We'll be outside in the hallway."

"Good to see you, too, Governor. Thanks, we shouldn't be long."

He winked, and both men left the room.

Sally moved forwards and smiled down at Craig. "How are you feeling?"

"Sore. It's nice to feel safe and warm for a change, though. How is the case going? Any news for me?"

She sighed and placed a hand over his. "I have good news for you, Craig. Well, actually, I have good and bad news for you."

He shuffled to sit upright in his bed and winced. "You better give me the good news first."

Sally's eyes welled up. "We've caught the culprit. The person who killed Anne. Which means that you will now be totally exonerated. I knew from the instant I laid eyes on you that you were innocent. I can't apologise enough for what my colleague put you through all those years ago and what you've suffered during your time in prison. No one will ever understand the devastation and trauma you've gone through, but I'm truly sorry you've had to endure everything that has been thrown at you."

Craig's bloodshot eyes were bulging out of his head. He moistened his lips several times as Sally shared the news with him. Finally, he cleared his throat and whispered one raspy word. "Who?"

Sally glanced at Jack, who nodded for her to go on. She turned back to face Craig again. "That's the bad news, Craig. It was Kenny!"

His brow furrowed, and his hand began to shake in disbelief. "Kenny? My brother? I don't believe it. How? Why?"

"Basically, he was envious of the love you and Anne shared. He was under the impression that Anne loved him. I asked him if she had ever shown him any reason to believe that, and all he could tell me was that she was different towards him when you weren't around."

"My God. I can't believe it. All the pain and grief he's put my family through. No wonder he moved away and I haven't seen hide nor hair of him since. How could he do that?"

Craig's anger was evident in his eyes and his twisted expression. Sally had something else up her sleeve that she knew would ease his pain. She patted his hand and walked back to open the door.

Standing on the other side, speaking to the Governor was Molly.

"Come in and see your dad, love."

Molly didn't hesitate. She barged into the room and flung herself on her father. "Dad, you're free. I always knew you were innocent."

Her father began to choke but managed to spit out the words, "Let me breathe, Molly, for goodness' sake."

Molly pulled away from her father and bit her lip. "Sorry. I'm over the moon that they're going to have to let you go now. You can come and live with me."

"That's kind of you, love."

Sally placed an arm around Molly's shoulder. "Hey, by the time the compensation board has paid out, you'll be living it up in a mansion."

Molly laughed, but Craig still looked bewildered by what had gone on. Jack coughed. Sally turned to face him, and he nodded at the doorway. She swivelled and stepped aside so Craig could see. Standing in the doorway was a reluctant Jamie. Sally crossed the room to draw him closer to his father.

With tears streaming down his face, he rushed to his father's side and smothered him. "Please forgive me, Dad."

Craig's own tears mingled with his son's on his chest. That was when Sally and Jack chose to leave the family alone.

Governor Wilkinson shook her hand again in the hallway. "You and your team did an exceptional job, Inspector. You should be proud of yourselves."

"We are, sir. Craig and his family deserve all the happiness heading their way. When do you think he'll be released from prison?"

"Within the next couple of weeks, I should imagine. As to your other dilemma, you'll be pleased to hear that Darryl is going to be transferred to another prison."

Sally's heart rate escalated. "That's wonderful news. May I ask where?"

"To Scotland. Is that far enough for you?" he asked, tilting his head.

Sally laughed and hugged the governor. "Bloody marvellous. I can't thank you enough."

"He dug his own grave, shall we say. He can expect his sentence to be extended due to what he sanctioned for Mr. Gillan. And if he refuses to mend his ways, I'll make sure his sentence is lengthened in years to come."

"Much appreciated. Thank you again, Governor Wilkinson."

Sally tugged Jack's arm. "Come on, partner, we have a double celebration ahead of us."

Suddenly, she skipped ahead of Jack and jumped up in the air to click her heels à la Eric Morecombe, not caring if she fell flat on her face in the process.

Nothing would stand in the way of her wedding to her soulmate now… nothing

THE END

NOTE TO THE READER

Dear Reader,

I hope you enjoyed the tangled web that was unveiled during Deadly Encounter, so glad that Sally and her team dug deep to solve this case.

But wait, there is another tough investigation lying ahead of them, actually there are two in LOST INNOCENCE. One of the cold cases will put everyone's emotions on edge while the other will demand Sally to be at her cagiest to seek the truth to the answers she craves.

Will you join the team in their search for long awaited justice.

Pick up your copy of LOST INNOCENCE.

https://melcomley.blogspot.com/p/lost.html

Thank you for your continued support, if you could find it in your heart to leave a review that would be excellent and give me the impetus to keep pounding away at my keyboard every day.

Happy reading,
M A Comley

Printed in Great Britain
by Amazon